Finding Home

Acclaim for Georgia Beers's Fiction

"Sales Call" (in *Erotic Interludes 2: Stolen Moments*)

"'Sales Call' is an artfully well-developed and credible vignette. So often there is a fantasy aspect to erotica, but this reviewer prefers a kind of reality wherein the story could happen to anyone in similar circumstances. Beers delivers that expectation in a delightfully satisfying manner." — *Independent Gay Writer*

Too Close To Touch

"Beers knows how to generate sexual tension so taut it could be cut with a knife…[in this]…tale of yearning, love, and lust." — *Midwest Book Review*

"*Too Close To Touch* is about a woman who has dedicated her life to trying to please 'Daddy' and lost herself in the process. Beers doesn't tie the story up neatly at the end either. She leaves some questions open, which is appropriate for her character. Gretchen herself becomes an open question looking for a lot of answers. This is a very satisfying and thought provoking book." — *Just About Write*

Lambda Literary Award Winner *Fresh Tracks*

"…a story told uniquely by Beers with a clear and strong voice. If you are looking for a story where two women fall in love, have some misunderstandings along the way, and then move on to a committed relationship, *Fresh Tracks* is not that book…It is a meaty and challenging story with an ensemble cast where the lines between lovers and friends are sometimes blurred. Beers…rises above the pack of romance novelists [and her] love of her craft shines through with this bold and successful move." —*J ust About Write*

"…the focus switches each chapter to a different character, allowing for a measured pace and deep, sincere exploration of each protagonist's thoughts. Beers gives a welcome expansion to the romance genre with her clear, sympathetic writing." — *Curve* magazine

Mine

"…Beers does a fine job of capturing the essence of grief in an authentic way. *Mine* is touching, life-affirming, and sweet." — *Lesbian News Book Review*

Bold Strokes Books by the Author

Too Close to Touch

Fresh Tracks

Mine

Finding Home

Finding Home

by

Georgia Beers

2008

FINDING HOME

ISBN 10: 1-60282-019-8
ISBN 13: 978-1-60282-019-7

This Trade Paperback Original Is Published By
Bold Strokes Books, Inc.
New York, USA

First Edition: June 2008

Credits
Editors: Cindy Cresap and Stacia Seaman
Production Design: Stacia Seaman
Cover Design By Sheri (graphicartist2020@hotmail.com)

Acknowledgments

First, always first, I've been blessed with the most amazing partner a girl could ask for, my wife, Bonnie. She's all that I want, she's *way* more than I deserve, and she's easily the most incredible human being I've ever known. I am eternally thankful for her never-ending, unconditional love and support, without which I don't think I could breathe.

Thank you to everybody on the staff of Bold Strokes Books. A group of more dedicated, hardworking women who love the genre of lesbian fiction, you'll be hard-pressed to find.

My undying gratitude to my trio of proofreaders, Stacy Harp, Steff Obkirchner, and Jackie Ciresi, who never fail to drop whatever it is they're doing to read over any little bit I send them. Their suggestions, corrections, questions, and compliments do more than they can possibly understand to keep this writer writing. I thank them from the bottom of my heart.

My editor, Cindy Cresap, has proven to me once again that we make a damn good team. I thank her for the ongoing lessons on description, as well as the pats on the back that came when I really needed them. My copy editor, Stacia Seaman, is the most amazing one-woman cleanup crew I have ever seen. I'm continually astonished by the last-minute things she catches (and thank goodness she does).

And last but not least, I want to express my love to my parents, Roseann Leege and Tom Beers, for rolling with the punches and accepting my sexuality without much more than a few surprised blinks. Along with my love, I also want to offer them my thanks for not only supporting my writing career with great verve by buying each and every book individually, but for actually *reading* them, love scenes and all, and not looking at me any differently afterward.

Dedication

To Pepper, Knute, Nexi, Niko, Mickey, Darby, Henry, and Finley, for showing me the indescribable joys of being loved by a dog.

CHAPTER ONE

Drunk-dialing was never a good idea. Ever. Any woman in her right mind knew that. Unfortunately for Sarah Buchanan, she had too many gin and tonics in her system to be in her right mind, so she went right on dialing, taking three tries before she hit the right choice from the selections in her cell phone and ignoring the seemingly faraway voice screaming for her to hang up, for God's sake, before it was too late.

Her dog, Bentley, sat on the floor, staring at her as she flopped backward onto the couch from the arm where she had been perched, and she was almost certain his blue eyes showed genuine concern for her. Or was it disapproval? Somehow, she couldn't be sure. Then the room tilted sickeningly and began to spin. Sarah slammed one foot to the ground, an old trick her father told her he used in college, referring to the spinning as "the BTs," or "the black twirlies." It didn't work this time, and she tried to push her foot down harder as her call went through and the phone began to ring. Once. Twice. Three times.

"Hello?" It was picked up on the fourth ring, the groggy voice on the other end hitting Sarah like a battering ram with its soft familiarity.

"Happy Valentine's Day." Emotion made an unexpected appearance, and Sarah tried to maintain a steady voice. She reached out to scratch Bentley's head, using him as a touchstone to keep her calm.

"Sarah? Is that you?"

"Yeah, it's me. Hi."

"Do you know what time it is?"

Sarah squinted at the antique clock mounted on the wall, but her eyes couldn't—or wouldn't—focus on the hands. "No idea."

"It's after midnight."

"Oh. Oops. I guess I'm a little late, then. My bad. But you know what they say. Better late than never, right?"

The frustrated breath Karen blew out on the other end of the phone was also familiar to Sarah, and she winced when she heard it. It had been a far too common sound during their last few weeks together, as if Karen's repeated attempts at an explanation for why she'd chosen Derek over her had been endlessly falling on deaf ears.

"What are you doing?" Karen's voice held the gentlest of reproaches. Maybe she'd been expecting this, especially today.

"I'm sprawled out on the couch," Sarah answered.

"No, Sarah, I mean what are you doing? We talked about this. Why are you calling me?"

The tears sprang up so fast, they surprised her. First she was dry-eyed, then she wasn't, just like that. "It's Valentine's Day. And I miss you."

"Sarah…"

"Don't. Don't do that."

"Don't do what?"

"Say my name with such pity." Sarah sat up, her unreasonably quick change of mood lost on her, her sudden movement startling Bentley to his feet. "Like you feel sorry for me."

"Have you been drinking?" Karen's tone remained steady, calm, rational. *Damn her.*

"Like a fish."

"I'm hanging up now."

"No, wait. Wait…please?"

Karen's end was silent, but Sarah could hear her breathing, knew she was still there.

"I just called to tell you I miss you," Sarah tried again. "I don't see anything wrong with that."

"And what do you want me to say, Sarah? What exactly do you expect me to say to that?"

Sarah could picture her ex, her reddish brown hair all sleep tousled, her brown eyes bleary, freckles sprinkled across her nose. Karen never woke up easily. She was like a kid that way. She loved her slumber and she was always adorable the way she looked forward to snuggling under the covers. Sarah smiled as she thought about how Karen was most likely wearing boxers and a tight-fitting tank top, her usual sleeping attire. That smile slipped, though, when it occurred to her that they were probably *his* boxers… Bile rose in her throat, but she choked it back down.

"Is he there?"

"Sarah." Warning was etched all over that one word.

"Are you with him right now?" Sarah couldn't help herself, the anger building too rapidly for her alcohol-addled brain to filter it out.

"Why do you have to do this?"

"Is he lying next to you?"

"I'm definitely hanging up now." As it always had been, the larger Sarah's anger became, the calmer Karen sounded, and it was obvious that this behavior wasn't new or unexpected. She sighed heavily. "Drink some water, take some Advil, and sleep it off. You're going to be hurting in the morning. Good night, Sarah."

The click seemed to reverberate through her head, and Sarah whimpered at the sound of it, feeling so utterly helpless and alone she didn't know if she could bear it. As if it were some foreign and unidentifiable object resting in her hand, she gaped at her cell phone. "God, what the fuck was I thinking?" She snapped it closed and tossed it none too gently onto the end table next to her.

There was no fighting it. She knew that. The second she threw her arm over her eyes, the tears came. Her crying jags were nothing new to her, nor to Bentley. She felt his wet nose nudge against her hand and she patted him absently on the head but made no move to get up. It wouldn't be the first time she slept on the couch, the combination of her screwed-up emotions and too much gin sapping her of any energy or the desire to get up and go to her bedroom. God, she used to have such control of her life, such a tight handle on everything. Of course, that was part of the problem, according to Karen. *Why are you such a control freak? Loosen up, for Christ's sake. You don't have to orchestrate every aspect of your life, you know.*

Sarah snorted. "If she could see me now," she whispered.

She felt Bentley move closer, his soft tongue darting out to clean the tears off her cheeks. He was worried about her and she knew it. It was his job, after all, to look out for his herd and to make sure each member was okay. She dug her fingers into his fur and murmured reassurances to him, telling him she was fine, not to worry. He lay down on the floor with a sigh. Apparently, he too understood they'd be sleeping in the living room again.

❖

"Oh, Christ."

Sarah felt like a freight train was blasting through her head at full speed. Squeezing her eyes shut against the overwhelming brightness of the bathroom lights, she braced herself against the vanity with both hands and tried hard to regulate her breathing and stave off a second bout of vomiting.

Nice and easy...

In...

Out...

In...

Out...

Slowly and carefully, she opened her eyes and attempted to focus on her reflection in the mirror. That proved to be a very large mistake.

"Oh, *Christ*," she said again, pulling the medicine cabinet open so she wouldn't be forced to look anymore. Fumbling for the bottle of ibuprofen, she turned on the water and filled a glass. After popping three pills, she closed the door of the cabinet and tried again. "Consider it your punishment for last night," she mumbled at herself in disgust.

The woman who looked back at her was a disaster of epic proportions. Her normally sleek and shiny dark hair, which had its own little zip of curl to it, hung limp and lifeless, not to mention tangled and matted, just past her shoulders. She had a normally creamy complexion that many admired, but that certainly wouldn't be happening today, not with the sallow gray shade of it and the purplish black circles underneath her eyes. Speaking of her eyes—which were definitely her best feature on any given day—Sarah hardly recognized them. Their usual cheerful blue was dull, and "bloodshot" didn't begin to describe the redness.

"God, what the hell is the matter with me?" The question was no more than a whisper, but Bentley lifted his head from the bathroom floor to look at her. "And you," she said, glaring down at him in mock anger. "How could you let me call her?" She squatted and dug her fingers into the impossible silkiness of his tricolored fur, scratching around the thick coat on his neck the way he liked it. "Hmm? How could you let me be that stupid?"

He was such a good dog. She couldn't have created a better one from scratch. She'd gotten that lucky with him. Bentley was a miniature Australian shepherd—a mini Aussie—and she would never have another breed as long as she continued to own dogs. He was smart, loyal, loving, and gorgeous, and he was really the only thing that would make what she'd decided to do today difficult. But it would be okay. She was sure of it. She just needed some time.

Showering and getting dressed were not easy tasks in her state. Despite the handful of drugs, her head continued to pound, and the idea of putting anything other than coffee into her stomach started it churning in revolt. Too uncomfortable to put much effort into her appearance, she twisted her hair back behind her head and chose the pantsuit that needed the least amount of preparation for wearing—the black rayon combination. Deciding on the usual simple royal blue silk shell for underneath it, she hoped it didn't accent her eyes too much this morning. Her makeup was doing next to nothing to cover the evidence of her rough night, and she didn't need everybody and their brother asking her if she was feeling all right. The truth was, she was *not* feeling all right, mentally or physically, and she hadn't been for a very long time. That didn't mean she felt the need to discuss it with anybody.

Self-deprecation was apparently going to be her close, personal friend for the day, as it followed her all around the house that morning, tossing out whatever snippets she could remember from her conversation with Karen the previous night, making her cringe at her own desperation. She still couldn't believe she'd called, although she had a vague memory of entertaining the idea as she sipped from her fifth gin and tonic. This was the fourth morning in less than six weeks that punished her with a brutal hangover, and she absently wondered if she should be worried about herself. She'd always enjoyed an occasional cocktail, but she never used to get toasted like she did last night. Drunk was unattractive. It was embarrassing. It meant no control, no filters. She was dreading the idea of hearing what stupidly personal things she'd spouted at the bar, though she was sure Patti Schmidt, her administrative assistant, would tell her. Patti always told her. Patti meant well but had no clue what it meant to keep business and personal separate, and Sarah certainly didn't help matters by going out and getting obliterated around somebody from work.

Patti was too naïve to realize that this wasn't exactly appropriate behavior. Sarah made a mental note to have a little talk with her admin, one that included an apology.

When will I learn my lesson? She scolded herself as she maneuvered her car into a spot around the corner from Valenti's. All she'd hear about all day was how much fun Patti had last night. And while she brought Sarah water and asked her how she was feeling and was her usual concerned and nurturing self, Sarah's skin would crawl with embarrassment. God, she should know better. She *did* know better. She felt like kicking herself. The car door took the brunt of her frustration as she slammed it with more force than necessary.

Valenti's was a bakery and coffee shop in the more eclectic section of Monroe Avenue that had evolved with the times. Sarah knew this because she'd been coming to it for nearly ten years—at lunchtime when it had been an Italian deli, and for the last three years, in the morning, since it had moved its focus to baked goods and coffee. As the neighborhood had become younger and younger, centered more and more on recent college graduates, the deli business had tapered off considerably. Sarah had noticed fewer people each time she stopped by and worried about the survival of such a traditional place. One Monday about three years ago, there was a sign on the door that said simply, "Closed for Renovations. Will Re-open Soon." Less than a month later, Sarah's favorite coffee shop was unveiled, and the coffee and homemade baked goods were so wonderful, she never even missed the deli for a second.

It had been a very smart move for the owners. Each morning, it was packed with a steady stream of yuppies and tech geeks ready for their first jolt of caffeine and a blast of sugar from the homemade confections that lined the glass case. Sarah would swear on a stack of Bibles that Valenti's had the best latte she'd ever tasted. It was a very rare morning that she didn't make it in for one. And today, she needed it more than ever.

Waiting patiently in line and trying hard to ignore the

pounding of her head, Sarah focused on the woman behind the counter. Woman? Girl? She looked young but had an air of professionalism and poise that told Sarah she might be older than she seemed. She was adorable, sexy even, Sarah had always thought, with her small build and energetic smile. She was terrific with the customers, always quick with a wink or a laugh, a little flirty, but not obnoxiously so. Her eyes were either a light hazel or a dark green, Sarah wasn't quite sure, and her hair color changed on a regular basis. Last summer, it had been short, spiky, and bleached blond with a bright pink streak in the front. Then she'd let it grow out and went nearly jet black, still with the pink streak. Now it was almost a bob, the ends skimming the tops of her shoulders in a warm chestnut brown, and Sarah speculated whether this was the closest to her natural color she'd been in a while. It seemed to suit her. She still had the pink streak that fell casually across her forehead and over her right eye, and Sarah felt the sudden urge to brush it out of the way. Clenching her hands into fists, she glanced toward the homemade cannoli. On any other day, she'd be tempted, knowing from experience how decadently delicious they were, but today she swallowed down the sudden urge to retch.

"Hi there," the girl said, flashing her usual flirty smile as Sarah reached the counter. At least, Sarah always thought of it as flirty. An extra-large latte was set in front of her before she even had the chance to respond to the greeting. She blinked at it in surprise.

"I usually just get the medium," she said finally, lamely, as she looked up to meet eyes that were definitely light hazel. They glittered back at her in what appeared to be friendly sympathy.

"I know." The girl blew the colored lock of hair out of her eye, then lowered her voice and leaned slightly forward. "You look like you could use a little extra help this morning."

Sarah grimaced, torn between being flattered that the girl knew her order by heart and embarrassed that her appearance

CHAPTER TWO

"Yikes. Hot Business Exec is late today. And I'm betting she had a rough night." Andrea Tisdale watched over the rim of her coffee cup as the tall, attractive—and obviously sick, hungover, depressed, or all three—brunette headed for the door of the bakery.

"I think you're right," Natalie Fox tossed over her shoulder in response to her best friend's comment. Then she smiled at the man at the counter and gave him his change.

"Doesn't take away her hotness, though."

"Don't you have to get to work?"

"I took a personal day."

"What for?"

"Shh. I'm enjoying the view."

Natalie shook her head. "You've got a one-track mind."

"You can't tell me you don't find her drool-worthy. I happen to know you do."

"I didn't say that. I said you have a one-track mind."

"That's what happens when you go for six months with no sex." Andrea bit into a jelly doughnut, the raspberry filling sticking to the corners of her mouth, her lips white with powdered sugar. "God, these damn things are sinful." As a petite older woman in a blue apron bustled over, Andrea asked, "What do you put in these, Mrs. V.? Some kind of drug to keep us all addicted?"

Mrs. Valenti tapped Natalie on the hip, signaling that she should take her break now. "Oh, I not tell you or I have to kill you," she said in an endearing Italian accent. She winked at Andrea before fishing three cream puffs out of the glass case for the next customer and then shooing the girls out of her way. "Go. Go. Sit."

Andrea followed Natalie through the kitchen to the break room, where they sat at a small, nondescript table. Natalie positioned herself so she had a clear line of sight to the front counter. As with every weekday morning at this time, the crowd was beginning to die down. Natalie wouldn't have let Mrs. Valenti take over the counter if it had still been busy. The woman was an always-moving bundle of energy, but it didn't mean she wasn't in her seventies. Natalie was careful to watch her and make sure to relieve her if it looked like she was getting tired, because the elderly woman would never admit it and ask for help. It was a quality that was as engaging as it was infuriating, and Mr. Valenti was just as bad. They were like family to Natalie, like her own grandparents, and she was always looking out for them, whether or not they realized it. Which she was pretty sure they did.

"So?" She turned her attention to Andrea, who was polishing off the last bite of her doughnut. "What's the scoop? Are you going to meet her?"

Andrea stared into her now-empty paper cup for several long seconds. When she looked back up at Natalie, all mirth and humor had fled from her brown eyes. She ran a hand through her short, dark hair and her cheeks puffed with the exhalation of a long breath. "Yeah, I think I am."

"That's great!" Natalie clapped her hands together in enthusiasm.

"I'm nervous, Natty."

"I know." Natalie reached across the table and flicked some powdered sugar from Andrea's cheek. "I know you are. But I'm proud of you. This is a big step. And you practically know the woman, right?"

"I guess so."

"What do you mean, you guess so? You've e-mailed with her for weeks. You've talked on the phone. You've exchanged pictures. You're attracted to her. She's attracted to you."

"As attracted as you can be to a photograph. What if there's no chemistry?"

Natalie shrugged. "Then there's no chemistry and you've got a new friend. You can never have too many of those, right?"

"You're always so damned logical." Andrea threw an affectionate grin at her.

"Hey, I've got to be good at something. My point is you know what to expect. This wouldn't exactly be a blind date. You've seen one another's pictures. You know you have things in common to talk about. You'll know what to expect."

"She's going to expect a woman with two breasts."

Natalie chewed on the inside of her cheek. She hadn't agreed with Andrea's decision to not be completely up-front about her breast cancer. She thought it was better to get the facts out on the table and weed out the potential pain causers, but it wasn't Natalie's choice to make, and Andrea was still too sensitive about the subject to lead with it. Having a mastectomy at such a young age had really messed with her self-esteem and body image, and even *thinking* about dating was a huge step for her. Natalie was proud. She loved Andrea and so supported her any way she could, even if she thought she might have made the wrong choice.

"So you cross that bridge when you come to it, right?"

"Right." Changing the subject, Andrea reached across the table, caught a lock of Natalie's hair on her finger, and tugged gently. "Your pink is fading."

"I know. I've got an appointment next week for a trim. I'll have Jocelyn re-dye it for me."

The warm, comforting smell of cinnamon suddenly blanketed the air and both women lifted their heads slightly, taking in the scent almost unintentionally.

"Cinnamon rolls are done," Andrea said needlessly.

"God, I never get tired of that smell."

"So, what about you, Natty?"

Natalie propped her chin in her hand. "What about me?"

"When are you going to do some dating? It's really not fair for me to be the only one going through the torture, you know."

"Solidarity, huh?"

"Absolutely. Tommy and Jenny have somebody they want to set you up with."

"I know." They were teachers at the school where Andrea taught…the school where Natalie used to teach until she'd had enough of the political bullshit and threw in the towel.

"And?"

"God, you're pushy."

Andrea winked. "Some say it's one of my better qualities."

"Yeah, well, I'm not one of those people." Natalie couldn't help but grin, though. She and Andrea had been best friends since high school and knew each other better than anybody else. Deep down, she knew Andrea was simply worried that Natalie was lonely.

"Are you at least thinking about it? Tommy says she's a hottie. And you know how picky Tommy is."

"Yes, Andrea, I'm thinking about it."

"Promise?"

"I promise." Natalie recalled the voicemail message Tommy had left her a couple of weeks ago, his voice plotting and the tiniest bit seductive as he rambled on about his cousin's lesbian and single friend and how good-looking she was. Natalie had to admit, he made her sound extremely desirable, and she was actually leaning toward taking him up on the offer, despite the fact that even the *idea* of a blind date made her nervous and jerky.

"Good." The scraping of Andrea's chair on the linoleum floor was loud as she stood up. "I've got to run."

Natalie teased, "Personal things to do on your personal day?"

"Always." At that moment, Mr. Valenti walked past them carrying a tray of half-moon cookies and Andrea waved at him. "Bye, Leo, you sexy beast."

A blush crept over his stubbly cheeks and he rolled his eyes good-naturedly. "You a bad, bad girl, Andrea."

"You wouldn't have me any other way."

She bade her good-byes and was gone like a whirlwind, as always.

Not one to be able to just sit, even on her break, Natalie got up and began pulling the trash cans that were on wheels toward the back door. She knew it would help Mr. Valenti if she emptied the morning's garbage so he didn't have to worry about it later. It was damn cold out and the chill of the air hit her like a slap in the face as she opened the door to the back of the shop and pulled the cans toward the small Dumpster, her mind wandering.

She wouldn't really consider herself lonely. Sure, there were times she wished she had the company of a lover, somebody to talk to over the first coffee of the day, somebody to snuggle up with in the crisp frostiness of the winter nights. That didn't mean she was lonely, or that she even wanted a partner. She was pretty happy with her life as it was. Some would scoff at that statement, she knew. How could she be happy? She had a job that paid her barely more than minimum wage. She lived in a tiny apartment above the bakery. She was single. What was there to be happy with about her life? She grinned then, because she'd had this exact argument with her father the last time she went home for a visit. He wanted her to "make something" of herself instead of slinging coffee and doughnuts to ingrates. Responses to all his points seemed to come unbidden and she knew then that she was in a good place in her life.

No, she didn't make a lot of money, but she was good at planning and investing and shopping, and she was careful. She didn't overextend herself; she didn't live above her means, so she had enough, even a modest amount of savings. And the reality was, one day the Valentis would want to retire. Somebody who knew the business might want to take over. It was a tidbit that sat in the back of Natalie's mind at all times.

Yes, her apartment was small, but she loved it, and it was actually bigger than it looked. The second floor above the bakery was hers, and the Valentis owned the building, so her rent was very reasonable because they trusted her and were happy to have her there. Plus, living above a bakery meant heavenly scents drifted up all the time. She'd told her father at least she didn't live above a bar.

Yes, she was single. She didn't plan on remaining that way for the remainder of her natural-born life, but she was okay without somebody. When her partner was ready to show up, she would. Natalie firmly believed that. Her father had rolled his eyes.

She hadn't been angry at him. After all, he just wanted what was best for her and he was concerned. She knew that. She was thirty-one years old, and he probably had expected she'd be more settled by now, more rooted, have a house, a partner, and two-point-five kids. But she realized as she defended her life to him that she was happy, which was all most parents wanted for their children, wasn't it? And when it was time to be happier, she'd be ready for it. Simple, maybe, but there it was, and she didn't second-guess it.

Blowing on her hands to warm them, she decided she'd better get her overfull brain out of the cold before Mrs. Valenti came looking for her and scolded her for not putting on a jacket first. She dragged the cans back into the bakery, the scents of homemade bread, cookies, and coffee wrapping around her as she entered, coating her gently with the warmth and aromas of what home felt like to her.

❖

"Are you absolutely sure?" Mary Buchanan asked. She brushed her graying hair back from her face with a slightly trembling hand. Her eyes were clouded. She was trying hard to disguise her worry. Sarah could tell. It was something she had done as long as Sarah could remember, and she'd always been bad at it.

"It's okay, Mom." Sarah reached across the kitchen table and laid a warm hand over her mother's. "It really is. It'll be fine."

"But…it's so long."

"It's three months. It'll fly by and I'll be back before you know it."

"And…it's so far away."

"It is."

They sat in silence for several minutes, and Sarah was almost certain she could hear the processing going on in her parents' heads. Her mother tapped her finger lightly on her coffee mug, her wedding band making a soft pinging sound that seemed inordinately loud in the quiet of the kitchen. Her father was chewing on the inside of his bottom lip, a habit he always took up when he was thinking hard.

"Dad?"

Richard Buchanan took a deep breath, very slowly, puffing up his big chest. Then he let it out just as slowly as he gathered his thoughts. "You're a big girl," he said finally. "You have to make your own decisions, and if this is what you think is right for you, we'll support you in any way we can." His expression softened as he added, "Plus, I have to believe this is a good opportunity for you at work or you wouldn't even be considering it."

"It is." Sarah flashed a small smile of relief his way, seeing her mother's slight nod of agreement out of the corner of her eye. "And I need to get away." She studied the burgundy fabric place mat on the table in front of her, toyed with a thread hanging from the corner. "I was hoping things would be a lot better by now, but they're not."

"Don't sell yourself short, honey," her mother admonished. "You and Karen were together for a long time. That doesn't just go away in a few months. Recovering from a breakup can take a long time."

"It's been almost a year, Mom."

"Still."

"I just need to get away from here for a while."

"Well," her father said. "You can't get much farther away than New Zealand. That's the other side of the planet. Literally."

Her mother grimaced with distaste at the specifics.

"I'll be back before you know it," Sarah said a second time, hoping to wipe away the expression of concern on her mother's face. "And I need you to look after Bentley for me. I'd really love to take him with me, but there's no way I'm putting him on a plane. I've heard too many horror stories."

"I don't blame you," her mother said, reaching down to ruffle the fur on the dog lying at her feet. "I'll be more than happy to take care of my grand-doggie."

"Try not to spoil him too much, all right?" Sarah sent a grin knowingly at her mother.

Putting a hand to her chest, her mother feigned insult. "Whatever do you mean?"

"Who are you kidding? I'll come back, he'll be lounging on the couch, eating jerky treats and making *you* fetch his ball."

"And I would."

Sarah was filled with affection for her mother. She knew most people thought she was a little strict with Bentley, not allowing him on the furniture, making him sit or lie down before he got treats or meals, keeping a close eye on his diet. No table scraps, very few treats, all natural dog food mixed with actual meat. Mentally rolling her eyes, she was unable to edit the thought that zipped through her mind. *At least I have control of something...*

"We've got our cruise in the middle of March," her father reminded her. "We'll be gone for three weeks."

"That's right." Her mother squinched up her face in thought, then settled on a solution. "We'll have Ricky watch the dog while we're gone."

Sarah made a mental note to call her little brother and threaten him with bodily harm if anything happened to Bentley while she was away. She loved Ricky, but he was notoriously irresponsible. She briefly considered speaking up, but her mother already looked so worried, she didn't want to add to the burden by expressing her reservations about Ricky as a dog-sitter.

"When do you leave?" her father asked.

"The end of this month. I'll be back in late May or early June, depending on how the inception of the new office goes over and how smoothly things are running."

"That's less than two weeks," her mother almost whined, and Sarah wanted to smile with the affection that filled her. She'd always been very close to her parents, and she knew having her away for such a stretch of time was going to be tough on them, but they were handling it like troopers.

"I know. I've got some serious preparations to make."

"We'll have a going-away party so your grandmother can say good-bye. And your aunts and uncles…" The wheels were turning in her mother's head. It was the best way she knew how to handle the emotions swirling within her: plan a party.

"Just don't go crazy, Mom. I'm not a kid going away to college, okay? It's just work."

"Shh." Her mother waved a hand dismissively at her. "I'm making a mental list."

Sarah and her father rolled their eyes in tandem.

❖

Sarah was crying again and she knew it agitated Bentley, but she couldn't help it. She hadn't expected it to be this hard. He'd be fine here, she knew. He liked to be at Grandma's. She'd made sure to bring several of his toys, his bed, and his food. He'd stayed here before on many occasions, he seemed to like it, and she knew her mother loved having him. She wondered for a moment if he realized how spoiled he was when he was there.

She squatted down and took his face in her hands, looking him right in the eye. "You be a good boy, Bentley. Okay? Be good for Grandma." She kissed his head and sniffled. "I know you're going to be worried and it might upset you that I'm gone so long, but trust me. I'll be back, all right? I'm not leaving you. I promise I'm coming back." She kissed him again and he licked at her tears as he always did, his way of helping. She swooped him up and squeezed him tightly to her chest. She hardly ever picked him up, having taught him that his place was at her feet, and part of her wondered if she was completely freaking him out with her out-of-the-ordinary behavior. He answered her question, though, when he gently rested his head on her shoulder.

She whimpered at that and squeezed him harder. "I love you, boy," she whispered in his ear, kissed him once more, then set him down. "Be good." She grabbed her shoulder bag, hugged her mother, who was also crying, and hurried out to the car. She knew without looking that Bentley stood at the screen door, looking out at her. He followed the vehicle with his eyes as it pulled out of the driveway and Sarah waved at him through the window, unable to stop the tears coursing down her cheeks.

Chapter Three

It was just after seven in the evening and Natalie mentally counted twelve customers buzzing around the Starbucks as she sat across the small, circular table from Andrea and sipped her peppermint latte. She was trying to run calculations in her head to determine whether or not twelve customers would make it worth the Valentis' while to stay open beyond five, but Andrea interrupted her before she could finish.

"What do you think?" Andrea used her chin to point to the cup in Natalie's hand.

"It's a little too minty," Natalie said, glancing into her drink. "But if they lightened up on the peppermint syrup and added a bit more milk…"

"Might be perfect?"

"Might be perfect."

"Good. You should work on that."

Natalie chuckled at Andrea's sarcasm. She knew full well that "work on it" was exactly what Natalie would do the next day. She was always trying to come up with new versions of coffee for the Valentis to sell. Some had been disastrous, but many had become regular menu items.

"Shouldn't they be done with the peppermint by now?" Andrea asked. "Wasn't it a Valentine's Day promotion?"

Natalie furrowed her brows. "I think it was."

"Well, that was weeks ago." Andrea paused, then asked, "What makes peppermint a Valentine flavor anyway?"

"How should I know? The colors? Because it's red and white? I have no idea."

Andrea waved a hand dismissively. "Whatever. I'm glad Valentine's Day is over."

Natalie grunted her agreement, still watching the clientele mill about the shop.

"I have a new goal for us for next Valentine's Day."

Natalie slowly brought her gaze back to Andrea. "This ought to be good."

Andrea took a playful swipe at her. "I'm serious. Next year, by Valentine's Day, we are both going to at least be dating somebody. *At least*. What do you say? Agreed?"

Natalie studied her for several long seconds. Finally, she sat back in her chair and folded her arms across her chest. "How exactly do you expect to reach this *goal*"—she made quotation marks in the air to emphasize the word—"if you can't even manage to make a date to meet your e-mail friend face-to-face after chatting with her for weeks?"

A flash of anger shot across Andrea's features so quickly, Natalie would never have seen it if she didn't know her so well. Andrea mimed picking up the handset on a telephone and dialing. Putting the invisible receiver to her ear, she said, "Hello, Pot? This is the kettle. You're black." She hung up her fake phone and went on. "Don't you dare give me your shit, because I happen to know for a fact that you haven't gotten in touch with Tommy or Jenny to meet the woman they mentioned."

Natalie studied her coffee, feeling properly chastised. "I'm sorry. That was out of line."

"Yeah, it was, Little Miss Waiting for My Princess to Come." Andrea snorted and sipped from her own cup.

"I just hate the whole dating thing, Andrea. I can't help it." It was the truth. Just the thought of sitting through endless dinners and drinks, chatting with somebody for the express reason of finding out whether or not she'd make a good mate, completely exhausted her.

"Guess what? We *all* hate the whole dating thing. But don't you think you should at least try? Do you really think the perfect woman is going to just drop out of the sky and into your lap?"

"A girl can dream, can't she?" Natalie asked, trying to lighten the mood.

Andrea wasn't falling for it. She remained serious, determined. "You have to put forth some kind of effort, Natty. You're going to make some lucky girl very, very happy, but she isn't going to magically appear. You have to go looking for her."

"I hate that."

"Join the club."

As they sat and watched the activity around them, Natalie reflected on their friendship. Spanning more than fifteen years, it had had its ups and downs, but they always came out holding on to one another, standing up for one another, and loving each other. Even Andrea being a year older than Natalie didn't keep them apart in high school or in college. It was as if they were destined to be friends. Nobody had been stronger during Andrea's bout with breast cancer than Natalie. Andrea was such a young case that she and her family spent most of her treatment shell-shocked that this could even be happening to a woman barely thirty. So while they sat in waiting rooms looking blank and helpless, Natalie questioned the doctors relentlessly, took copious notes, and spent a huge percentage of her time at Andrea's apartment. The day she'd walked in with the pink streak in her hair signifying breast cancer support, Andrea had cried.

After a few minutes of silence, Andrea suddenly asked, "Hey, have you seen Hot Business Exec lately? I haven't noticed her."

"Me, neither," Natalie said. Unexpectedly, she was hit with a mental image of the attractive brunette, always in some gorgeous designer business suit, always looking so elegant and professional and put-together. Natalie had entertained more than one fantasy that involved seriously wrinkling those perfect clothes and tousling that expensive hairstyle. Furrowing her brow, she said, "Now that I think about it, I haven't seen her in quite a while. I hope I didn't piss her off with my comment to her that day."

"About her hangover?"

"I didn't actually use that word, you know."

"Yeah, well, you didn't have to."

"True." She took a sip from her cup, then added, "I suppose maybe she's found a better cup of coffee elsewhere."

"Not possible."

"It's too bad, though. She was definitely fun to look at."

"Amen to that."

They returned to sitting silently, people-watching and enjoying one another's presence, something they'd done ever since Natalie could remember. She didn't really see any of the patrons after that, though. She found her thoughts strangely preoccupied by a tall, sexy business executive with dark hair, a designer suit, and legs to die for.

❖

Sarah felt good and it surprised her, so much so that she almost lost that good feeling by worrying too much about why she was suddenly feeling good. She shook her head at herself, wondering how she had managed to survive the past year as such a freak, and took a slug of her Steinlager. It was okay as far as beers went, but she mentally decided she would switch to something else once the bottle was empty.

She'd found the little lesbian bar online, pleased that it was so close to the complex of suites in which she was staying. It made stopping by after a long day in the office easy, once she managed to dodge the almost daily dinner invitation from Patti Schmidt. She liked the woman well enough and felt bad turning her down as often as she did, but there were times when all Sarah needed was a little time to herself, and the last thing in the world she wanted to endure was Patti accompanying her to a gay bar. *God, I'd rather stick needles in my eyes*, she thought as she took another sip. Though she didn't keep her sexuality a huge secret at the office, she also didn't walk around with a rainbow on her forehead. Being dragged to a gay bar by her boss seemed well beyond the requirements of Patti's job description. At the same time, Sarah hadn't wanted Patti to know she was going out on the town without her. They were both strangers in a strange land and Sarah felt a little guilty for leaving her to her own devices.

As she sipped her beer and let herself unwind, she wondered, not for the first time, if she was finally beginning to come back to herself, and it was a pleasantly positive thought. The key, though, was going to be *how far* back. Until the whole Derek issue, the most common argument Sarah and Karen had had was about Sarah's need for control, her need to have everything run on her clock, on her schedule, to her liking.

"When did you become so rigid? So predictable? Don't you get bored with being in command of every single thing in your universe?"

When Karen had asked her that, she'd reeled back as if she'd been slapped, astounded by how much it stung. Was she that bad? She knew now that she was, and Sarah was reasonably sure that after that particular argument, Karen had decided she wanted out. Derek had simply been another fun wrench tossed into the gears of Sarah's neat and orderly life. After that, all semblance of control was ripped away and Sarah had felt like she'd been set adrift in a vast ocean of nothingness.

But now…now there was land in view and she could almost touch bottom with the tips of her toes. Taking this trip to the other side of the world, throwing herself into her work, exploring a new country, had been the smartest thing she'd done in ages, and she was immensely proud of herself. And while she was looking forward to finding the old Sarah Buchanan again, the woman who was solid and familiar and competent, she was also very cautious about letting her take over. She'd be more careful this time. She had to be.

"Here you go, love." The bartender was a large woman with smiling eyes and cropped salt-and-pepper hair who'd begun calling Sarah by name when she came in. She placed a shot glass upside down in front of Sarah and gestured toward the other end of the bar with her chin. "That lovely blonde down there'd like to buy you a drink."

"Would she now?" Sarah drained her beer. "I think I'll let her. Bombay and tonic. With a lime, please."

"Coming right up."

Sarah had been in New Zealand for more than a month and this wasn't the first drink somebody had sent her way at this bar. It was, however, the first time she considered the fact that it was a Friday night and maybe spending it in the company of a beautiful blonde would be preferable to spending it alone. The bartender slid the drink in front of her and Sarah wrapped her hand around the cool moistness of the glass. She held it up in a salute to the blonde. Then she gestured with her eyes to the empty stool next to her. The blonde smiled, picked up her purse, and headed in Sarah's direction.

Yes, a little company might be just what the doctor ordered.

CHAPTER FOUR

Natalie banged the back door open much more savagely than necessary, taking her anger and frustrations out on the innocent building rather than on her coworkers or customers, much to her own relief. She knew the drill, had been working in retail long enough to understand that no matter what her mood might be, if she gave out rudeness, she'd get rudeness back in spades. So she swallowed her foul disposition until she got a chance to let it loose on something that could take it with no hurt feelings…in this case, the door.

She needed to calm down. She took a couple of deep, cleansing breaths, trying to remind herself that people were often assholes and she couldn't let the assholes get the better of her, even if they were completely and unnecessarily rude.

Hauling the wheeled garbage cans across the back lot to the Dumpster none too gently, she muttered angry words under her breath, wishing she hadn't let the guy get to her. *Am I PMSing?* she wondered, thinking that would explain why a customer who claimed she'd screwed up his order completely had sent her so dangerously close to the verge of tears. She inhaled again, willing herself to calm down and let it go.

A rustling behind the Dumpster stopped Natalie dead in her tracks. Garbage pick-up was due this morning, and between Valenti's and the pizza joint next door, the Dumpster was filled to overflowing. Despite being in a well-populated area of the city, it wasn't unheard of to have a raccoon or a possum rooting around in your garbage. Even a skunk was a possibility.

Not wanting to worry the Valentis and bring them out in the chilly almost-spring air but uncertain exactly what to do, Natalie stood there, one hand on the edge of a garbage can, one hand pressed firmly to her chest, as if making sure her heart wouldn't beat itself clean out of her body. *Okay, moron, do something. Be that tough dyke who was going to knock another person senseless just a minute ago.* She squinted, trying to see what was making the noise. What if it was a raccoon? What exactly did she think she was going to do about it? Ask it nicely to be on its merry way? She rolled her eyes at herself as the rustling continued, but nothing appeared.

"Psst!" She made the sound loudly, feeling like an idiot. Under her breath, she mumbled, "Oh, good. Hiss at it, whatever it is. That'll help. Maybe it'll think you have a secret and come out to see what it is."

The rustling stopped and both Natalie and the rustler remained still and silent for what seemed like hours. Then the sound began again and Natalie repeated her hiss.

"Psst!"

Unaware of the fact that she was bent almost totally forward at the waist, she jumped back and straightened up at the startling sight of the blue eyes that peered around the steel Dumpster to take her in.

They stared at one another, blinking, and Natalie could only see its head, finally figuring out that it was a dog making all that noise, a much smaller one than she would have expected. It was chewing on what looked like a dirty piece of pizza crust and eyeing her warily, as if it expected her to pounce at any second and it wanted to be able to sprint away in a flash. When she moved, the dog flinched, so she was careful to move slowly, not wanting to frighten it away.

"Hey, there," she said softly as she squatted to be closer to the dog's level. It continued to chew slowly, its unexpectedly colorful eyes never leaving her face. "Are you lost?" She held out her hand as it contemplated her and she cooed soothingly at it. "Come here, buddy. It's a little chilly to be out here all alone, don't you think?"

The dog licked its lips as it finished the crust and continued to study her. As it inched slowly out from behind the Dumpster, its gaze shifted from her eyes to her outstretched hand, then back to her eyes again. Remembering a documentary she'd seen recently on the Discovery Channel, she shifted her gaze away, then back, then away, not wanting to issue any kind of challenge by staring directly in the dog's eyes. This seemed to ease its tension just a touch and it took a step toward her. Its moist black nose twitched, and Natalie knew she was being sized up by smell as well as sight.

Despite the eventual tingling in her bent legs, she did her best to remain still, to let the dog set the pace and decide when to approach, which it did with painfully slow progress. It wasn't a very large animal at all, maybe twenty or twenty-five pounds, and looked scrawnier than Natalie suspected it normally was. Its coat was matted, a mishmash of white, black, gray, and a few dabs of brown, and she had the feeling that when clean and brushed, it would shimmer and shine like silk. One ear was black, the other a speckled gray and white, and if it didn't look so wary and cautious, Natalie knew it would be a beautiful, possibly loving animal. She had the sudden, almost irresistible urge to find out.

The dog continued to inch, his eyes leaving Natalie's only briefly for quick checks around to make sure it wasn't about to be pounced on from another direction. When it got close enough to touch the tips of her fingers with its nose, it stopped.

"It's okay," she whispered, wanting desperately to stand up and ease the prickling caused by the lack of circulation to her feet, but wanting more for the dog to trust her enough to relax.

"It's okay. Are you hungry? I bet Mrs. Valenti's got something inside for you. Want to ask? Hmm?"

The dog cocked his head at her and she was sure she could see it debating whether or not she could be trusted. Before she could say anything else, a warm, pink tongue licked her fingertips tentatively.

"Yeah, you taste that? Cinnamon and flour and stuff? You want some more? I bet I can find you a roll or something. You look like you haven't eaten in a while. I might even have some chicken up in my apartment. What do you say? Hungry?"

Still wary, the dog suddenly seemed more exhausted than anything else as it crept slightly closer to her, close enough to allow her to dig her fingers into the thick fur around its neck and scratch it. Natalie wondered how long it had been a stray. It looked like a purebred to her and she found it hard to believe it wasn't simply lost. But there was no collar or identifying tags under her fingers, and the condition of the dog's coat and build told her it had been a while since it had been inside. The idea of somebody abandoning a helpless animal and leaving it to fend for itself made her blood boil.

A quick bend of her neck and glance underneath the animal told her it was a male. "Okay, handsome," she said to him soothingly as she continued to stroke his fur. "You're all right. I'm not going to hurt you, I promise."

The dog seemed to be relaxing by the second, she was relieved to notice, and he inched closer to her until he curled his body between her bent knees so she could scratch more of him. She laughed at this.

"Oh, sure. Pegged me as a sucker already, did you? You're a pretty smart guy."

The sound of the bakery door made him stiffen and Natalie quickly soothed him with her voice as she turned to see Mrs. Valenti standing in the doorway, hands on her hips.

"Natalie, is cold. You catch your death," she said.

"I know. I know. But..." Natalie stood so that Mrs. Valenti could see the dog.

"Ohhh...*turchino*," she said, her voice almost reverent as she stared.

"*Turchino*?" Natalie frowned and looked down at the dog, who glanced up at her with the unmistakable question on his face of whether or not he could trust the older woman. "They're not turquoise, they're blue." She took a step toward the building and gently called for him to follow, which he did, with trepidation. "It's okay, buddy. She's a nice lady."

"You say blue. I say *turchino*," Mrs. Valenti said, using her apron to wipe her hands.

"Well, maybe you need new glasses," Natalie teased her. She and the dog stopped at the door.

"He too skinny."

"He was rooting around the Dumpster."

"He looks hungry."

"I thought so, too."

"Come." She gestured for them to follow her inside. "I have idea."

❖

Half an hour later, the dog was stretched out on the floor in the break room, gnawing happily on the beef bone Mrs. Valenti had used to flavor her vegetable beef soup the day before. Natalie watched him as she sipped a cup of coffee, reaching down occasionally to stroke his head. He had relaxed considerably.

"It's a good thing you use this kitchen to make your own stuff here for home," she said to Mrs. Valenti. "I don't know if he would have been all that fond of a cannoli. I think he's happy now."

"He need bath."

Wrinkling her nose in agreement, Natalie nodded. "Yeah,

that Dumpster smell sort of clings, doesn't it? I'll take him up to my place when he's done and see if I can clean him up a bit. We shouldn't have him in the kitchen anyway." It would be just their luck to have a surprise inspection happen when a filthy stray dog was lounging on the floor in the back room of the shop.

"What you going to do about him?"

"I don't know." Resting her chin on her folded hands, she watched him chew, marveled at the way he used his white paws to hold the bone still so he could get to the good parts. "He's got no collar, no tags. He's obviously been on his own for quite a while. Makes me think some jerk gave up on him or got tired of taking care of him or something."

Mrs. Valenti grunted in concurrence as she swept the floor around the table. "He good dog."

"He is, isn't he?"

Since they'd come inside, the dog hadn't barked, hadn't messed or lifted his leg, hadn't jumped up on anything or anyone. He'd slurped down an entire bowl of water and when Natalie showed him the beef bone, he sat handsome and straight, waiting patiently for her to hand it over. He was as well behaved as he could possibly be, despite the fact that he glanced toward the door at regular intervals, as if expecting somebody to arrive looking for him.

Natalie felt a strange sort of kinship to the animal, not that she'd mention such a thing out loud because she knew it sounded hokey. But there was something about him. His icy blue eyes were kind and he hadn't exhibited even an inkling of an aggressive cell in his body. If anything, he projected hesitancy and loneliness, and despite all her pronouncements of how happy she was, Natalie could relate to both.

"We're kindred spirits, aren't we, buddy?" she whispered to him. He looked up at her and smacked his lips, making her grin.

❖

"Oh, my God, I think I'm in love." Andrea sat lounging on Natalie's futon in the small living area of the apartment above Valenti's. The dog was lying along her leg, his head resting on her torso in a pose that was both relaxed and protective. Andrea stroked her hand along his soft and silky fur.

"Isn't he amazing?" Natalie squinted at the monitor of her laptop, editing text on the flyer she was making. The ginger-peach candle that glowed softly next to her on the marred desk filled the room with a warm, cozy fragrance.

"I think you should just keep him."

"Much as I'd like to, I can't do that." Natalie grimaced because keeping the dog, which she had affectionately begun calling Chino in honor of Mrs. Valenti's color perceptions, was exactly what she wanted to do. He was sweet and lovable and she instantly enjoyed having him around. She suddenly felt needed. Guilt hung over her like a cloud because she had yet to call any of the local animal shelters to see if he'd been reported missing, even though she knew she should. But when she felt the guilt was about to get the better of her, she thought about when she found Chino a few days earlier and how skinny and hungry and dirty he'd been, how frightened and hesitant he'd been to have anything to do with a human being. He was obviously neglected, had been on his own for a while, and with no collar or tags, it wasn't likely that his owner was all that concerned about recovering him. Still, she felt she had to do *something*.

"What happened here?" Andrea ran gentle fingertips over Chino's back leg where a strip of gauze had been wrapped lovingly around it.

"When I got him in the tub, I noticed that. It's a cut or a bite of some kind. I wonder if he got into a fight or something."

"Did you call a vet?"

"Not yet. It wasn't that deep, just needed cleaning." She grimaced. "And vets are expensive."

"Mmm." Continuing her petting, Andrea remarked, "I can't get over how soft he is."

"Isn't he? Once I bathed him and brushed all the snarls out of his coat, he just glowed." She watched as Andrea stroked him and Chino burrowed closer to her. "He likes you."

"Of course he does."

Grinning at the unspoken "duh" in Andrea's tone, she continued to work as Andrea hummed softly along with the Diana Krall CD emanating from the small stereo on the bookshelf. Finally finishing with an exaggerated flourish, Natalie announced, "There. Done. What do you think?"

"Can't see it." Andrea grunted and pretended to crane her neck, but made no real move to get up and look.

"You're such a lazy ass." Natalie sighed and carried the laptop over to the futon where she knelt down next to it.

"I'm not lazy. Look at this." Andrea gestured to Chino, who had stretched his back legs out behind him and was sleeping comfortably against her. "Would you move if you were me?"

"No, probably not." Natalie stroked the dog's back as she held the laptop for Andrea to see.

The flyer was simple but complete. The phrase "dog found" was printed at the top in big, black capital letters across the top. Beneath it was a vague description of Chino, along with the general vicinity where Natalie had discovered him. She purposely left off such pertinent information as his eye color and small size.

"Where the hell is his picture?" Andrea asked. "Did I lug my digital camera over here for nothing?"

"Yep. Sorry about that. I decided not to include a picture. If his owner wants to claim him, they should be able to describe him to me well enough to prove to me that he's theirs, you know?"

"I guess that makes sense."

"It does." Natalie stood back up and popped her memory stick into the USB port to copy the flyer over to it. "Can you print ten or fifteen of these off for me tomorrow? Then I'll post them around the area, and wait and see what happens."

"I hope it doesn't work," Andrea said, bending awkwardly so she could place a kiss on Chino's furry head. His eyes opened just enough to take a quick glance around the room, then closed again as he sighed with great contentment. "I hope nobody claims him and you get to keep him."

Me, too, Andrea. Me, too. Natalie was too worried about what kind of person that made her to say it out loud.

CHAPTER FIVE

How could this have happened?

Sarah sat blinking in disbelief at her family, trying unsuccessfully to absorb and process what they'd told her.

How is it even possible?

Her mother was crying. She had been for a while. Her father looked worried and had his arm protectively around her mother's shoulders. Ricky looked sheepish. More than that, he looked guilty. As well he should. Sarah turned to glare at him and felt the tiniest sliver of satisfaction when he flinched, as if her gaze was physically sharp.

"You just…lost him? You *lost* him?"

Ricky swallowed. "I think so."

"You *think* so?"

"I came back here and he was just…gone." Her brother's eyes shifted, darted around the room, looked anywhere but at her deadly stare.

"He was just gone." Sarah almost curled her upper lip in a snarl.

"I don't know how he got out."

"No idea?"

"No."

"Uh-huh. And did you bother to look for him?"

Her father cut in, obviously seeing the violent path the conversation might possibly be taking. "We all did. Believe me, honey, we all did." Her mother stifled a small sob and her father tightened his hold on her. "We've searched high and low for weeks. We've called all the animal shelters half a dozen times. We've driven around and around every single night. We just…" He blew out a frustrated breath. "We haven't found a sign of him. He's just gone. We're so sorry, baby."

"I can't believe this." Sarah's anger left her in a whoosh as she absorbed the news that her dog had run away—or been stolen—over a month ago and not only was he nowhere to be found, but nobody had bothered to tell her. Her eyes filled with tears. "I wish you would have called me."

"So you could do what?" Her father's voice was gentle, but factual, and she knew he was right. What could she have done? Her job didn't allow her the time to fly home for anything less than a family emergency, and her missing dog would not have been considered such by the higher-ups at her company. So she would have been filled with worry, which would have taken her focus off her job and kept her from thinking of anything else. No, her father had been right not to call her. Had she been here, she wouldn't have done anything any differently than her family did and she most likely would have gotten the same results.

"I can't believe this," she said again, feeling suddenly deflated and completely, utterly helpless.

"Honey," her mother said, her voice cracking, "I am so, so sorry. I know you trusted us and we let you down and I don't know how we can ever apologize enough for that." The tremendous burden of guilt that sat on her looked so heavy, it would be obvious from across the street, and Sarah felt bad for being so angry. She knew her mother well and was certain this had been eating her alive since it happened and would continue to do so for a long time to come. She also knew her parents would never do anything to purposely hurt her, nor would Ricky, despite his lack of maturity or responsibility. It was evident that this had been some kind of fluke accident and her family had done everything in their power to repair it. Their efforts simply hadn't been enough.

Those facts didn't keep her heart from aching, though.

"I've got to get home. Unpack. Do laundry." She rubbed at her forehead. "I'm tired."

"I'm sorry, Sarah." Her mother's voice was barely a whisper.

"I know, Mom. I know."

Once back in her townhouse, Sarah felt like every ounce of energy had drained out of her and she flopped onto her leather couch, staring off into space. She really needed to get up and open a few windows to air the place out, but she just couldn't manage to summon the energy. Instead, she just sat.

She knew exactly what had happened, didn't need much of an explanation to figure it out. Bentley had wanted to get home, it was that simple. He'd been worried about her. She'd learned when she got him about the herding instincts of his breed, about his need to be aware of his herd at all times, how it was his job and was in his blood. After so long without her, he must have been a nervous wreck, feeling like he'd failed her. Her idiot brother had probably forgotten to latch the door properly, a bad habit he'd been guilty of since they were kids, and it wouldn't have taken long for Bentley to push his way through. The fact that Sarah had Bentley's collar tucked into her purse—Ricky had taken it off one night because Bentley was scratching and it made too much noise—only served to make her grind her back molars. Her brother was lucky she hadn't throttled him then and there in their parents' kitchen.

In the past twelve weeks, she'd become used to living completely alone, so she didn't feel the emptiness blast her the second she walked in the door without Bentley, and that surprised her. She'd left at the end of February. It was now the first week in June and things had changed for her, just as she'd hoped. She felt stronger. She felt slightly more in control of her life. She felt a little less vulnerable. Once she'd gotten past the idea of how much Karen would like the lush New Zealand countryside with its thick green forests and rocky, gorgeous beaches, she was able to push her ex into a dark corner of her mind and leave her there. To be honest, she hadn't even thought about Bentley all that much. She'd forced herself to focus on the job at hand and she'd done so quite well.

She dragged herself off the couch for the sole purpose of opening a bottle of wine—a nice, hearty red. Though gin and tonic was her cocktail of preference, she'd been surprised to find her latent enjoyment of wine brought to the fore during her trip. The wineries in New Zealand were really coming into their own and making big bucks, and Sarah had partaken of many, many wonderful Chardonnays and Sauvignon Blancs during her stay. But the climate there wasn't all that helpful when it came to growing the grapes needed for a good red, and though the vintners were working diligently on them, Sarah found herself missing some of the delicious Napa Valley Zinfandels she'd grown so fond of over the years. She poured herself a generous glass and admired the deep crimson color of it as she returned to the living room and sat down with a world-weary sigh.

Remarkably, Sarah had called Karen only once while she was away, and though she'd hung up like a coward the second Derek had answered, she was pretty proud of herself. She'd thrown herself into her work and—when she'd been able to sneak away without Patti knowing—she'd picked up a drink on occasion and a warm body once or twice. Yes, the trip had been very good for her, just as she'd hoped. She'd felt like she'd finally recaptured some of the control and direction of her life that she'd somehow misplaced after her breakup, like she was finally on her way back to being a woman she at least recognized.

It depressed her to understand that losing her dog made her feel uncomfortably like she'd taken a backward slide since returning home to upstate New York. She wasn't sure what to do with that.

❖

Sarah's return to work a few days later wasn't so much work related as welcome back related. There were flowers and cookies and balloons, and an overall feeling of celebration. She was genuinely touched by the thoughtfulness of her coworkers and they spent the majority of the day asking her questions, both business and personal, about the exotic country of New Zealand, what she'd learned, whom she'd met, what she'd eaten and drunk, and what it was all like. Having gone a little crazy with the digital camera she'd purchased specifically for the trip, she hesitantly showed them some of her pictures, all the while being painfully cognizant of the possibility of becoming a tourist stereotype, boring people to tears with endless photographs and stories. At least she wasn't subjecting them to a slide show.

Patti was excited to share her adventures with the staff and did so in the shy, somewhat uncertain way she did most things. Sarah's previous secretary had retired a little over a year ago, an old battle-axe of a woman who took no prisoners and practically finished Sarah's sentences, and Sarah had hated to see her go. She was replaced by Patti just as Sarah's relationship with Karen was reaching critical mass, her life spiraling out of control. Patti was the niece of the founder of the company, but despite the obvious nepotism, she had promise. She just needed some intense training in the ways of Corporate America and a little polishing in the department of Business Savvy. Sarah'd had no qualms about taking her on as an assistant because she could see the potential shimmering just below the surface. Unfortunately, she'd barely had the energy or the willpower to drag herself from home into her office. There was no way she was up for endless hours of training with her support staff. Karen's departure had completely drained her, and poor Patti had been dropped into a position where her boss was preoccupied a good percentage of the time. To her credit, she'd managed to teach herself a lot of things and she'd kept herself and Sarah afloat while Sarah had worked on recovering. For the first time in a year, Sarah entertained the idea of actually thanking her admin for hanging in there when she was certain many others would have thrown in the towel.

Back in the present, Patti was going on about some park she'd discovered on her own one Sunday when Sarah "didn't answer her phone for some reason." Only from months of practice was Sarah able to school her expression and keep from looking as guilty as she sometimes felt about evading the poor woman, but it wasn't easy.

Thank God for Caller ID, she remembered thinking more than once during the last three months. *Whoever invented that was a friggin' genius.* Then she felt guilty again.

It wasn't until the day was coming to a close that she finally had a chance to sit at her desk in her own empty office. She was suddenly bone tired with the annoying beginnings of a killer headache gnawing at the outer reaches of her awareness. As she spun in her chair and fumbled in the top drawer of her credenza for the trusty bottle of Motrin, her gaze landed on the framed 8x10 perched on the mahogany surface. Stopping the search for ibuprofen, she simply looked, her eyes running over every curve of Karen's smiling face, the sun-kissed bronze color of her skin, the way the sun caught the red highlights in her hair. Next to her was Bentley, his tongue lolling out of his mouth, the expression on his face as close to happiness as a dog's could get. Sarah remembered the day as clearly as if it had been yesterday and not three years earlier. They'd been on a walk through the park. Bentley was just a puppy, but that was the day they realized how smart and obedient he was. Against Sarah's wishes, Karen had taken him off his lead and thrown a tennis ball for him. He ran, fetched it, and brought it right back to her over and over and over, as if it never once occurred to him to run off into the nearby woods to explore or sprint up to the other visitors in the park and jump on them to get some attention. Sarah had been experimenting with a new camera and had snapped dozens of photos, but this one had been the best. It was as if she'd caught them both unawares, Karen hugging Bentley with such pride and love, and Bentley looking like he was actually smiling. Sarah had immediately had the snapshot enlarged and professionally framed, and here it had sat ever since.

Chewing on her bottom lip, Sarah ran a finger along the glass, tracing Karen's face, then Bentley's ear, certain that if she concentrated hard enough, she could actually feel the texture of each. Then she blew out a breath of utter exhaustion and shook her head. *What the hell am I doing? They're both gone.* Long ago, she had vowed to stop being one of those pathetic people who wallowed, who couldn't let go, who refused to move on from their heartbreak, and she was disgusted with herself for taking even one step down that path. Despite a detailed list of every pound and organization her parents had contacted, Sarah had contacted them all again, hoping against hope that somebody had her dog. Every avenue had led her to a dead end, with no sign of Bentley. She knew she had to try to convince herself that he now had a good home with somebody who loved him. It was the only thing that brought her even a modicum of peace. With a growl, she quickly tossed the picture into a drawer and pushed it shut with a slam, wishing there was some way she could close the door on her past once and for all.

"Everything okay?"

The voice startled Sarah and she flinched in her chair before spinning back around to face the front and the concerned visage of her boss, Regina Danvers, who stood in the doorway. As always, Regina was impeccably dressed in a chocolate brown pantsuit, her auburn hair pulled back into a French twist.

"Yes." Sarah pasted a smile onto her face. "Everything's great."

"Your first day back go all right?"

"Fine. Just fine."

"Well, we missed you around here, but word is you did a fantastic job overseas." Regina tossed her a genuine smile and

Sarah suddenly felt like a third grader who'd just pleased her favorite teacher. "It seems like the Sarah Buchanan we know and love might actually be back, hmm?"

Before Sarah could respond, her intercom buzzed and Patti's voice came on the line. "Sarah?"

"Yes, Patti?" She shot an apologetic look at Regina, who simply smiled knowingly.

"A bunch of us are going to happy hour across the street at Joe's. Want to go?"

Sarah forced herself to wait a couple seconds to give the impression she was at least thinking about it. "You know, Patti, I'm really tired. I think I'm just going to go home tonight. But thanks."

"Oh." Patti tried unsuccessfully to hide her disappointment. Then she perked right back up. "Well, I guess I'll have to be the one to talk about being a Kiwi for three months."

"You do that," Sarah said, pushing the button to end the call. She turned her gaze back to her boss. "Sorry about that. She forgets to check and make sure I'm not with somebody before she starts talking. We're working on that."

"Is she driving you nuts?" Regina's eyes twinkled in amusement.

Sarah shook her head and smiled good-naturedly. "No. No, not at all. She's doing fine. Just needs some fine-tuning."

"As I was saying, word on the street is that you went above and beyond overseas." As she turned to look toward Patti's empty workstation, she added, "And I imagine you did the majority of the work single-handedly."

Sensing Regina's disapproval of the way Patti had gotten her job, Sarah tried to defend her admin without sounding like she was doing so. "Actually, we worked quite well together."

"Well." Regina focused on Sarah with such intensity, Sarah had to fight the urge to squirm. "Nicely done. The managers are impressed. I wanted you to know that it's nice to have you back."

Certain that the line held a double meaning but too tired to ask, Sarah inclined her head once in gratitude. “Thank you, Regina. I appreciate that.”

“Now, go home. You look exhausted.” Regina waved a hand at her as she turned away. “And stop worrying about your ex. You can do far better. It’s her loss.” With that, she was gone, her heels clicking a staccato rhythm down the hall until they faded away completely.

Sarah sat blinking, replaying the last three minutes in her head. *Her loss, huh?* Though Sarah certainly didn’t hide her sexuality in the workplace, she’d never realized that Regina Danvers paid even the slightest bit of attention to the personal lives of her employees. That she not only knew about Sarah’s preferences but seemed up to date on the status of her relationship made her feel something she couldn’t put her finger on. Flattered? Proud? Embarrassed?

Seems like the Sarah Buchanan we all know and love might actually be back, hmm?

Sarah knew she didn’t have the energy to analyze exactly what Regina was saying. Truth be told, it wasn’t all that hard to figure out considering Sarah had spent a good six months of the last year as a shell of her former self. Now she felt like she might actually be taking some baby steps toward the tough, successful woman she’d once been. *Finally.* Were other people noticing as well?

Regardless, Regina was right about one thing. It *was* Karen’s loss. And it was high time Sarah started thinking that way, too.

CHAPTER SIX

The long July Fourth weekend was upon Sarah before she even realized it, but she was relieved, which was very unlike her. In the past, she'd never looked forward to time off, had never planned vacations ahead of time. Karen had always tried to get her to be more spontaneous, but her attempts were fruitless most of the time. Sarah wasn't one for surprises. She needed to be fully aware of everything going on around her. But here she was now, alone. She had three days off and she was free to do whatever she wanted. Her parents were having a cookout on Saturday and she would go to that, but otherwise, she had nothing planned. It was a fact that would have freaked her out completely less than a year ago, because back then, she was a woman who had to have each day planned down to the second, and most of it involved work. But when Karen left, Sarah found herself to be a woman with no plan, and that had scared her to death.

Now the quiet pleasure she felt at the idea of having time to herself surprised her. Maybe she'd go see a movie. Maybe she'd go shopping or hit the Memorial Art Gallery. Maybe she'd lose herself in a good book. The possibilities were endless, and for the first time in as far back as she could remember, she was looking forward to just playing it by ear. It was a very different feeling for her and she wanted to sit with it a while, turn it around in her mind, really study it.

Friday was beautiful. Not too hot, not too cold, not a cloud in the sky, a great day to have off from work. Pulling her bike out of the back storage area was something Sarah hadn't done in ages. She wasn't even certain whether or not she'd done any riding last summer, though she had her doubts. If memory served, last summer had been spent moping, crying, and living in a general state of self-pity. She grabbed a wet cloth from the kitchen and gave the bike a thorough wipe-down, eliminating the accumulation of dust, cobwebs, and dead spiders, and feeling a strange sensation of anticipation. She'd always loved to go bike riding when she was younger because it was a great way for her to clear her head. She'd purchased this bike expressly for that reason and had hardly ridden it. *That's about to change*, she thought with determination as she swabbed the last vestiges of storage off the metal and chrome. The deep green color of it sparkled, and she had the weird sensation that the bike was happy to see her. It could probably use a good tune-up and Sarah made a mental note to drop it the following week at the local bike shop where she'd purchased it.

Rather than allowing it to collect insect fossils like the bike, Sarah stored her matching green helmet in the hall closet. She retrieved it and strapped it on, tucking her hair in as best she could and avoiding mirrors at all costs. She knew wearing it was a necessity, especially when riding in traffic. She also knew that if she caught a glimpse of her own reflection, she'd feel like she had a salad bowl buckled to her head and take it off immediately.

After locking the front door and the back, she pocketed the key and set off for a nice, relaxing ride around town.

The location of Sarah's townhouse complex was ideal. Technically "in the city," it felt more like the suburbs, with lots of trees and quiet cross streets, but she was, quite literally, ten minutes from everything. The art gallery, the George Eastman

House, the Rochester Museum and Science Center, the Little Theater, Park Avenue, the planetarium, Cobbs Hill Park—everything was within a quick walk or drive, and Sarah wouldn't have it any other way. Rochester wasn't a big city, but it had a lot to offer and access was a cinch. She'd decided to zigzag up and down some of the neighborhood streets of the Park Avenue/Monroe Avenue area before stopping off to grab some lunch or something when the mood hit.

The houses there were old and huge and gorgeous. If she were the handywoman type, the type who could build things and fix things and design things, she wouldn't think twice about finding a house in the area to remodel and live in. They were so large that most were either broken into apartments or split in two so the owner could live on the second and third floors and rent out the first floor to a tenant. There were issues, of course. Most were poorly insulated and had old windows and doors, so heating and cooling could get expensive. They were old structures, so oftentimes the repairs needed to keep the houses safe could be outrageously expensive. Those that boasted garages had ones that were in serious disrepair. But these houses also had beauty and character and loads of charm, and as Sarah coasted easily up one street and down another, taking in the leaded glass windows, original chimneys, and carved wooden porch railings, she thought this was the most magnificent area around, glorious and elegant.

They just don't build homes like this anymore.

After more than an hour, when she started to feel slightly fatigued, it occurred to her that she should be sure not to overdo it. It had been a long time since she'd taxed her leg muscles, even gently, and she didn't want to end up so sore tomorrow that she could barely move. Making a right turn onto Monroe, she decided to grab a snack and sit at an outside table to enjoy the sunshine. She locked her bike to the steel rack next to a telephone pole and headed into Valenti's.

Cinnamon seemed to coat her like an invisible snow, filling

her nostrils with the warm, homey scent that took her immediately back to her childhood. Her mother used to make her cinnamon toast when she was a kid, and the smell of it would always remind her of those carefree days. She inhaled deeply, a sudden relaxation falling over her as she strode toward the counter.

"Hi, there." The cute girl at the counter did a double take and then looked genuinely pleased to see her, which made Sarah smile, as she felt the same way. "I didn't recognize you out of your business suit. Out for a ride?"

Realizing belatedly that she still had her stupid helmet on, Sarah fiddled with the buckle and removed the cap quickly, smoothing her hair and hoping it wasn't too much of a rat's nest. "Yeah, it's a gorgeous day." She felt suddenly self-conscious.

"The usual?" The girl's rosy streak was darker than Sarah remembered the last time she'd been in, but the rest of her hair was the same light chestnut and had gotten a little bit longer. She looked good, Sarah realized, surprised by the tingle it caused. She looked very good. The girl's eyes searched Sarah's warmly, waiting for a response.

"That'd be great. And I need one of those cinnamon rolls, too." Sarah gestured to the glass case where a dozen rolls sat, their white frosting dripping slowly off the sides. They looked sinfully delicious.

"Oh, good choice," the girl said from the coffee machine. "Mr. Valenti just brought them out of the oven about ten minutes ago. I may have one myself." Then she winked.

Feeling herself blush, Sarah turned away and looked around the small shop, noting that it was fairly quiet at the moment. She was used to being there at the peak of the morning rush, zipping in and zipping out, and she'd never really taken the time to check things out. It was a long, narrow space, which had worked well when it had been a deli. Tables lined the wall on the right, and the counter and bakery case were on the left. The floor was a durable beige tile that probably cleaned easily, and the walls were decorated with old signage from classic baking materials like flour and brown sugar. It was a simple yet tasteful décor, and Sarah gave it a mental nod of approval.

"I haven't seen you around in a while," the girl said, bringing Sarah's attention back to the matter at hand.

"Oh." Sarah handed over a five. "I was out of town on business for a couple months. I just got back a few weeks ago. I guess I haven't quite gotten back into my old routine yet."

"Well, I missed seeing your smiling face."

At that, Sarah did smile.

"See? Now all is right in the world." As the girl grinned and handed Sarah her change, somebody called out something in Italian from the back of the shop. She grimaced. "Duty calls." Nodding at the goods on the counter in front of Sarah, she said, "Enjoy." And she was gone, leaving Sarah grinning like an idiot who'd just been sprinkled with fairy dust.

Balancing her coffee, cinnamon roll, and bike helmet was no easy feat, but Sarah managed to get out the door without dropping any of them. Finding an empty outdoor table, she took a seat and spent some time just watching the world go by. To say the street wasn't busy would be an untruth, but there was definitely a different attitude in the air and it was obvious that many of the strolling pedestrians were not working today. The pace was more relaxed, the laughter was more plentiful and spontaneous, and the atmosphere was one of general happiness. Sarah sipped her coffee and chewed her cinnamon roll and marveled over how she'd never noticed such things before—mainly because she'd never taken the time to. She wasn't really sure what had changed in her lately, but she seemed to be paying more attention to smaller things, slowing down a little bit, trying to no longer be the kind of person who wants nothing more than to get from Point A to Point B as quickly and efficiently as possible.

A woman walked by pushing a stroller. A couple strolled along, hand in hand. A young man passed with his Rottweiler, who took a sniff in Sarah's direction as he went by, his sleek, black fur shining in the sun. Sarah followed him with her eyes, suddenly missing Bentley and wondering if she would ever be ready to get another dog. Her gaze stopped at the telephone pole that stood near the bike rack and she squinted against the glare of the daylight. Shading her eyes with her hand, she saw the words: DOG FOUND.

Moving closer for a better look, she saw that the sheet of paper stapled to the pole was a makeshift flyer of some sort. It was battered and faded and she wondered how long it had been there. She could make out most of the verbiage, as well as the phone number to call at the bottom. The details were vague. It basically just said this person had found a male dog and to call if you thought he might be yours.

"I suppose keeping a description a secret would keep the crazies from claiming him," she muttered aloud. Tugging gently, she pulled the flyer down and read it again. Her parents lived in Penfield. Though it wasn't more than a twenty-minute drive from where she stood, she found it hard to believe that there was any way Bentley could have run away from their house and made it this far. With a sigh, she folded the paper up and stuck it in her pocket anyway. She had no illusions that this would have anything at all to do with her dog, but she knew if she didn't at least give it a shot, she'd wonder forever if she should have. Besides, what would it hurt to call?

❖

The tattered sheet of paper sat on Sarah's dining room table for most of the weekend. Every time she walked by, she glanced at it, but for some reason, she couldn't seem to bring herself to simply make the call.

What the hell is wrong with me?

She wasn't sure exactly what the issue was. It was nothing

more than a phone call. Maybe she was worried that she'd get her hopes up? She had done a pretty reasonable job getting used to Bentley's absence. She supposed she might have an underlying concern that she'd slide backward, fall back into the depression that had threatened to overtake her at the realization of her complete aloneness. It made sense. It did. She was sure any therapist worth her salt would agree.

So just make the damn call already.

With a grunt of determination, she picked up the handset of her cordless phone. It was Sunday evening and she'd stared at the beaten-up piece of paper for more than two days. It was time. She dialed.

❖

"You are such a good boy, Chino." Natalie smiled exuberantly at the little dog, then giggled as the fur on his backside began to shake, indicating that he was wagging his nub of a tail. They had just returned from an afternoon of romping in the park, and Natalie had decided to try taking the dog off the leash for the first time. She suspected he was some kind of herding dog, judging from his coloring and his build, and she hoped he'd stick around. Much to her delight, he'd never left her side, except for when she threw the ball for him to fetch. He brought it right back to her every time and she praised him with enthusiasm. Once or twice, he'd noticed another dog or a person who, for whatever reason, interested him, and he stopped what he was doing and focused on them. Natalie gave a firm warning of, "No, Chino. Stay." It seemed to work.

As she refilled her water bottle in the kitchen sink and tucked it into the small fridge, she noticed her answering machine light blinking a bright red. She took a modest piece of beef bone from the freezer and set Chino up on a large towel on the floor, hoping to protect the throw rug from meat stains.

"Here you go, buddy. For being so good today." The dog went to town, gnawing and smacking as he enjoyed his treat, his stumpy tail still wagging furiously. Hitting Play on the machine, Natalie said to him, "I bet it's Aunt Andrea."

She was wrong and she frowned when she didn't recognize the voice.

"Hi, my name is Sarah Buchanan and I saw your flyer this weekend about the dog you found. I have no idea if he could be mine, but I thought I'd give it a shot. My dog ran away from my parents' place in Penfield about three months ago. He's a miniature Australian shepherd, maybe twenty-five pounds. He's a blue merle, which means his fur is a multicolor mix of white, black, brown, and gray. One ear is solid black and the other is sort of gray and sticks up a little bit. And he's got beautiful blue eyes." The woman paused, seemed to collect herself. "Anyway, if you still have him and he fits this description, would you please call me?" She left her name again and her number and the machine clicked, signifying the end of the message.

Natalie swallowed, a sudden discomfort settling in the pit of her stomach. She looked over at Chino, who was chewing happily across the room, and absently wondered if dogs recognized voices after long periods of time. He didn't seem to be paying her any mind and for that, Natalie was grateful.

My dog ran away from my parents' place in Penfield about three months ago.

"Well, how irresponsible are you and your parents?" Natalie said aloud to nobody. "I mean, seriously. Three months ago?" She did some quick math in her head and realized that Chino would have been on his own, wandering around the city with no food or water at his disposal, for over two weeks before she found him. No wonder he was so frightened.

The smell of beef assaulted her as she stretched herself out on the floor next to him and stroked his fur as he chewed. After a couple minutes, he shifted slightly and adjusted his positioning so she couldn't quite reach him, making her laugh. "Oh, excuse me, Mr. I'm Chewing a Bone Right Now So Don't Bug Me by Petting Me. Forgive me for distracting you." Becoming serious again, she sighed as she watched him, thinking how much she adored having him around, how much he'd brought to her over the past two months. She'd never had a dog growing up, and though she came from a loving home with wonderful parents, she'd never really fully grasped the concept of unconditional love until she had Chino in her life. Now she got it, got what dog lovers were always talking about. Chino didn't care if she was in a rotten mood or had PMS or bad breath. He loved her regardless, without limits and without specifics, and she was loath to give that up, especially as she was just beginning to get used to it.

The ringing of the phone saved her from more wallowing, but then her heart began to pound. What if it was this Sarah Buchanan again? Cursing herself for being too budget-conscious to splurge on Caller ID, she held her breath until the machine picked up.

"Hey, it's me." Andrea's voice filled the room and Natalie exhaled in relief. "Where are you? Pick up."

Natalie snatched up the handset. "I'm here."

"You're screening? That's new."

"Yeah, well, I just walked in."

"I'm coming over. What do you feel like on your pizza?"

Forty-five minutes later, they sat in Natalie's tiny living room, stuffing themselves with a mushroom-and-green-pepper pie and replaying Sarah Buchanan's answering machine message.

Andrea grimaced. "Maybe it's not him."

Natalie blinked at her.

"Okay, okay. It is him. Those ears are a dead giveaway. But…it's been three months. *Three months*. And remember what kind of shape he was in when you found him."

"I know. I can't get it out of my head."

"How do we know she's not abusive to him? I mean, how do we know *she's* not the one who starved him? Maybe she's some whacko, animal-cruelty person."

"Anything's possible." Natalie studied Chino as she chewed her pizza. He dozed contentedly on the braided rug at their feet. "He doesn't even beg. He's so good."

"He is." Andrea rubbed her bare toes over his silky fur and he sighed.

"He sits, he lies down, he shakes hands, he comes when he's called."

"He's a miracle doggie."

"My point is somebody trained him. Somebody—probably this Sarah Buchanan—spent time and energy teaching him. Does that sound like an abusive person?"

Shifting on the futon so she faced her, Andrea stared at her for several long beats. "You know what sounds abusive to me? Leaving your beloved pet in the hands of an idiot stupid enough not only to allow it to run away, but then not be able to find it. Given all the technology and animal rights activists today willing to help, don't you think they could have looked a little harder for him?"

Natalie scratched at her forehead. She knew Andrea was trying to help. She also knew Andrea loved Chino as much as she did and was unwilling to give him up. When she finally spoke, her voice was soft and pained. "What kind of person does this make me? If I keep this woman's dog from her, what does that make me?"

"Sweetie, look at me." When Natalie obeyed, Andrea continued. "It makes you somebody who cares about the welfare of this animal. He was starving, Natty. *Starving*. He was filthy. His leg was gashed open. He was terrified. He'd been on his own for a long time. You rescued him. You *saved* him."

"Yeah, I guess."

"He loves you. You deserve him."

Natalie wasn't sure she looked totally convinced and Andrea confirmed that by jumping up and crossing the room to the answering machine. With one swift push of a button, the machine's robotic voice announced, "Message erased."

"Andrea!" Natalie's eyes were wide with disbelief.

Lifting one shoulder in a half-shrug, Andrea responded, "There."

"I can't believe you just did that."

"Now you don't have her number and you can't call her back. She probably won't call you again, so it's done. Everything's fine. Okay?" She returned to the futon and plopped down. "Have some more pizza. You shouldn't be skinnier than me. I had cancer, remember?"

CHAPTER SEVEN

Sarah's feel-good attitude lasted slightly longer than a week. Work had become nuts, and she always found herself the most depressed when she worked late and came home to a dark and empty house. It never failed to cause an ache in the pit of her stomach and send her scrambling to the liquor cabinet to mix herself a Bombay and tonic. It had happened almost every night this week.

On Saturday, Sarah slammed the phone down, annoyed by her own annoyance and trying not to notice that her temper seemed to be getting shorter and shorter by the day. She was starting to feel like her old self—and not in a good way. She wanted to be able to control everything around her and she couldn't, and it was driving her crazy.

Who the hell does this Natalie person think she is anyway?

She'd left five messages for the woman—named Natalie according to her answering machine—who had posted the flyer about the dog she'd found. Five messages in less than a week. Now it was Saturday and not one of them had been acknowledged, no return phone calls, and Sarah was irritated that the woman didn't even have the decency to call back and say, "Sorry, not your dog."

In reality, the dog was probably not Bentley. She knew that and she wanted to be able to just leave it alone and let it go. She'd even been checking the newspaper for ads with puppies for sale, thinking that maybe if she got another one, she could eliminate the niggling feeling about Bentley that she couldn't explain. And maybe she could stop calling this poor woman.

On the other hand, who didn't return a phone call like that? There was something a little fishy, some kind of weird inkling that she couldn't seem to shake, and it had been driving her nuts for several days now. Suddenly flashing on an idea, she took the steps of her townhouse two at a time and entered the third bedroom that she used as an office.

Aside from her own bedroom, this room was the one that looked the most lived in, the most comfortable, probably because she spent the most time in it. Her plan had always been to work on the rest of the house in order to give it the same warm appeal. The office got a ton of sunlight, so she had several plants scattered about. The personal, cozy touches—like family photographs on shelves and throw pillows for the overstuffed reading chair in the corner—were things she wanted to spread around the rest of the place, but just hadn't gotten to. Every time she entered the office, she kicked herself for not following through, it was such a snug and relaxing room in which to be.

Falling into her big leather desk chair with a sigh, she squinted at the computer monitor and moved the mouse to wake things up. Clicking to Google, she typed in the phone number from the flyer. The information came up so quickly, Sarah blinked at it for several seconds, stunned by how easy it was to track somebody down.

Natalie Fox. 217 Monroe Avenue, Apartment 1, Rochester, NY 14607.

She was even more astounded to see the little "map" icon next to the address. She moved the mouse and clicked on it.

Within two seconds, a detailed map to Natalie Fox's residence popped up.

"Good Lord, is it really this easy to stalk somebody?"

she asked aloud, appalled by the facts and shaking her head in disbelief. "That's *so* scary."

Despite her distaste, she found herself printing the map. Maybe she'd just go have a quick look. She didn't want to actually knock on the door. That would be creepy and she didn't want to frighten the poor woman. But maybe she'd just go peek, take a ride over on her bike and see what she could see about this Natalie Fox. If she got lucky, maybe she'd find the answer to why the woman couldn't return a simple phone call. At least it would keep her occupied for a while, give her something to do on a balmy Saturday evening.

❖

"You've got to be kidding me," Sarah muttered to herself. "What are the chances?"

217 Monroe Avenue turned out to be Valenti's. She coasted to a stop on her bike and stood there looking at the shop, which was closed, and the small two-one-seven stenciled on the window above the glass door.

Her gaze traveled upward to the floor above the coffee shop. *That's got to be where Natalie Fox lives. Okay, Nancy Drew, what are you going to do now?* She rolled her eyes at herself.

Monroe Avenue was bustling on this weekend evening, people strolling the blocks, entering or exiting various restaurants, sitting at outside tables with bottles of beer and glasses of wine. It was a festive, happy atmosphere, as residents soaked up the too-short summer weekends. Wheeling her bicycle across the street, Sarah found an unoccupied black metal table outside an ice cream parlor. Toeing the kickstand, she propped the bike nearby, took a seat, and set her helmet on the surface in front of her, trying to ignore the fact that she was actually staking somebody out. She had no idea what the hell she was doing. Having nary a clue as to what the person looked like made spying on them just a tad difficult, but for some reason, Sarah felt the need to sit and wait. She knew it was stupid, knew she was being ridiculous and wasting her own time, but the weather was nice, the people-watching was interesting, and she really had nothing better to do. So she sat.

When the intoxicating aromas drifting through the air from the Italian trattoria a few doors down had her worried that she might actually drool all over the front of her shirt, she scooted into the ice cream parlor and got herself a chocolate almond cone that was magnificent and heavenly. She sat back down to savor the flavor combination of the sweet ice cream and the salty nuts, and that's when she saw them.

Or rather, that's when she saw Bentley.

He came walking out from around an alley that apparently led to the back of Valenti's. He was on a leash and was walking with two women who were chattering to each other and had smiles on their faces.

Standing up so fast that her ice cream rubbed against the front of her and left a long, brown streak on her shirt, Sarah race-walked across the street, narrowly avoiding getting flattened by a FedEx truck, the driver of which laid on his horn for an unnecessarily long beat. Glancing over her shoulder, she was painfully aware that her bike was unlocked, but she couldn't stop. People had turned to look when the horn honked, including the women walking Bentley. As Sarah got closer, she recognized one of the women, and her feet faltered as if trying all on their own to stop her progress.

The counter girl from Valenti's—the one with the pink streak—looked uncertain and then smiled. "Oh, hey," she said, furrowing her brow, probably at Sarah's agitated state as well as the chocolate ice cream on her chest that must have made her look like a five-year-old. She cocked her head to the side and began to ask a question. "Are you o—"

"That's my dog," Sarah blurted, pointing at Bentley.

The kind expression slid right off the girl's face as if made of wet paint, and suddenly changed to worry and near panic. Before she could respond, her companion stepped directly in front of her, eyes glaring, nostrils flared. She was taller than the coffee shop girl, and she waved her on.

"Keep walking, Natty."

Natalie did as she was told, albeit hesitantly, coaxing Bentley along with her, glancing over her shoulder more than once with an apprehensive grimace.

The taller woman suddenly filled Sarah's vision, preventing Sarah from following by using her body as a roadblock. The way she protected the coffee shop girl and turned on Sarah made her seem even bigger and broader than her slender frame suggested. Despite her attractive features, everything about her screamed *Back off!* and her casual Abercrombie and Fitch outfit seemed more like body armor. The look on her face actually made Sarah pull up short. Not one to be easily intimidated, Sarah simply blinked at her in confusion.

"That's my dog," she said again, trying to keep her voice steady, even though she felt a weird combination of joy, panic, anger, and fear.

"I don't think so." The woman's voice was a near growl. "You certainly don't deserve to have him. Do you have any idea what kind of shape he was in when Natalie found him? Do you?" Her dark eyes flashed with fury and she spoke through clenched teeth, her voice low enough so passersby couldn't hear her, but vicious enough to keep Sarah rooted to her spot on the sidewalk.

"I was away," Sarah said. "Overseas. For work." She sounded pathetic even to her own ears.

"Yeah? Well while you were away? Overseas? For work? That dog was on the street. He was starving. He had no water. He got in fights. His hair was missing in clumps. His leg was sliced open. He was afraid of people. And did I mention the starving part?"

Sarah swallowed down the bile rising in her throat. "It wasn't my fault," she said, her voice like a small child's. "I…my brother…" Her voice trailed off. "It wasn't my fault," she said again, this time with even less conviction.

"It was somebody's. Natalie found him. She fed him. She nursed him back to health. She loved him. She put up flyers to find his owner. And you know what happened? Nothing. And tthree months have gone by and now? That is *her* dog. Her. Dog. He's happy with her and *she* deserves him." Stepping another inch closer, she poked Sarah in the chest as she snarled, "You leave her alone." She turned and left so quickly that Sarah wasn't sure she'd even seen her go. She was just—not there anymore.

Head spinning, Sarah stood on the sidewalk, ice cream all over her shirt, hair matted from her bike helmet, and watched as the taller woman jogged to catch up with Natalie and Bentley. Both woman and dog glanced over their shoulders as they continued on. Both looked worried.

What the hell just happened?

It was the only thought in Sarah's head. Her feet seemingly fused to the cement, she could do nothing but stand there like an idiot and shake her head in disbelief.

What the hell just happened?

❖

"I really should call her."

"No," Andrea said, her tone firm. "No, you shouldn't. And stop it. You look like a little old lady. Plus, you're weirding him out."

Natalie was nervously pacing the floor of her apartment, wringing her hands. Chino was obviously picking up on the tension, because though he was seemingly lounging on the futon with Andrea, his stance was bowstring taut and it was clear that he could spring to his feet in a split second. Natalie went to him, ruffled his fur, and kissed the top of his head.

"It's okay, buddy. I'm sorry if I'm acting strange." She

looked up at Andrea as she continued, "It's not every day that I steal somebody's dog."

"You didn't *steal* him." Andrea's voice was surprisingly gentle, especially given that Natalie was expecting to be scolded. "He was hurt. He was lost. He was hungry. You took him in, you fed him, you took fantastic care of him, like he was your own, and you loved him. And you know what? After a certain amount of time, that makes him yours."

"I don't know, Andrea." Andrea had always been the stronger one, since as far back as Natalie could remember. Though Natalie would never consider herself a pushover by any means, she was the quieter and more polite one who preferred not to rock the boat. Andrea was the outspoken one who would never allow herself or her friends to be taken advantage of, no matter what. Most of the time, Natalie wished she had the balls Andrea did, that she wasn't the kind of person who always thought twice before speaking her mind, especially if the result would be to piss somebody off. But there were also times that she felt Andrea went too far, spoke too harshly, like today. The look on Sarah Buchanan's face was a combination of surprise and hurt that Natalie could see clearly even from down the street, and when she thought back on it, her stomach did flip-flops of nerves and guilt. She shook her head now as she took a seat next to Chino so he was sandwiched between the two women. His body language changed immediately and she could feel him relax. Natalie wished she could do the same thing, but the uncertainty was still coursing rapidly through her veins.

"See?" Andrea gestured to the dog, as if to prove her point. "Look at how much better he feels with you sitting by him." On cue, Chino settled his chin on Natalie's thigh and she couldn't help but laugh.

"Oh, very subtle. She is so coaching you, isn't she?"

He responded by sighing.

"Nice," Andrea said with a laugh. "Way to blow me in."

They sat in companionable silence for long moments, each lost in her own thoughts. Then Andrea snorted.

"What?" Natalie asked, wanting to be in on the joke.

"I'm still trying to absorb the fact that it was Hot Business Exec."

"God, I totally forgot, it's all been so crazy."

"I mean, what are the odds? Really?"

"Very, very slim."

"I guess I've blown any chance of asking her out, huh?"

"Um, yeah." Natalie gave her a sly grin. "I'd say that's a given."

"It's really too bad. She looked great in her biking attire."

It was true. Natalie couldn't pretend she hadn't noticed. Though she was a complete sucker for a woman in a business suit, she had to admit Sarah Buchanan painted a delectable picture in snug shorts and T-shirt. Mentally playing back the sight, Natalie let her eyes roam upward from the white sneakers to the bare legs that were long and sexy, despite needing a little more sun, to the torso that said Sarah kept herself in shape. Her tummy was flat and her hips pleasantly curved in exactly the right way. The cotton pulled just enough across her chest to convey that her breasts might be a bit more of a handful than expected—something that made Natalie bite her lip in anticipation. The pained expression on Sarah's face, however, stopped the cerebral once-over so quickly, Natalie was surprised she didn't hear the sound effect of a screeching halt.

As if reading her thoughts, which she did far too often and with way too much accuracy, Andrea squeezed Natalie's shoulder. "Stop worrying. It's all right."

Digging her fingers into the thick fur around Chino's neck, Natalie wanted to ask him, wished he would answer her, tell her what to do. *I don't know, Chino. Is this right? How can it be? She doesn't seem like the kind of person to abuse an animal. Maybe her story is true. Who am I to decide she's a liar? What makes me better than her?* Try as she might to channel her thoughts into Chino's head, to make him understand her, he remained in the same position. His head rested warmly on her thigh and his eyes drifted closed as she massaged him. *Yeah, you're a big damn help*, she thought with a sigh.

Chapter Eight

Sarah was unraveling fast. She could feel it.

Her precarious grip on her control was slipping just as obviously as if she'd been dangling from a cliff face and felt the rock skidding under her fingertips and cutting into her skin. The more determinedly she tried to convince herself she was fine, the louder the voice in her head screamed, "You're losing your mind!" She felt wobbly and unbalanced, like her solid life had gone from being made of stone to being made of water and, try as she might, she couldn't keep her fingers pressed tightly enough together to keep it from seeping out of her hands and onto the floor with a messy splash.

Things had been going so well. The past few weeks, she'd finally started to feel like herself again, not some shell of the woman she'd been before Karen left. Losing Bentley had been a blow—to her identity as much as anything else—but she had picked herself up and trudged forward, hard as it had been, and for that, she was proud. She'd been learning to relax, to ease up, to take deep breaths every now and then.

But now…

Who does this Natalie Fox think she is? You don't get to just take somebody's dog, for Christ's sake. That's called stealing, plain and simple. And what's with the damn bodyguard? She shook her head, disgusted with herself, as she recalled how thoroughly the dark-haired woman had held control of things, how small she'd made Sarah feel. Very few people in the world had ever been allowed to do that, and Sarah was embarrassed now that she'd let a total stranger make her feel like crap on the street in the space of a few small seconds.

Proof.

That's what she needed. She needed the correct papers to prove that Bentley was hers. Scrunching up her face, she tried to remember if Karen had taken that batch of files or if she still had them upstairs in the file drawer. Regardless, she definitely had receipts from vet bills. Would those work? Maybe. Maybe not. The receipt of sale from when they'd actually purchased Bentley would be better. Wouldn't it? *Should have had him microchipped when I had the chance.* Having to prove that her own dog was, in fact, hers was beginning to grate on her. Rubbing angrily at her forehead, she wondered if she should call a lawyer. Immediately assaulted by visions of her hard-earned money flying right out the window in alarmingly large denominations, she thought better of that idea, at least for the time being.

At the liquor cabinet, she pulled out the Bombay and fixed herself a ridiculously strong drink, not happy about it but feeling the undeniable need for it in order to calm her nerves as well as the ire that was making her hands shake. As she took the first sip, she noticed the red light on the phone blinking, an indicator that she had a voicemail message waiting. Hoping maybe to take her mind off things even for a few minutes, she picked up the handset, dialed into her voicemail, and listened.

"Hi, Sarah. It's, um…it's Karen. How are you?" There was a pause and Sarah could almost hear the wheels turning as Karen tried to plan out her next words. "Ugh, I really didn't want to do this on the machine, but…I'm not sure when I'll get you and I wanted you to hear it from me and not somebody else, one of our friends or something. Plus, it's been a few months since we last talked, and I'm sure you're in a better place by now. Emotionally, I mean. Than you were in February. Right?" She cleared her throat. “Wow. I’m rambling. Sorry. Okay. Um…” She paused and then blurted, “Derek and I are getting married in November.” There was a whoosh as she obviously blew out a relieved breath. “Like I said, I just wanted you to know from me and not from somebody else. I’m sorry to leave it on a message, but I didn’t want to wait.” This time, the sound was an audible swallow. “Okay then. I hope you’re doing well and that you’re okay with this information. Give Bentley a kiss for me. Bye.”

Sarah held the phone to her ear long after the robotic female voice told her that was the last message.

Derek and I are getting married in November.

She felt like an ant, like Derek was a giant and she was a tiny insect and he simply walked along, squashed her under his foot as he did so, and continued on without a care in the world, completely oblivious to how he’d just crushed another living thing.

Okay, it was a ridiculous analogy and Sarah knew it, but she couldn’t swallow down the pain and nausea that bubbled up as she listened to Karen’s voice. She’d sounded nervous, absolutely. But she’d also sounded happy. Underneath the jitters and the worry over telling Sarah, she was a typical, giddy bride-to-be, and that made Sarah glad for her and miserable for herself, both at the same time.

Like a five-year-old, she slid down the wall until her butt landed on the kitchen floor, the phone still in one hand, her drink in the other. The progress she’d made over the last month had seemingly evaporated over the past few hours, and she suddenly felt like Karen had left her only yesterday…except this time, there wasn’t even any Bentley to give her comfort as the tears rolled down her face.

❖

Natalie was restless. It wasn’t late—barely nine thirty—but she could no longer readjust her sleeping schedule from workweek to weekends. She had to be awake and downstairs in the coffee shop ready to work by five thirty during the week, so she usually hit the hay by nine thirty or ten at the latest on weeknights. The weekends used to be different. She used to stay up until after midnight, just enjoying her time, going out with friends or channel surfing on the tube. Apparently, those days had gone away with her twenties.

Tonight, however, her brain would not shut off. She wanted to sleep, but her body told her that wouldn't be happening. She couldn't get the confrontation with Hot Business Exec out of her head. Mentally chuckling without humor, she told herself she shouldn't refer to her as such any longer. She was a real person and had a name. Sarah Buchanan. She frowned as she glanced toward the foot of the bed where Chino lay chewing on a Nylabone. *And apparently, this is Sarah Buchanan's dog.*

Despite the fact that Natalie thought Andrea had been a little harsh with the woman, she also thought Andrea was right. There was no way to be sure that Chino belonged to Sarah. Was there? He had been a wreck when Natalie found him and now she loved him more than she thought possible, and there was no way she was going to send him back to a living situation that might land him in the same circumstances. No way. She cared about him too much. Ruffling his furry butt, she thought Sarah Buchanan would just have to fight her.

And what if she did?

Sarah looked like the kind of woman who had money and resources…or at least powerful friends. Natalie had a little over four grand in her savings account, and all her friends were teachers. How would she possibly be able to stand up to somebody with so much more?

The thoughts swirled around and around in her head until she felt like screaming. Concentrating on a book didn't even seem to be an option, and after she read the same paragraph of the latest Lisa Gardner novel three times without absorbing a word of it, she slammed it facedown on the small nightstand next to her bed. With an irritated sigh, she picked up the remote to the little television that sat on her dresser and clicked it on, flicking through the limited channels until she found a *Law & Order* rerun. She was all prepared to swoon over Angie Harmon when her phone rang, startling her.

Assuming it was Andrea, as it usually was if the phone rang after nine p.m., she grabbed the handset from off the nightstand and said in a low, sexy voice, "Miss me that much?"

A beat of silence followed, then an uncertain female voice said, "Um…Ms. Fox?"

Natalie sat up in bed and frowned. "Yes. Who's this?"

A throat cleared and Natalie swore she could almost hear the woman thinking. "This is Sarah Buchanan."

Closing her eyes in dread, Natalie swallowed, waiting for the barrage of curse words and shouting, but it never came. Instead, there was a silence that wasn't really silent. Natalie strained to hear, but was fairly certain she detected a soft sniffle. "Ms. Buchanan?" she ventured. "Are you okay?"

The snort that came next was laced with sarcasm. "No. No, I don't think I am."

"I'm sorry." It sounded so lame, but it was all Natalie could think of to say.

"I believe you." The words were just slightly run together, and Natalie found herself wondering if Sarah Buchanan had been drinking. "My ex is getting married."

Eyebrows raised, Natalie wondered at the statement and the way it was just blurted out to her, essentially a total stranger. "Oh."

"Yeah. She left me for him and now they're getting married. In November. And I didn't expect it to feel like she just ripped my heart out all over again, but that's exactly what it's like."

Trying hard to keep up, Natalie could latch on to only one thing: Sarah Buchanan's ex was a woman. Annoyed at herself for wanting to grin like an idiot, she tried to focus on what was being said. "I'm sorry," she said, and she meant it. "That sucks."

"Doesn't it?" The gentle tinkle of ice cubes against glass came over the line and Natalie heard Sarah swallow.

"Are you okay, Ms. Buchanan?" she asked again.

"Call me Sarah. Ms. Buchanan is my mother."

The smile came unexpectedly. "Okay. If you call me Natalie."

"Natalie. That's a pretty name."

"Thanks."

"Can I ask you a favor, Natalie?"

Here it comes, Natalie thought, and braced herself. She had the mental image of Andrea shouting at her to hang up, to stop talking to the enemy, to yell at Sarah to leave her alone. But something in the tone of Sarah's voice sounded…defeated, and Natalie couldn't allow herself to abandon the poor woman, even if she'd wanted to. She prepared for the worst as she replied, "Sure. What do you need?"

"Could I just…visit him?" Sarah's voice was so small and heartbroken that Natalie had to remind herself she was talking to a grown woman. She felt tears welling up in her eyes and was at once annoyed by her own empathy and saddened by the pathetic tone of the question. "I won't try to take him, I promise. I just want to see him. I need to see him." Her voice cracked and Natalie swallowed the lump in her own throat. "I feel like my entire life is falling apart, that everything I knew is gone, and if I could just see him, pet him, maybe I can get a grip on…on…oh, God, I don't know what the hell I'm saying." She sniffled again and then sighed. "It's stupid, I know. This was stupid. Forget it. I'm sorry I called."

"Wait." What was it? The sadness in her voice? That she sounded so utterly alone? That of all the people in the world, Sarah had called her? Natalie couldn't put her finger on any one reason—maybe it was a blend of all of them—but she didn't want to let Sarah go. Not like this. Not when she was such a mess and the cure was lounging across Natalie's bed chewing on a hunk of plastic. "Don't hang up."

Sarah didn't respond, but she also didn't hang up. They remained on the phone in silence, the only sounds being those of their tandem breathing and Natalie's television.

"Is that *Law & Order*?" Sarah said after a few minutes.

"Yeah." Natalie grinned. "I'm a junkie."

"Me, too."

Wetting her lips, Natalie plunged ahead. "Listen, we go for a walk in the park on Sunday mornings over at Cobbs Hill. Why don't you meet us there tomorrow and you can hang out with us. Okay?" Andrea was going to kill her. She knew it already.

There was obvious hesitation as Sarah said, "Will your girlfriend be there?"

"Who?" Natalie was baffled.

"Your girlfriend. The scary dark-haired one?"

A ripple of laughter burst forth from Natalie's chest as she realized not only that Sarah thought Andrea was her girlfriend, but also that she found her scary. Surprising herself, she kept the details under wraps and said simply, "Andrea? No. No, she won't be there." Sarah seemed to be weighing her options on the other end of the line. "What do you think? Want to join us?"

"I think I'd love to. What time?"

"We're usually up and about by six or six thirty. Just come on by the park. We'll be there."

"Okay. That sounds great." Sarah was quiet for several seconds before continuing. When she did, she sounded like she had a better handle on herself. "I'm really sorry I bugged you."

"You didn't bug me."

"Well. Good. Thanks for listening."

"You're welcome."

"I'll see you tomorrow."

"Okay."

"Good night, Natalie."

"Night."

The click seemed gentle somehow and Natalie held the phone in her hand, replaying the relief in Sarah's voice, the slightly embarrassed tone of her thanks. She knew she'd done the right thing for this woman and that made her feel good. Glancing at Chino, though, she wondered if she'd done the right thing for him. He looked up at her like some wise old man, blinked his blue eyes at her once, as if he knew something she didn't, then went back to his bone.

Only then did she wonder if she'd done the right thing for herself.

❖

Sunday was overcast and gray. The sky was the color of a dull nickel and looked as if it might split open at any second and drench everyone and everything on the ground below. Still, Cobbs Hill Park was surprisingly populated. The summers were far too short-lived in upstate New York and the residents tended to milk every single second from them that they could, threat of rain or not.

Sarah shifted her car into Park and sat quietly in the lot for several long moments, scanning the visitors that had pets, looking for Natalie and Bentley, but at the same time frightened of finding them. Still unsure about whether this was a good idea, still feeling like she was fighting in a battle of emotions inside her own head, she studied her hands on the steering wheel and tried to calm herself. Nervousness warred with anger, which slapped at sadness, all clashing inside her skull as if they had clanging swords and suits of armor. She'd taken a handful of Motrin when she'd opened her eyes, blaming the headache on her mixed feelings, but knowing deep down it had a lot to do with the alcohol she'd consumed the night before.

"God, I've got to ease up on that," she whispered aloud. If anything made her feel out of control, it was too much alcohol, and she wondered, not for the first time, if her psyche was trying to tell her something. Had Natalie had any idea she'd been well on her way to sloshed during their phone conversation?

Sarah's anger simmered slowly as she continued to peruse the grounds. Cobbs Hill wasn't a small area and she was annoyed with herself for not thinking to ask for a more specific location. With an irritated grunt, she got out of the car and began to walk farther into the park, away from the street.

The promise of rain made the air thicker than usual, close and damp, the scent of vegetation as prominent as if it were something solid. Sarah had dressed in a simple pair of black Adidas shorts and a white tank top and still, she broke into a mild sweat almost immediately. Glad she'd thought to pull her hair back into a ponytail and slap a hat on her head—her only defense against the frizz that humidity caused—she wiped at the clamminess beaded along her upper lip as she walked.

"Heads up!" somebody shouted, catching her attention just as a bright orange plastic Frisbee went whizzing past her face. It was followed almost immediately by a running college-age man who apologized while simultaneously giving her a quick once-over and grinning on his way past. His expression was so self-deprecating, so *I know that was really rude, sorry about that, but hey—not bad*, that she couldn't help but grin back at him as she kept on walking. She was thirty-eight years old and if somebody who was at least fifteen years her junior thought she was attractive enough to check out, who was she to judge?

Not seeing the pair she was seeking, she continued on, following a short trail through some woods, knowing it would spit her out onto another large section of the park. Maybe Natalie walked Bentley around that section. Of course, she was also a little late, so maybe she'd missed them altogether. Still aggravated by the situation, she tromped through the trees. When she reached the edge, she stopped in her tracks, the sight before her keeping her hidden behind the branches so she could watch without detection.

The first thing that struck her was that Bentley was off leash, and her heart did a quick jump, as it always had when she worried he'd go tearing off and never come back. Sarah knew his breed was a herding breed, that they were border dogs that would generally stick around and didn't need a constant tether, but she'd always been too nervous, too much of a control freak to allow him that freedom. Now as she watched, Natalie threw a red rubber ball across the large field and Bentley sprinted after it, obviously in his glory.

My God, he's fast.

He sprang into the air and his jaws snapped shut on the ball while it was in mid-bounce. Sarah couldn't help but smile at the grace of it. Then he turned on a dime, sending up a shower of grass and dust, and ran back to Natalie like his rear end was on fire. She squatted as he reached her. She praised him and showered him with hugs and kisses, his little stub of a tail wiggling a mile a minute, causing his entire butt to shake. In the time he was with her, Sarah was never, ever bad to him. She never treated him in any disparaging way. He was fed and exercised and loved. But she'd never seen him look *this* happy. Never. He was having the time of his life and Sarah wasn't sure what to do with that.

Unable to move just yet, she continued to watch as Natalie threw the ball again, and Sarah had the sudden thought that Natalie must have played softball at one time. Maybe she still did. She definitely did not throw like a girl. The realization made her chuckle until she suddenly recalled part of the previous night's conversation. She distinctly remembered referring to the dark-haired woman who'd belittled her on the street as Natalie's girlfriend. She also realized that Natalie hadn't denied it.

What are the chances that my lost dog was found by another lesbian?

Slim to none should have been the correct answer, but Sarah wasn't so sure as Natalie threw the ball yet again. They weren't far away, maybe fifteen yards, but the trees kept Sarah obscured fairly well. She took the opportunity to really look at Natalie—her nemesis, as she was beginning to think of her. It was something she'd never been able to do for longer than a few seconds at the coffee shop without being obvious. She wasn't a big woman, nor was she tall. Sarah would almost venture to call her petite, though compared to her own 5'9" frame, lots of women seemed petite. She guessed Natalie to be maybe 5'4". Today, she wore navy blue workout pants that reached to mid-calf and looked well worn, as though they were made just for her, and Sarah tried in vain not to linger on Natalie's well-shaped behind as a little jolt of arousal hit her right between her legs. Natalie's light blue T-shirt was cropped, and a flash of belly winked teasingly each time she threw the ball. Sarah swallowed and wet her lips, wondering why all her saliva was suddenly gone. Natalie's chestnut hair was pulled back off her face, but the lock of bright color waved loosely, refusing to stay tucked behind an ear, despite her constant attempts. *Maybe it's rebelling*, Sarah thought sarcastically, trying to shake off the pull of physical attraction. The entire package was undeniably pleasing, but the pink streak seemed like a last-ditch effort to remain a teenager or something, and it made her roll her eyes.

When Natalie's backside threatened to steal Sarah's attention once again, she moved her gaze forcibly back to Bentley. He was absolutely in heaven—it was apparent to anybody who chose to take three seconds and look—and Sarah felt a blanket of depression settle over her. Of course he was in heaven. Why wouldn't he be? Everybody else who left Sarah ended up happier than they had been with her. Why should her dog be any different? Pushing a loose rock around with the toe of her sandal, she wondered why on earth she thought coming here was the right thing to do. *This was a stupid, stupid idea.* But before she could turn and escape back to her empty, lonely townhouse, a familiar voice caught her attention just as solidly as if a hand had gripped her arm.

"Sarah?"

Her eyes closed in resignation and she swore under her breath before looking up and seeing Natalie smiling at her. Damn her. Smiling that smile, the one Sarah looked forward to every morning when she stopped to get coffee. *Used to look forward to.* Along with the smile, her expression was questioning, only this time instead of wondering what she'd like with her coffee, she was probably trying to figure out why Sarah was lurking in the bushes and staring at her.

"What are you doing in there?" Natalie asked, squinting at the trees and confirming Sarah's suspicions as she walked toward her. "Did you just get here?"

Nodding vigorously, Sarah pushed herself into the open feeling like a child caught peeking at something forbidden. "Yeah. Yeah, I wasn't sure where in the park you'd be, so I decided to come this way."

"Good thinking." Natalie's voice faltered ever so slightly and she looked away. It was at that moment that Sarah realized maybe she was nervous, too. *Good. She should be.*

Their awkward silence was interrupted by Bentley, who skidded to a halt near Natalie's feet, ball firmly clamped in his teeth. He looked up to meet Sarah's gaze and cocked his head to the side, as if trying to figure something out. His stump of a tail continued to wag as Sarah squatted down so he could see her.

"Hey, Bentley," she said, her voice soft and gentle. "How're you doing, buddy?" He dropped the ball and sat, his head still tilted and his expression looking as if he was actually smiling. Sarah wasn't sure he remembered her. Could he? It had been nearly five months, after all, and people were always talking about dogs having no concept of time and no long-term memory. She'd never believed that. Her parents had a dog while she was growing up that could remember when a kernel of popcorn had skittered under the stove. For days on end, he got up each morning to lie across the linoleum with his nose pressed to the bottom of the stove and whine softly. Sarah had finally used a wooden spoon to retrieve the morsel. Only then did the dog actually leave the kitchen and get on with life.

Bentley, however, seemed like any other dog she might run into in the park—friendly, wanting to be petted, hoping she'd throw the ball for him. She couldn't tell if maybe he actually knew who she was but was too caught up in the ball game to give her a proper hello. The thought depressed her and she felt deflated. She ruffled his fur, then picked up the ball and hurled it, unable to bear looking at his adorable face, not wanting to continue wondering. Natalie was watching her carefully, obviously trying to figure her out.

"Maybe I should just go," she said softly, tearing her gaze from the hold Natalie seemed to have on her.

"Overseas where?" Natalie asked as Bentley skidded to a halt and dropped the ball at her feet.

"Excuse me?"

"Andrea said you were overseas." She threw the ball an impressive distance.

Sarah nodded in recognition. "Ah. Andrea. The girlfriend."

"She's not my girlfriend."

"No? She certainly protected you like one." The snippiness crept in before Sarah realized it.

"She loves me." At Sarah's raised eyebrow, Natalie stumbled on, trying for an explanation. "Like a sister. She loves me like a sister. I don't have a girlfriend."

Sarah couldn't help the small grin that appeared because the look on Natalie's face very clearly said she'd revealed something by accident. She looked almost mortified, and Sarah's satisfaction at having the upper hand lasted all of four seconds. Then she wanted to make Natalie feel better, so she said, "I don't have one, either." And then she was annoyed at herself. *I shouldn't be making her feel better.*

"And your ex is getting married." Sarah whipped her head around to glare at Natalie, who had the good sense to look chagrined. "You mentioned it last night."

"Yeah, well, it's none of your business and I don't want to talk about it."

"I'm sorry."

"Fine."

By unspoken agreement, they'd begun to walk the perimeter of the large field, Bentley alternately chasing the ball, bringing it back, and following next to Natalie.

"So," Natalie said as they strolled. "Overseas where?"

Apparently, not talking wasn't an option for her. Sarah answered grudgingly. "New Zealand."

"Really?" The hazel of her eyes twinkled merrily as Natalie looked up at her. "Wow. That's amazing. I'd love to go there someday. What was it like?"

Sarah found herself torn. She didn't want to be talking to this woman. This woman was a thief as far as she was concerned and didn't deserve the time of day from her. At the same time, there was something about her, something that drew Sarah, something she had no intention of exploring or thinking about, so answering the questions was probably the best way to keep the weirdness at bay. She took a deep breath, then blew it out loudly before speaking, making it clear that she didn't really want to be talking in some friendly, hey-look-at-us-we're-pals kind of way. Not to Natalie.

"It was nice."

The grimace on Natalie's face was followed by the narrowing of her eyes, as if she'd been issued a challenge by Sarah's lame description. She picked up the ball and threw it for Bentley.

"What was nice about it?"

Sarah shot a glare her way. "It's a cool country. Very similar, but very different."

Obviously still not satisfied, Natalie tried a different tack. "You were there for work?"

"Yep."

"What do you do?"

"I work." Unnecessarily snotty, Sarah knew, but she couldn't help it.

"I see." Natalie didn't miss a beat, didn't flinch at the insulting tone, and didn't take the hint and stop with the questions. She kept right on as if they were two old friends having a chat. "What were the New Zealanders like?"

"Kiwis."

"They were like kiwis?"

"No, that's what they call themselves. Kiwis. Not New Zealanders. A Kiwi is a bird."

"Oh. Well, what were they like?"

"Nice."

"Nice?"

"Uh-huh."

"Friendly?"

"Yep."

"What about the food?"

"Not bad."

"The coffee?"

"*Strong*." Natalie laughed at that, a sound Sarah loved, then immediately became annoyed by. *No laughing. I should not be making you laugh. I don't like you, remember?*

"How was the weather?"

"Starting to cool. It was their fall."

"Did you get much chance to explore? Or did you work the whole time?"

"I wandered a little, but it was mostly work."

"That's too bad. Did you see anything cool? Go to any fun bars or anything? Meet any interesting people?"

Feeling suddenly and inexplicably uncomfortable by the line of questioning, Sarah made a show of looking at her watch. "Wow, is it that late? I need to get going."

"But it's barely eight o'clock in the morning."

"I have somewhere to be." Unnecessarily snotty yet again.

"Oh." Was she mistaken or did Natalie sound disappointed? "Okay."

"Um…" Sarah squatted down to pet Bentley, who was panting like crazy and didn't seem at all affected by any of this.

He was all about the ball. It was news to her that he liked this game so much, and the thought made her sad. She glanced up at Natalie, who was watching her closely, and had no idea what to say to her. She wanted to hate her, wanted to glare and be angry and spit and swear and yet somehow, she just didn't have the energy. To add insult to injury—and much to her own horror—she felt tears suddenly spring into her eyes. *Jesus Christ, what is happening to me?* Dropping a quick kiss on the top of Bentley's head, she muttered, "I've got to go."

She heard Natalie call out from behind her, asking if she was okay as she nearly ran back to the trail and stomped into the trees like some jilted lover from a romantic comedy. Her heart was pounding like a jackhammer and she couldn't seem to catch her breath, but that didn't stop her. When she reached the car, she didn't even pause to collect herself. She keyed the ignition, slammed it into gear, and streaked home as fast as possible, feeling like something she couldn't name—her past? her fears? her self-doubt?—was chasing her and any second now would have her in its cold and unforgiving grip forever.

CHAPTER NINE

I feel bad for her. I can't help it."

"Why on earth do you feel bad for her?" Andrea was clearly annoyed, still trying to absorb the news that Natalie had actually met with Sarah in the park that morning.

"I don't know. I just do." Natalie took a sip of her Diet Coke and watched the people below. The biggest perk to living in her bitty apartment above Valenti's was this, the tiny square of rooftop to which she had full access. All summer long and through much of the fall, Natalie and Andrea sat in lounge chairs, ice-stuffed cooler between them, and watched the neighborhood go by. The thermometer reading of ninety-three degrees had prompted her to leave Chino in the coolness of the air-conditioned apartment, which he didn't seem to mind, given that he was completely wiped out from their morning in the park and was currently napping on the futon. "She just seemed so…sad."

"Maybe we should put some rum into that Coke, huh?" Andrea made a swipe at the can.

"Why?" Natalie held the drink out of Andrea's reach. "Why is it so appalling that I feel sorry for her?"

"Because she's trying to take your dog away, Natty."

"She's trying to get her own dog back, Andrea. Big difference."

Andrea shook her head in frustration.

"She called him Bentley," Natalie said softly.

"Well, that's a stupid name."

"He did seem to know her."

"But he didn't go with her."

"No."

"See? He's happy with you. He wants to stay with you."

"I think she's lonely." Natalie gazed off into the bright blue of the sky, remembering the faraway, cheerless expression on Sarah's face, trying to put a name on it. Turning to Andrea, she continued. "I mean, think about it. She's gone overseas for work for God knows how long. She probably didn't know anybody there. She comes home to what I can only assume is an empty house. Her ex tells her she's getting married. And while she was gone, her dog disappeared. She's got nothing and nobody to keep her company. How could she not be lonely?"

Andrea stared at her, a combination of admiration and frustration clearly etched across her face. "That is your blessing and your curse, you know that, right?"

"What is?"

"Your damn compassion."

Natalie shrugged.

"Wish I had a fraction of it," Andrea muttered, only half-jokingly. "Wish *everybody* had a fraction of it. The world would be a better place."

"I should just give him back to her."

"What?" Andrea sat up and swung her feet off the lounge so she was facing Natalie. "No. No, you shouldn't. Are you crazy? First of all, just because this Sarah chick might be lonely, that doesn't mean she's good to him. You know? Do I have to remind you yet again what kind of shape he was in when you found him?"

Natalie shook her head just once while studying her own lap.

"Somebody caused that. Let's not forget that little fact, okay?

Second of all, you love him. And he loves you. He's happy here. Do you *want* to lose him?"

"No, of course not."

"Then leave it alone." Andrea returned to her lounging position and lay back, closing her eyes against the sunshine. "You did a nice thing today, allowing her to join you guys on your walk. Now let it go."

Natalie lay back, too, feeling the heavy burden of indecision weighing her down, the only clear thought in her head not something that was much help at all: *I have no idea what to do.*

❖

Raking along the edges of her parents' yard, Sarah couldn't help but compare the jumbled mess of grass clippings, leaves, and twigs to the mixed-up mess that was rolling around in her own head. Feeling this out of sorts was not something she was used to, nor did she like it. As a matter of fact, it was pissing her off, and she took her anger out on the unsuspecting lawn, raking it to within an inch of its life.

Yard work was something she enjoyed, found cathartic, but rarely had time for, given her busy work schedule. Thus, she'd purchased a townhouse so she wouldn't have to be bothered with normal outdoor upkeep. Every now and then, however, she felt the urge to rake or mow or plant or dig just to help work out whatever was clogging up her brain. Her parents were more than happy to accommodate her with their own yard. Plus, her father wasn't getting any younger, and any strenuous work she could take off his shoulders made her feel like she was helping out at least a little bit.

She'd told her parents about Karen's message, and she'd even managed to do it without bursting into a raging river of tears, which she half expected to happen. Her father had pulled her into a hug—which had almost started the waterworks for her—and as she glanced at her mother over his shoulder, she saw only one thing on her face: relief. Mary Buchanan was not the kind of woman who could hide her feelings. Sarah's father often playfully accused her of being made of Lucite—strong, but see-through—because whatever was going on in her head was clearly visible on her face. At that moment, relief was the most apparent emotion there and Sarah finally understood why. She swore she could almost hear her mother's voice in her head.

Maybe now she can get on with her life.

Sarah's reactions to that realization were mixed. At first, she was angry, which seemed to be the only sentiment she was capable of lately, and frankly, one she was tired of. Then the guilt set in. She hadn't really taken the time to see how worried her mother had been about her since Karen's departure, and she felt sort of stupid about that. Her mother was nothing if not a worrier. She'd been known to worry about things that had nothing at all to do with her, and Sarah suddenly found herself embarrassed it had never crossed her mind that her depression and inability to pull herself out of this slump might be weighing as heavily on her mother as it was on her.

Now she found herself feeling almost indifferent, and that was the weirdest sensation of all. If she let herself dwell—something that, in general, she worked very hard *not* to do—she'd realize that the ambiguity was akin to giving up, throwing in the towel, calling it quits. On everything. Life, love, any kind of concern at all. Her shoulders slumped as she raked, and she blew out a breath heavy with frustration and emotional exhaustion.

Fine. Whatever. I don't care anymore. I'm just tired of feeling everything in such extremes. I really didn't think wishing for a normal life where everything's not *falling apart at once was asking for too much. Apparently, I was wrong.*

Pushing thoughts of Karen from her mind somehow only allowed space for Natalie Fox to squeeze in. *From one pain to another. Terrific.*

Why did she have to be so nice? That was the unanswerable

question that popped into Sarah's head immediately. She flashed back to walking in the park, to Natalie trying her very best to engage Sarah in some kind of conversation, of her refusal to be deterred by Sarah's refusal to participate. Almost smiling about it, Sarah knew she never would have tried that hard had the roles been reversed. She just would have walked along quietly, deciding she wasn't going to waste her breath if Natalie didn't find her good enough to talk to. But Natalie was obviously much stronger, much more determined than Sarah. She definitely got an A for effort, that was for sure.

Still, a large part of Sarah wanted to cut into her, to really give her a piece of her mind, to let her know exactly how she felt about how Natalie had taken somebody else's dog and made him her own. Nodding to herself as she shoved yard debris into a garbage bag, she felt a new resolve. If nothing else, Natalie Fox was going to get an earful. She was going to be undeniably clear on how Sarah felt.

The next morning, bolstered by steely determination and a healthy dash of indignation, Sarah stalked into Valenti's ready to do battle. She was wearing her favorite, kick-some-ass-and-look-good-doing-it black pantsuit that she knew made her look intimidating as well as sexy. Her opponents never knew what hit them when she wore that suit, and that's exactly how she wanted it.

Straight-backed, she stood in line, just like always. She watched Natalie wait on customers with a friendly and warm smile, just like always. When Sarah finally reached the counter, Natalie's smile faltered ever so slightly, and the only thing that gave her away was the way her eyes took on a panicked blinking.

"Hi, Sarah," she said, and there was an uncertain quaver to her voice, like she was anticipating bad news.

"Good morning," Sarah said, fixing her steely gaze on the face of her foe. As if made of vapor, her determined demeanor instantly left her, just dissipated into the air, leaving her standing there in front of an attractive, uncertainly smiling woman with no idea what to say. She felt like an idiot.

They stood looking at one another, and though it was only a couple of seconds, it seemed more like hours. Sarah felt as if they were each trying to read the other, trying to determine exactly what was going on in the other woman's head, certain that if she knew, she could decide the next course of action with no doubts. Then they both tried to speak at once.

"Do you—?"

"Could I—?"

Both women laughed quietly as the man behind Sarah huffed with impatience and went around her to the second register so somebody else could wait on him. She could feel his annoyed stare, but she ignored him, and when she looked up at Natalie, she was pressing her lips together in an obvious attempt not to smile. Sarah cleared her throat and gestured to Natalie with a slight nod.

"You first."

"Okay." Natalie cleared her throat and pushed the colored streak of hair away from her eye. "I was wondering if you would be interested in joining Chino—er, Bentley—and I for a walk later."

Sarah stood still, blinking in surprise, not at all sure she had heard Natalie correctly. "Um…a walk?"

Natalie nodded quickly, and like a person who didn't know what to do with her hands, began making the latte that Sarah had ordered every morning before she'd left for New Zealand. "After work? Say six?"

As if she had no say in the matter at all, as if her body and brain did their own thing and Sarah's consciousness was simply there to observe, she felt her head begin to nod. "That sounds great. I'll meet you out front?"

"Perfect." Natalie set the latte down on the counter and took the money Sarah robotically handed to her.

"I'll see you tonight."

"Great."

Sarah took her latte and headed out the door, just like always. When she looked back into the shop from the street, her own face reflected back at her in the glass and, much to her own dismay, she was sporting a goofy grin.

"Oh, for crying out loud," she muttered at herself in disgust as she headed off to her car.

❖

I used to be tough. I used to be strong. What the hell happened to me?

Sarah sat at her desk later that morning, gazing unseeingly out the window, replaying her visit to the coffee shop over and over in her mind, trying to figure out exactly where she'd screwed up and lost her nerve, her killer instinct that had gotten her so far in the corporate world.

"Am I that much of a sucker for a pretty face?" she asked herself out loud.

"Are you talking to me?" Patti Schmidt was suddenly standing in the doorway.

"Oh." Sarah shifted in her seat, sat up straighter. "No. No, I was just muttering to myself."

"What's going on with you?" Patti asked, plopping into a wooden chair across from Sarah and propping her elbows on the desk to regard her curiously. "Are you okay?"

"What do you mean? Nothing's going on with me," Sarah tried to play down the immediate indignation she felt at the question, mostly because she'd been read so easily by somebody who really didn't know her all that well.

Patti snorted, clearly telegraphing that Sarah was full of shit. "You've been staring off into space all morning." She picked a pen out of the cup on the desk and began to click the plunger.

"Yeah, well."

"Something's definitely on your mind." *Click. Click. Click.*

"Maybe."

Click. Click. "Want to talk about it?"

"Not really."

"Sometimes it really is better…" *Click. Click.* "To talk to somebody about stuff." *Click.*

Sarah's jaw was beginning to ache because of how tightly she had her back molars clenched together.

"Come on." *Click.* "Talk to Aunt Patti." *Click. Click. Click.*

Sarah snatched the pen out of Patti's hand with a growl. "I miss my dog, all right?" she said, snarling the words in a much louder voice than necessary. "Jesus."

Patti blinked at her, eyes wide. "Bentley's gone? Oh, no! What happened?" The genuine concern in her voice made Sarah's initial irritation with her dissipate into the air like steam and she was suddenly sorry she hadn't told her sooner.

"He ran away while we were gone." She knew the lack of information would only keep Patti asking questions, but she was loath to give up the whole story. The whole thing made her feel irresponsible and stupid.

"Well, did you call animal control? Put an ad in the paper? Drive around the area where he was?" She ticked off the suggestions on her fingers.

"Gee, Patti, what great ideas. I wish I'd thought of them." At the flash of pain that zipped across Patti's face, Sarah gentled her tone just a bit, realizing the woman was only trying to help. "Yes, we did all that. It's fine. I know where he is."

"You do?"

"Yeah."

"Where?"

"He's fine. Somebody found him and is taking care of him."

"What do you mean?" Patti's barrage of questions kept on. "Don't you want him back? Do you want me to call my cousin? He's a cop. And my brother's buddy works at animal control. I'll call him right now." She stood up to leave, obviously ready to call in the cavalry to rescue Sarah's dog. Her determination to lend a hand made Sarah grow a little more fond of her.

"No." The quickness of Sarah's reply stopped Patti in her tracks. The sudden image of a bunch of large, burly authority figures barreling down on Natalie was just too much for Sarah to bear. "No. It's fine. Really. I appreciate your offer to help, but I've got it under control."

Patti blinked at her and scratched at the part in her hair. "Mmm." Her tone was drenched in doubt.

"Seriously, Patti. It's fine." Sarah gave a genuine smile. "Really. Thank you so much for wanting to help. It's good."

Patti's skeptical expression clearly stated that she wasn't totally convinced. "All right. If you say so." She left the room uncertainly, glancing back at Sarah twice, as if hoping to catch her at a moment of weakness, ready to tell Patti the truth.

Sitting back in her chair and returning to her contemplative state, Sarah spent a long while staring off into space again, rolling the current events of her life around and around. The idea that slowly began forming in her mind seemed totally off the wall but somehow comforting, which didn't seem like it should even be possible. She wondered if she was crazy.

❖

What the hell was I thinking?

That same question had been scrolling through Natalie's mind like CNN's streaming news at the bottom of the screen since Sarah had walked out of Valenti's that morning. She felt like her brain had taken a break and her mouth had seized the opportunity to wreak a little havoc in its absence. Since that moment, she'd screwed up seven coffee orders, put salt into the cannoli filling instead of sugar, left a batch of cinnamon rolls in the oven to burn while she was staring off into space, and let a dozen eggs slip out of her hands and onto the floor.

"You." Mrs. Valenti pointed at her as she stood staring

down at the broken eggs, her face a combination of irritation and concern. "Come." Gesturing Natalie to her with a rolling of her work-callused hand, she grabbed her by the back of the neck, none too gently, and slapped a palm against her forehead. "You sick? You not feel well? What?" She touched her cheek on one side, then the other, then went back to her forehead.

"I'm sorry, Mrs. V." Natalie rubbed at her eye, embarrassed. "I'm just having an off day."

"No sorry. S'okay. You always work hard for me. Why don't you take a break and go upstairs? Take a nap or something. Rest."

"But I'm okay. I swear." Natalie hated the idea of letting her bosses down.

"No. S'okay. You go. No more burning buns today." The gentle snap with a dish cloth she gave to Natalie's backside helped take any sting out of the words. "Go."

Like an eight-year-old, Natalie lifted her arms and let them drop back to her sides in frustration. Maybe Mrs. Valenti was right. She'd done enough damage for one day.

Upstairs for more than three hours, she took Mrs. Valenti's advice and took a nap, something she rarely did. But the summer sun was beaming in through the windows and Chino was used to sleeping away his afternoons, and she couldn't resist the pull. So she cuddled up with him on the futon, and they drifted in and out of a lazy doze for almost two hours. Rather than cranky and more tired—the way she usually awoke from a nap—she felt rested and energized. A timid knock on her door revealed Anthony, Mrs. Valenti's twelve-year-old great-grandson, carrying a bowl of homemade minestrone.

"Nana said to give you this." His voice was soft, he was blushing, and his deep, dark eyes never met hers. Andrea always teased her that Anthony had a crush on her and for the first time, she wondered if Andrea was right.

"Oh, that's so sweet." She took the bowl gingerly from his outstretched hands, careful not to spill.

"She said to tell you to make sure you eat it all. So you get better." He still avoided her eyes. Chino poked his head around her legs and Anthony's face lit up. "Hi, boy. How are you?"

"Do you want to come in, Anthony? Play with Chino while I eat?"

"Nah." He grimaced, telling Natalie he'd love nothing more than to take her up on her invitation. He squatted and held a hand out to Chino, who licked it, his nubby tail wiggling uncontrollably. "Papa's got some stuff he needs my help with."

"All right," Natalie said, smiling. "Well, if you change your mind, come on up, okay?"

"Uh-huh." He turned and headed down the stairs.

"Thanks for the soup, Anthony."

"Welcome," he called over his shoulder.

She followed him with her eyes, thinking how much she adored the Valenti family, how lucky she was to have them as part of her life, especially given that she lived a couple of hours from her own folks. Mr. and Mrs. Valenti treated her like one of their own, and the steaming bowl of minestrone was as much proof of that as anything else.

And it was indescribably delicious.

By six o'clock, Natalie was fighting an attack of the guilts. Despite the fact that she'd been trying to talk the Valentis into staying open for an extra hour to catch the after-work crowd that might be interested in fresh bread with dinner, she was glad they closed at five. By the time she and Chino were ready to head outside and wait for Sarah, the shop was closed up and everybody had gone home. There was nobody left to wonder why Natalie had been too "sick" to stay at work, but seemed healthy enough to go for a stroll with her dog. Not that anyone would have really thought that way. It was more likely Natalie's guilty conscience was making her feel weird. She donned a pair of black, seen-better-days nylon shorts and a pink T-shirt with a faded Old Navy screen print across the front. Strapping on her Tevas, she asked Chino if he was ready to go. He began to wiggle his butt emphatically and spin in circles, something that never failed to make Natalie laugh.

The temperature still hovered in the mid eighties and Monroe Avenue was busy with people soaking up the too-short season. Natalie and Chino hung out in front of the shop, Natalie reclining on an iron bench and watching the world go by as they waited for Sarah, and she absently wondered what the hell she'd been thinking inviting Sarah on their walk. The woman hated her, and frankly, Natalie was a little bit afraid of her. *God, I make some stupid spur-of-the-moment decisions, don't I?* She shook her head ruefully.

Chino knew by now that the next step was that they would head for the park and his little body thrummed with anticipatory energy as he paced in front of Natalie, unable to completely relax, his doggie brain probably preoccupied by visions of chasing a red rubber ball through the grass. Natalie scratched his head absently as she kept a lookout for the third member of their threesome and her heart thumped a nervous rhythm.

She'd been looking to her right and Sarah's face registered belatedly as she swiveled to look in the other direction. That's when she noticed Andrea coming from her left.

"Oh, crap," she muttered, cursing the bad timing and feeling like she was about to be tossed into a box with a snake and a mongoose. Steeling herself, she stood up and waved to Sarah, who actually smiled and looked happy to see her. *Interesting,* she thought, not unhappily. But Natalie could pinpoint the exact moment when Sarah recognized Andrea coming up behind her because Sarah's warm expression dissolved like a sidewalk chalk design in a rainstorm. "Crap," Natalie said again.

"Hey, Natty," Andrea said from behind her.

Natalie turned to face her. "Hey, yourself. What are you doing here?"

"I called the shop this afternoon, but Mrs. Valenti said you were upstairs napping. I called, but you must have been screening or something, so I thought I'd better check on you, see if you needed anything."

Just as she had with Sarah, Natalie knew immediately that Sarah had come up behind her simply by the irritated look that settled itself on Andrea's face. Keeping her sigh of frustration as silent as she could, Natalie turned and pasted on a smile for Sarah.

"Hi."

"Hi," Sarah said warily.

Natalie introduced the two women formally, though she was well aware that *they* were well aware of who the other was. Sarah held gazes with Andrea for what seemed like hours, then squatted to scratch Chino, obviously uncertain exactly what she'd just stepped into and not happy about that uncertainty.

Turning back to Andrea, Natalie said too loudly, "We're going to the park. Want to come?" The overabundance of feigned cheer in her tone actually made her wince.

"Um, no thanks. I think I'll pass." The disdain in Andrea's voice was crystal clear and her eyes drilled into Natalie's, their unspoken message just as unmistakable: *What are you doing?*

"Okay, well, we should get going, then." She gestured down to the dog with her eyes. "He's getting antsy. Thanks for checking on me."

"Are you sure you're all right?" Andrea seemed reluctant to let her go, and Natalie felt her aggravation over the situation growing.

"Yep. I'm sure. Promise."

"I'll call you later, then?" Andrea narrowed her eyes at Natalie, as if squinting might help her see things more clearly.

"Cool." Looking down at Sarah, Natalie said, "Ready?"

Sarah nodded, meeting Andrea's gaze one more time before following Natalie up the street. Natalie could feel Andrea's eyes on her for more than a block. She and Sarah walked in silence for several long minutes before Sarah finally spoke.

"Well, that was fun."

"I'm sorry about that." Natalie made a face that portrayed her embarrassment over the situation. "I didn't know she was coming."

"You're *sure* she's not your girlfriend?"

Natalie laughed. "I'm sure."

"Ex?"

"Nope."

"Just loves you like a sister," Sarah said, using Natalie's previous phrase regarding Andrea.

"Exactly."

"Why was she checking on you? Are you sick?"

Pushing the lock of pink hair out of her eye, Natalie shook her head. "No. I just had sort of a weird afternoon." Laughing in self-deprecation, she added, "I dropped a lot of things."

"Oh, one of *those* days."

"Right. Mrs. Valenti thought I was sick and needed to go take a nap. Like I'm three."

Sarah smiled. "An Italian grandmother. We should all have one."

They walked along, the three of them, like they'd been doing it for years. Natalie handed the leash over to Sarah without comment and Sarah took it the same way. They continued up Monroe Avenue, stopping several times so passersby could pet Chino, oohing and ahhing over his gorgeous eyes and friendly demeanor. Once they arrived at the park, they searched for an area that was less crowded than most of the place and began taking turns throwing the ball for him.

"So, how was your day?" Natalie asked, feeling Sarah's eyes on her as she threw the ball, surprised by how pleasant things had been so far.

"It was okay."

Natalie nodded and tried to internally gauge how much work she wanted to put forth to get this woman to talk, and whether or not it was even worth it. Chino brought the ball back and Sarah took the slobbery thing from him, made a face, and wiped it on the grass with a *blech*, which made Natalie smile. *She's really very pretty*, Natalie suddenly thought about Sarah. It wasn't that she hadn't always thought of her as incredibly attractive, but she'd never really had a chance to look at her openly. Pretty wasn't a word she had ever used to describe Sarah. It had always seemed too…soft, somehow. She was attractive, definitely. Sophisticated and focused. Imposingly sexy. But now Natalie realized that "pretty" was actually very accurate. Sarah Buchanan was a very pretty woman. Watching her, Natalie tried to decide which way she looked better to her, all decked out in her business clothes, or like this: casual yet classy in nice khaki dress shorts and a flatteringly clingy black T-shirt. Her dark hair was pulled back into a perfectly smooth ponytail, which made the blue of her eyes stand out even more than usual. Natalie absently wondered if she ever looked disheveled. When her thoughts began to veer toward how much fun it might be to actually do the disheveling, Natalie shook her head quickly, hoping to dislodge that sensual image. She didn't have a lot of luck.

"You don't say much, do you?" she finally asked Sarah, a question which seemed to surprise both of them momentarily.

Seeming to honestly contemplate the query, Sarah took several seconds before answering, finally saying with a half-grin, "Well, I think the circumstances are a little…special. Don't you?"

"Circumstances? What circumstances?" Natalie asked with a matching expression on her face. "Oh! You mean the ones about me having your dog because I'm not sure if you abused him, not to mention that I love him to pieces, and you wondering if you should show up on my doorstep with a bunch of lawyers and police and take him away from me? Those circumstances?"

There was a beat of uncomfortable silence during which Natalie waited to see if Sarah would catch on to her gentle teasing, to her desire to keep things light even though she knew full well that they were in a weird and tenuous situation. Sarah glanced at her and must have caught something in her eyes because she smiled back at her.

"Yeah, those are the ones."

"Do you think we could set them aside for the time being? Or is that a silly request?" Natalie asked the questions honestly, not quite knowing where she stood and not liking the feeling at all.

"It is a silly request." Sarah winked at her and then threw the ball for Chino. "But I think we can do it for now."

The relief that swept over her caught Natalie off guard. "Cool."

"One condition, though."

"What's that?"

"I get to ask a few questions."

"Oh." Natalie raised her eyebrows and then gave a single nod. "Okay. What do you want to know?"

Sarah made a contemplative face, but Natalie got the distinct impression she already had a list in her head and was just faking the pensiveness. The idea made her feel warm inside.

"How old are you?"

"Wow, right for the jugular, huh?" Natalie laughed outright, wiping her hand on her hip after throwing the ball for Chino. "Thirty-one." She felt rather than saw Sarah's head whip around in surprise.

"Seriously?"

It wasn't the first time somebody had been stunned to learn she was older than twenty-five. "Thirty-one, swear to God. And yes, I still get proofed at bars."

"I can see why."

She squinted at Sarah. "I'm trying to decide if I should be insulted by that."

"Not at all. I'm just saying you look younger, that's all."

"All right. I'll let you off the hook this time."

Chino plopped down at their feet, directly between the two of them, his chest heaving in a rapid pant, his tongue lolling out the side of his mouth, and his nontail wagging continuously. "Pooped already?" Natalie teased him. "You're out of shape, boy."

"I hardly ever let him off the leash." Sarah said it quietly, almost as if she was embarrassed by the fact.

"How come? He's very good."

"I think I'm just a worry wart."

"Or a control freak." Natalie said it lightly, jokingly, but could tell from the flash of pain that crossed Sarah's face that she'd hit a nerve.

"That could be it." She sat down next to Chino and Natalie followed suit. They soaked up the evening sun and lounged in the thick grass in silence for a long while.

"Can I ask you a question?" Natalie said after a while, almost hesitant to break the spell of the quiet that had woven around them.

Sarah nodded once, looking off into the distance.

"Where did the name Bentley come from?"

A gentle smile just touched the corners of Sarah's mouth. When she finally turned to look at Natalie, her eyes were sparkling. "I figured that was closest I'd ever get to owning one."

"The car?"

Sarah inclined her head. "Yep."

"I have no idea what a Bentley looks like."

Sarah scratched the dog's head, just behind his ears. "Like this," she said with affection. He settled his chin on her thigh and sighed in contentment.

The feeling that hit Natalie was a weird combination of unpleasantness and admiration as she watched Chino and Sarah simply enjoying one another. "Maybe I should be calling him that instead," she said softly.

Sarah looked up, obviously trying to read her tone. "Where did you get Chino?"

"Mrs. Valenti." Natalie fondly recalled the day they'd found him near the Dumpster. "She called him *turchino*, which means turquoise in Italian. I told her his eyes weren't turquoise, but the name sort of stuck."

"I like it," Sarah said.

"Yeah?"

"Yeah. It's different."

Natalie nodded, inexplicably pleased that she'd met with Sarah's approval on something. "But Bentley's good. It is." She tried it out on the dog a couple times, laughing as his ears perked and he cocked his head as he listened.

"Okay, so here's my next question," Sarah said, and the quirk of her eyebrow told Natalie it would probably be something smart-assed. She didn't mind at all. She liked Fun Sarah and was secretly trying to figure out how to get her to come out and play more often. To Natalie's surprise, Sarah leaned over Bentley and reached toward her, tucked her finger under the lock of pink hair, and tugged gently at it. "What's with this?"

"My pink? It's for Andrea," Natalie said with a tender smile. Seeing Sarah's confusion, she elaborated. "She's a breast cancer survivor. When she was diagnosed, I wanted to do something to show my support, something everybody could see. I don't have a lot of money, so my meager donation wouldn't have meant much. Wearing a pink ribbon is one thing, but this"—she rolled her eyes up in an attempt to see her own hair—"this was something that worked, that did what I wanted. Plus, I think it helped Andrea. Every time she sees me, she knows she's got me in her corner in whatever way she needs. You know?" When she met Sarah's gaze, she couldn't really read her expression and she felt suddenly self-conscious, wondering if she'd revealed too much.

"That's really amazing. And something to be proud of. I can't believe she was diagnosed so young. Wow. Andrea's lucky to have somebody like you."

"Now maybe you see why she's so protective of me?" Natalie raised her eyebrows in question.

Sarah grimaced. “Yes. And I owe you an apology.”

“For what?”

“The hair.”

“Let me guess,” Natalie said with a chuckle. “You thought I was rebelling or having some punk flashback, right?”

Sarah grinned at her. “Something like that.”

“I’m afraid I’m just a boring, conservative kind of girl.”

With a snort, Sarah said, “Yeah, well, that makes two of us.”

A young man and his German shepherd walked across the field about thirty yards from them. Chino’s head lifted and his ears perked up, his whole body suddenly alert. He stood and Sarah flinched, her body language matching his as she stretched a hand toward his collar.

“No,” Natalie warned in a low and gentle voice, halting Sarah in mid-reach. “You stay.”

Though his eyes followed the twosome until they were out of sight, the rest of his body relaxed at Natalie’s command. Then he lay back down. Sarah had observed it all. Natalie could feel her eyes and was suddenly self-conscious.

“He’s very good off the leash,” Natalie said quickly, suddenly feeling the need to explain. “But there are times when he’ll bolt. Squirrels. Other dogs sometimes. He always comes back when I call him, but…it can be a little nerve-wracking. So we’ve been working on ‘stay.’” She dug her fingers into the fur on his neck and massaged him. “Good boy,” she said softly. “That was very good.”

“I want to talk to you about something,” Sarah said, unexpectedly serious.

Uh-oh. Here it comes. She’s going to take him away or threaten to sue me or… Natalie had to make a great effort to shut off her mind, the possibilities sending her careening toward panic mode. The idea of losing Chino was a tangible pain in her gut, and she grimaced.

Sarah must have recognized her injured expression because she placed a warm hand on Natalie's thigh and said in a reassuring voice, "Hear me out."

Swallowing hard, Natalie nodded, not looking at Sarah, her body tensed as if waiting for a physical blow.

"How would you feel about sharing him? With me?"

Natalie looked at her then, blinked, wondering if she'd heard right, having trouble understanding. "Sharing him?"

"Like a joint custody thing."

Natalie blinked some more.

"Look, let's be honest. He's my dog. You know it and I know it, and if I wanted to fight you and get him back, I could." The gentle and nonthreatening tone of Sarah's voice didn't make her words any less scary to Natalie. "But…" She faltered for the first time, looked down at her hands, pulled some grass out by the roots. "But he seems really happy with you. You took him in when he needed somebody, and you take good care of him. You love him, he loves you, it's obvious to anybody who sees you together. And despite the whole legal ownership part of it, I don't think taking him away from you completely would be a good thing or the right thing. I don't want to do that to him. Or to you."

Natalie didn't know what to say. She felt clogged with emotions: joy, gratitude, hesitation, wonder, confusion. "Joint custody?" she said for clarification.

Sarah lifted one shoulder in a half shrug. "I couldn't think of a more appropriate term. I think it would work well, plus it will be good for us as well as him. If I have to go someplace, you could watch him. If you have to go someplace, I could watch him. We'd each have a built-in dog-sitter and he'd never have to go to the kennel again."

"He'd still get to stay with me sometimes?"

"Absolutely. We can work out a schedule so I have him some nights and you have him some nights."

Natalie had begun to nod slowly as Sarah talked, the idea of sharing Chino—er, Bentley, which she was going to have to start calling him—sounding not altogether bad. And the idea of not continually worrying about whether or not Sarah would wake up one day and decide to come take him away sounded even better. She must have been quiet longer than she realized. Sarah's voice prodded her.

"So? What do you think?" Surprisingly, Sarah looked almost anxious as she waited.

"Like I'm going to say no?" Natalie said.

"Good." Sarah's entire face lit up, her smile showing perfectly straight white teeth. "That's great. We'll want to keep in contact, make sure we're feeding him the same food and the same treats so his system doesn't rebel."

Natalie nodded. "Makes sense."

Growing serious, Sarah said, "Look, Natalie, I know you were worried. About his state when you found him and whether or not I'm…mean to him." It seemed hard for her to say the words, and at that moment, as Sarah lovingly stroked Bentley's furry back, Natalie knew she couldn't have been more wrong, that Sarah would never abuse him. "But this way, you can keep an eye on him and make sure I'm not. Right?"

Feeling terrible about her unfounded assumptions but elated at the unexpected turn of events, Natalie couldn't speak. She simply smiled in agreement. Sarah held out her hand.

"Deal?"

Natalie took it, surprised by the warmth of it and Sarah's firm grip. "Deal."

CHAPTER TEN

July slipped away in a wave of heat, and August arrived in just as steamy a fashion. By the middle of the month, Natalie and Sarah had fallen into a gentle and easy routine of sharing custody of Bentley. Sometimes he stayed with one of them for a couple nights in a row. Sometimes they alternated nights and he took turns at their places. They walked him together almost every evening, unless Sarah had to work late or it was raining. It was working out very well for all involved.

Sarah sat at a large oval conference table and made what could only be considered a valiant effort to stay attuned to the words being spoken in the meeting. The marketing consultants were making a good presentation. It wasn't that. It was simply that Sarah had found herself feeling restless lately, a symptom of what, she didn't know. She also had no idea how to pull herself out of it. Maybe she just needed to relax a bit. Or maybe she was relaxing too much and needed to get more involved in… something. A sport? A book group? Something. Scowling at the incompleteness of her thoughts, she turned her attention back to the meeting.

Suzanne Kennedy was fun to look at, so at least there was that. As she went on with her presentation, relaying to Regina Danvers, Sarah, and four other members of upper management why her marketing promotion was the way to go, she made eye contact, stopping on Sarah more than anybody else. Something about the penetrating gaze made Sarah squirm as if Ms. Kennedy could see right through her clothes and Sarah was sitting there nude before her. Shockingly, the feeling wasn't altogether unpleasant for Sarah. When her assistant, Mike Something-Or-Other, took over, Sarah could still feel Suzanne Kennedy's eyes on her. She hazarded a glance once or twice, each time finding herself held temporary prisoner by a jade green intensity that sent a tingle down her spine like gentle fingertips.

When the presentation was over, Sarah found herself lingering in the conference area, unnecessarily shuffling papers and organizing already organized memos, covertly studying this woman who'd so easily captured her attention. She was tall and lean, definitely athletic, and Sarah wondered not *if* she played any sports, but which ones. Her short blond hair was cut stylishly, tapering into a gentle V at the back of her neck. Though she carried off the business suit look very well, it was apparent to Sarah that Suzanne Kennedy's outfit of choice would be jeans and a T-shirt any day of the week, and that she'd look femininely powerful in them.

As if sensing the pheromones floating in the room, Mike told Suzanne he was going to grab a bottle of water and meet her in the lobby. With a quick tip of his chin to Sarah, he took his leave. Sarah had paid so little attention to him that if he robbed the front desk at that moment, she'd be of no help to the police, unable to even pick him out of a lineup, but his exit left the two women alone in the room, and for that, she was inexplicably grateful.

"Great presentation," she ventured, addressing her comment to Suzanne Kennedy's back as she packed her materials into her wheeled case. When she turned to meet Sarah's eyes, Sarah found herself once again captured.

"Thanks. Glad you liked it." She smiled, sort of a half-grin, the same type of casual, self-confident expression that the star athlete in high school might sport, knowing he had the head cheerleader in the palm of his hand.

"Very impressive. You made some good points."

"Did I?" Suzanne took a couple steps toward her, briefcase in one hand, handle of the wheeled case in the other, sexy smile still caressing her face. "Maybe you'd like to discuss them further? Over drinks tonight, perhaps?"

Sarah hoped the heat rushing through her body didn't show on her face. Quirking an eyebrow, she said, "My, my. Impressive again. You could be taking your future working with our company into your hands right now." She winked to take any threat out of her words.

Suzanne simply grinned rakishly. "True. But I realized once I hit forty that life is too short to hesitate. I see something I like, I go for it. Besides," she lowered her voice just slightly, "my gaydar hasn't failed me yet."

At that, Sarah laughed outright.

"So? What do you say?" Suzanne asked. "Meet me at McGinty's at six?"

Sarah liked the location, a casual but not dumpy Irish pub only a few minutes from the office. "I'll be there."

"Great."

Sarah watched as Suzanne and her paraphernalia left the conference room and headed down the hall to meet up with Mike What's-His-Name in the front lobby. She felt inexplicably energized, like she'd been asleep and suddenly woke up, ready to face the world. How long had it been since a sexy woman had made a play for her?

Too long! came the loud answer, as if somebody shouted it through her head.

The restlessness and uncertainty that had bathed her earlier was abruptly nowhere to be found and she giggled like a schoolgirl.

"I have a date," she said to the empty room, then headed toward her office to call Natalie. They were supposed to meet tonight and walk so that Natalie could take Bentley home. She'd just have her pick him up instead.

"Why?" she asked herself aloud.

"Because I have a date," she answered herself, unable to keep the grin off her face.

❖

Natalie liked the way things had worked out. It was funny when she thought back on all of it, on how panicked she'd been about finding Bentley, then over maybe losing him, about facing Sarah, how angry she'd been with her, how determined she was to hate her, and now…how much she actually liked her. Life was strange. Strange in a good way, and she was okay with that.

Andrea, however, hated the whole thing. She'd been scowling since she entered the coffee shop through the back door ten minutes earlier, making it apparent to the whole world that she was ticked off today.

"Want to see a movie tonight?" she asked Natalie. "That new Jodie Foster one just opened in Pittsford."

Natalie shook her head as she wiped down the front counter between the cash registers. "Can't. It's my night with Bentley and I have to go get him." She could almost hear Andrea roll her eyes.

"Now she's got you going to pick him up?" The disgusted disbelief in her voice apparent, Andrea punctuated it with a snort.

"She got stuck at work. She called a few minutes ago."

"Figures."

Natalie stopped working to rest her eyes on her. "What exactly is that supposed to mean?"

Andrea sighed. "Nothing."

They stared at each other for several seconds before Natalie decided she wasn't in the mood for an argument and went back to swabbing the counter. She knew Andrea was becoming frustrated with her inability to find enough courage to date, that she was going through a period of feeling worthless and unwanted, which happened to her on occasion, and Natalie vowed to cut the girl some slack. But not if it meant she had to argue with her.

"You spend an awful lot of time with her," Andrea stated after a few minutes of silence.

"It's for Bentley," Natalie responded matter-of-factly, as she did every time Andrea made the same comment—which was every other day at this point.

"Yeah, well, I don't like her."

"I know you don't."

Andrea flopped down into a wooden chair as Natalie lifted the others and placed them seat-down on the tables they surrounded. She heaved a mighty sigh, so "oh, woe is me" that it made Natalie laugh out loud.

"Okay," Natalie said, still chuckling. "I get the hint." Taking on a sweet, girly voice, she asked, "Whatever is the matter, Andrea, darling?"

Andrea smiled in spite of herself. "I feel like shit."

Natalie grew serious. "What? What is it? Have you called the doctor?"

Shaking her head, Andrea said, "No, no, not that kind of shit. I feel like shit up here." She tapped a finger against her temple.

Relieved but still sympathetic, Natalie kissed the top of Andrea's head. "I know, sweetie."

"I'm lonely, Natty."

Natalie nodded, having no solution for her problem and not knowing what to say to make it any better.

"Internet dating really isn't all it's cracked up to be."

"I can only imagine," Natalie scoffed. She knew it worked for a lot of people. She had friends who'd met online and had fallen instantly in love. But Natalie also knew how her own mind worked, and she needed to be around somebody, be near them physically, in order to develop feelings. Pretty words on a screen weren't going to make her heart go pitter-patter. She was sure of that. Despite her own misgivings, though, she'd hoped it would work for Andrea instead of depressing her further.

"I need to get laid!" Andrea shouted at the ceiling. Her statement was immediately followed by a loud clang coming from the kitchen, the unmistakable sound of a stainless steel mixing bowl crashing to the floor. Natalie turned wide eyes to Andrea, who in turn pressed her lips together in an effort to keep from giggling.

"You're going to give poor Mr. Valenti a heart attack," Natalie whispered, barely able to keep from laughing.

Andrea lowered her voice as Natalie headed to a nearby closet. "I can't help it. The vibrator just isn't doing it for me anymore."

Returning with a broom, Natalie commented, "Maybe you need a bigger vibrator."

Andrea snorted a laugh and Natalie could tell by her expression that she was feeling the slightest bit better. *Thank God,* she thought. It could be nearly impossible to pull Andrea out of a funk if she was determined to stay there, and Natalie just didn't have the energy for it tonight, something that made her feel guilty.

"I can't wait for that damn camping trip," Andrea said after watching Natalie sweep for several minutes.

"Good. It'll be fun. An entire weekend of nothing but drinking and friends and eating and drinking and playing cards and drinking."

"But will there be drinking?"

"As a matter of fact, there will. You can forget everything for a while."

"I like the sound of that."

Half an hour later, Andrea had headed home and Natalie was navigating her beat-up Toyota Corolla to Sarah's townhouse, using the directions she'd scribbled on a piece of scrap paper. It was a nice section of town, not far from the shop at all, in a buried treasure of a development, which couldn't be seen from the road and which Natalie hadn't even known was there.

"Nice," she said softly to the interior of her car as she coasted along the road scanning the house numbers. Finding 1228, she swung into the short driveway outside the garage and turned off the ignition. It was a gorgeous place, bringing to mind a bungalow along the coast of Maine. The siding was blue-green and all the trim was a rich-looking off-white that was so creamy, Natalie was tempted to taste it. Finding the extra key hidden on one of the decorative pieces of wood that trimmed the entryway right where Sarah had said it would be, Natalie let herself into the foyer and shut the door behind her.

The silence was immediate and so complete that for a split second, Natalie thought she'd lost her hearing. Then she adjusted and could hear the gentle sniffling sound of Bentley in his crate in the kitchen. Personally, she didn't think the crate was necessary, but she was beginning to get the impression that control was an important thing to Sarah, so she simply went along good-naturedly. In the kitchen, she released the catch so Bentley could come out.

"Hi, baby," she cooed at him as he waggled his butt and bathed her face with dog kisses, obviously happy to see her. "Mama's working late, so it's you and me tonight. Okay?" He went directly to the sliding glass door off the kitchen and Natalie peered out to see the chain lying on the cement patio. Knowing he didn't need it, but clipping it to his collar anyway, she let him out to do his business, and turned back toward the empty townhouse, wanting to explore a little bit, knowing she shouldn't, but sure she was going to anyway.

The living space had an appealing open design, with the sink and part of the glossy granite counter overlooking the living room. Trying to picture Sarah fixing snacks or a meal for guests while they chatted near the fireplace, she realized she had no idea whether or not Sarah could cook. Natalie could, but spending the majority of her day in a kitchen, cooking was the last thing she wanted to do when she got home. Still, there was something about the smell, the taste, and the atmosphere created by a home-cooked meal, and this was a terrific space for hosting company. The visual of Sarah in a sexy apron stirring up some concoction in a bowl was alarmingly appealing, and Natalie turned abruptly away from the kitchen.

Sarah's tastes in colors tended toward what Natalie would call "earthy," not surprisingly. She would never peg Sarah for a hot pink or electric blue kind of girl. Her couch was taupe and her carpet was almost the same shade, but the throw pillows, afghans, and curtains in various shades of deep eggplant and gentle lavender softened it all to form a very inviting and livable appeal. The thick, so-purple-it-was-almost-black throw rug in front of the gas fireplace seemed especially alluring and Natalie pictured herself lying on it, propped against a pile of pillows, reading a favorite novel and sipping a hot toddy on a brisk Sunday afternoon in the winter.

The place was spic-and-span, right down to track marks in the thick carpeting from the most recent run of the vacuum, and Natalie found herself speculating whether Sarah even lived there. Recalling the disarray in which she'd left her own apartment—last night's clothes in a heap on the bedroom floor, dirty dishes on the kitchen counter, hair in the bathroom sink—Natalie was almost embarrassed. She made a mental note to be sure to scour from ceiling to floor and everything in between if there ever came a time when Sarah would see the interior of her living space.

Built-in bookshelves took up one corner of the living room and Natalie stepped closer, curious as to what books and photographs Sarah thought were important enough to display. Noting there wasn't a trace of dust anywhere in the room, Natalie figured Sarah must have a cleaning woman or something. With her crazy schedule, there was no way she had time to keep her own house so spotless, and the image of Sarah dusting and vacuuming just seemed…wrong somehow. Turning her attention to the items on those dust-free shelves, she scanned an entire hardcover collection of Sue Grafton's mystery series, pristine and lined up in such a neat row that she had to wonder if Sarah had used a ruler and level when placing them. Natalie smiled at the precision but nodded in approval at the choice of books. She had the same series herself, albeit in paperback.

Framed photographs of all sizes decorated the shelves, sprinkled among and around the books and knickknacks, and Natalie was surprised. She didn't see Sarah as a knickknack kind of girl, but there were several little trinkets taking up residence in the living room, from a ceramic dog that looked like a replica of Bentley to some weirdly shaped brown bird made of wood that didn't look at all familiar to her. She picked it up—it was heavy and about the size of brick—and turned it around in her fingers, but didn't recognize the long bill or squatty build. She went to set it back in its place when her eyes fell on the 5x7 photograph that had been tucked in the back. Gingerly, she pulled it out and studied the two women, standing side by side with their arms around one another. The woman on the right was Sarah, obviously several years ago judging by the complete difference in hairstyle. She was smiling widely, her eyes dancing, her cheeks rosy, evidently having a wonderful time. The woman on the left was smaller, maybe three inches shorter than Sarah. Her reddish brown hair skimmed her shoulders, and the joyous sprinkling of freckles across her nose did nothing to brighten the faraway look in her dark eyes. She was smiling, yes, but it was apparent that she wanted to be anywhere else.

The ex, Natalie thought, certain. *She was gone even before she left. Poor Sarah. I bet she never saw it coming.*

Bentley chose that moment to jump at the door, and the sound caused Natalie to flinch where she stood. Feeling suddenly and inexcusably intrusive, she quickly put the picture and the weird bird back in their places and then let the dog in. As she passed back through the kitchen, she noticed a notepad and pen near the phone on the counter and decided to jot Sarah a note.

"All set?" she said to Bentley after setting the pen down. "Let's go for a ride."

At the mention of the R-word, Bentley began waggling and bouncing, making funny noises and causing Natalie to laugh.

"Come on, goofball."

❖

Good Lord...

It was the only coherent thought that came to Sarah's mind, given the situation and the dazzlingly erotic buzz her body was experiencing.

Good Lord...

She could hardly believe the situation. It was so…*unlike* her. She stood in a darkened corner of McGinty's parking lot, out of the glare of the overhead lights. Her back was pressed firmly against the side of Suzanne Kennedy's black SUV, and she was trapped between the vehicle and Suzanne's body. Her arms were wrapped around Suzanne's torso, holding on for dear life because Suzanne's tongue was buried deep in Sarah's mouth, exploring every inch of it, doing swirling, twirling things that only set Sarah's blood to racing and her heart pounding when she thought about where else those oral talents might be applied.

Suzanne Kennedy didn't say much once the kissing had begun. Frankly, she'd taken Sarah by surprise with her assertiveness. Sarah was used to being the one in charge, the one in control, the one to make the moves, and now the roles were reversed. It was no easy feat to force herself to relax, but she'd had no idea how sensual and sexy it could be to let somebody else take the wheel for a change, to be led…*to be felt up*, she thought with a jolt as Suzanne's hand slipped deftly up her blouse and cupped her breast. Her nipple stiffened in painful attention at the touch, and Sarah tried unsuccessfully to recall the last time she'd been handled with such promise, such ownership. *Not by Karen. Never by Karen.* Suzanne Kennedy knew what she wanted—and was obviously prepared to take it right here in the parking lot, Sarah realized as Suzanne's knee pushed between her own, forcing her legs apart enough so she could push a thigh against Sarah's hot and drenched core and then groan into Sarah's mouth at the feel of it.

Releasing Sarah's lips, Suzanne moved down her chin and forged a steaming wet assault on her throat and the pulse point in her neck, nipping just enough to make Sarah flinch, but not enough to make her pull away. Reveling in the touch of another woman after so long, realizing how much she missed having somebody want her, Sarah let herself drift along on the waves of pleasure Suzanne created with her tongue, her lips, and the fingers that were squeezing and pumping her nipple through the fabric of her bra, nearly making her cry out in ecstasy, it felt so blissfully good.

"Jesus Christ almighty, you're fucking sexy," Suzanne whispered, her first words since she'd begun kissing her.

Sarah opened her eyes to smile at the compliment and then noticed a handful of people coming out the back door of McGinty's. She was reasonably sure they couldn't be seen where they stood, but still. *I'm not some eighteen-year-old who's going to allow herself to be fucked in the parking lot of a bar.* Grasping Suzanne's head in both hands, she lifted her face so she could look into her eyes—eyes with pupils so dilated with desire they were nearly all black. She needed to gain some sort of a hold on the situation so she didn't feel like she was totally adrift.

"I've had a fabulous time tonight," she said in a low voice, then kissed Suzanne softly on the mouth.

"I'm sensing a but," Suzanne said with a half-grin.

"But I have to get home."

"We could continue this there, you know."

"I'm aware of that. But—"

"But you don't sleep with a woman on the first date."

"That's right." Sarah arched an eyebrow. "Point for you."

Suzanne leaned in close so her lips were butterfly soft against Sarah's ear. "What about on the second date?" she whispered, her hot breath sending a shiver down Sarah's spine. She flicked her tongue over Sarah's earlobe, causing a literal swoon, Sarah's knees practically buckling on her as she gripped Suzanne's shoulders for support.

"God," Sarah breathed. "The second date is an entirely different story."

"That's what I was hoping. I have to go out of town tomorrow. Are you busy late next week?"

"I believe I may have some free time," Sarah said with a wink.

"Terrific. Call me." Suzanne held up her business card so Sarah could see it, then lowered it, slipped it slowly down the front of Sarah's pants, and tucked it snugly into her panties, giving the crisp hair there a quick caress with her fingertips before withdrawing her hand. "To remember me by."

Sarah felt light-headed as Suzanne stepped away, and her body felt suddenly, achingly cold. She took a step backward and watched as Suzanne got into the driver's side and clicked her seat belt into place, then started the engine. With a wink and a wave, she backed out of the space and drove away.

Deciding she was fond of—and a little turned on by—the rough scratchiness of the rectangle of paper tucked into her underwear, Sarah left it there as she walked around her own car, astounded by the sopping state of her crotch as she took the wheel, certain she was going to leave a wet spot on the seat. God, when was the last time she'd been that excited? That ready to just whip off her clothes and go at it? It had to be the very early stages of her relationship with Karen, when they were newlyweds and doing it on every piece of furniture they owned. She gave herself a quick check in the rearview mirror, noting her disheveled hair and seriously flushed cheeks, and began to giggle.

"Good Lord," she said aloud, over and over as she drove home.

Despite the events of the evening, she found the silence of her townhouse to be a little depressing. She'd never been able to fully adjust to coming home to an empty place, although now that she had Bentley several days a week, it was better. But she remembered that she'd asked Natalie to come get him earlier and now she was truly alone, the dark and the quiet seemingly closing in on her, quelling her giddy mood.

Squinting in the kitchen light she'd flicked on, she stood still for several seconds, allowing her eyes to adjust, then reached into the refrigerator for a bottle of Gatorade. She always vowed to drink water alongside her cocktails when she went out, but the idea seemed to slip her mind once she was seated on a bar stool. She'd been proud of herself tonight. She'd only had two Bombay and tonics and she'd sipped them slowly, not wanting to drive Suzanne Kennedy away with any loud, drunken antics—or worse, talk of her ex. So she'd nursed her drinks and ended up making out in the parking lot with an incredibly sexy woman as a reward.

Not a bad deal, she thought with a grin.

Taking a slug of the sports drink directly out of the bottle, Sarah noticed a piece of paper near the phone with some unfamiliar writing on it.

Hi, Mama –

Just wanted to tell you that I miss you and hope you didn't have to work too late. Get some rest and come to meet me and Natalie tomorrow at the park. I love you!

Love, Bentley.

PS: Natalie says hi!

Sarah grinned widely, feeling suddenly much better. She admitted to the tiniest sliver of guilt over having lied to Natalie about the reason she would be late, but the truth was, she hadn't really known what would happen. Suzanne Kennedy might have stood her up and then she would have ended up going back to the office and working late. So it wasn't really a lie, just a tiny twisting of the truth. Right?

Regardless, it wasn't any of Natalie's business. They shared the dog, that was all. Still…she fingered the note in her hand, thinking it was a sweet gesture and surprised by how much she'd actually ended up liking Natalie, despite the foot they'd gotten off on. She was sweet and kind and fun to be around. With a gentle grin, she tacked the note to the refrigerator door with a whale-shaped magnet she had purchased on a trip to Cape Cod, then took her Gatorade and headed up to bed, Suzanne Kennedy's business card still rubbing provocatively inside her panties.

Chapter Eleven

Natalie and Bentley were frolicking in the park for about half an hour on Friday evening when Sarah appeared, looking like the cat that ate the canary. Natalie said hi, then squinted at her as if trying to see further in.

"What?" Sarah asked, taking the slobbery ball from Bentley's mouth with a grimace and tossing it for him.

"You're all smiley," Natalie replied.

"I'm all smiley?" Sarah said the word with a raised eyebrow.

"Yeah. You're usually more…I don't know…intense. More serious. Today, you're smiley. How come?"

"Are you saying I'm not allowed to be smiley?"

Playing along at Sarah's obviously teasing tone, Natalie answered, "No, not at all. I'm just saying it's rare that I even see your teeth. And today, there they are, in all their pearly whiteness. I'm just curious."

Sarah laughed outright and the sound made Natalie grin even wider. Bentley plopped down at their feet, panting and wagging his nubby tail, apparently happy as a clam. Natalie loved seeing him like that and hoped Sarah did, too. Judging from the look on her face, it was a shared sentiment.

Sarah squatted down and gave Bentley a thorough neck-scratching, murmuring sweet words to him as Natalie watched.

She'd apparently gone home to change before joining them, donning a pair of khaki shorts and a navy blue polo shirt. Her dark hair was pulled back off her face and a fine sheen of sweat sprinkled the back of her neck. The unexpected urge Natalie felt to touch her fingertips to it was interrupted when Sarah looked up suddenly, catching Natalie by surprise with the blue of her eyes.

"I had a date last night, if you must know."

Natalie's eyebrows shot up into her hairline. "You did? That's great. I'd ask how it went, but I can see by your expression and mood that it went well."

Sarah nodded. "I think it did."

"Where did you meet her?" By unspoken pact, they began their usual stroll around the perimeter of this section of the park, alternating who threw the ball for Bentley. He fetched it and brought it back to wherever they were at the time.

"She gave a marketing presentation at my office yesterday."

Natalie did a double take at her. "You asked somebody out who's trying to get your business?"

Sarah's face told Natalie she knew that wasn't necessarily ethical. "I didn't ask her out. She asked me out."

"Okay, well, that makes a difference." A teasing snort accompanied the comment.

"I know!" Sarah whined. "You're right, I know. I'm bad. I probably should have said no. But she was so sexy and…it's been a long time since somebody asked me out and…I wanted to go! Sue me. I wanted to go. Do you know what I mean?"

Natalie tempered her laugh by putting a warm hand on Sarah's back as they walked, rubbing it reassuringly. "Hey, you don't have to explain to me. I totally understand that. Us single girls have to stick together. I probably would have done the same thing. Did you have a good time?"

"I did." Sarah took the ball from Bentley, who was standing at red alert, his gaze focused on another dog coming into the area. He took off at a dead run before either of them could stop him.

"Bentley! Come!" Natalie shouted at him. His step faltered and Natalie yelled to him again. The springer spaniel that had entered the park was leashed and his owner looked questioningly at the two women, pulling tightly on the nylon lead. "He's okay," Natalie called as they crossed toward the newcomers and Bentley inched forward to sniff the springer. "He just wants to say hi. He's not aggressive."

"Yeah, but mine is," the woman warned just as the springer snarled and snapped at Bentley. He jumped back, obviously surprised, and retreated back to his owners.

"Sorry about that," Sarah said to the woman, who led her dog off in the opposite direction, shaking her head in irritation.

Natalie grimaced. "I forget about that," she said, feeling suddenly foolish and inadequate. "Bentley's so sweet and friendly that I forget there are dogs who just aren't, and I shouldn't assume everybody's okay with him running up to them like that." She sighed. "Sorry."

"It's okay, but how 'bout we leash him now?" Sarah said with a note of concern. Seeing Natalie's embarrassed expression, she added, "You know, at least he gets exercise with you. I told you I never had him off the lead."

"Well, then, I guess that means you never had another dog try to take a chunk out of him."

"True," Sarah said. "We'll just have to be more careful." Then out of the blue, she blurted, "Hey, want to go get some dinner? It's Friday night, I'm ready for a glass of wine, and I'm starving. My treat."

Natalie looked at her, thinking that having a date had actually done Sarah Buchanan a whole lot of good in the mood department. "That sounds great. We can drop Bentley off at my place and eat around here. Would that work?"

"Perfect."

❖

It didn't occur to Natalie until she slid her key into the keyhole that she was about to let Sarah see her apartment. She did a quick mental scan and wanted to slap herself in the forehead for not *thinking* before she suggested. She knew the place wasn't a complete disaster, but it wasn't as clean as it could be and it sure wasn't classy and elegant like Sarah's townhouse. Resigned to her fate, she swallowed back a sigh and climbed the stairs to the second floor of the building, Bentley scooting up in front of her and Sarah following behind.

"The Valentis own the whole building?" Sarah asked.

"Yeah. They rent the second floor to me for a really good price. It's not much as far as apartments go, but it works." She keyed the second door, the one at the top of the stairs, and pushed it open. Bentley shot directly to his water dish and began slurping away. "Welcome to my humble abode," she said, making a grand sweep with her arm. "Such as it is."

"This is adorable," Sarah said, wandering into the small living room. She stopped and looked at each photograph and knickknack, making Natalie shift uncomfortably from the kitchen as she made a lame attempt to clean up the tiny area. Stooping to snag a sweatshirt off the floor, she hurled it into the bedroom before it could be seen.

Sarah stopped near the futon and looked out the windows. "This is great. You can see right down to Monroe. I bet this is a cool place to sit and read, in the sun like this." The setting sun cast red-hued light beams through the opened miniblinds and across the furniture and floor.

Natalie glanced up quickly from the dirty dishes she was piling into the sink. "It is." She was pleased Sarah had picked out her favorite spot and her demeanor eased up just a touch. Hating that she was feeling so self-conscious, she noticed Sarah reading the back of the Ann Patchett book she'd been absorbed in last night. "Have you read that?"

"Not yet, but I saw that it's gotten fabulous reviews."

"The woman writes like a goddess, I swear. She's truly magical. You're welcome to borrow it when I'm finished."

Sarah looked up and met her gaze across the small space. "I'd like that. Thanks." Bentley had sprawled across the floor like roadkill, tongue lolling, still panting. He looked like somebody had tossed him there and that's how he'd landed. Sarah laughed. "Well, I see he's already missing us terribly. You ready?"

Hanging the dishcloth over the faucet, Natalie nodded. "Ready. Where do you want to go?" she asked as she grabbed her keys.

"What about that little place on the corner of Park and Oxford? The one that's been there for ages?"

Natalie scrunched up her face as she thought. "Logan's?"

"That's the one. We can walk there from here, can't we?"

"Absolutely. Be a good boy, Bentley."

Bentley barely lifted his head to look up at them as they exited, his tongue still hanging out the side of his mouth.

❖

Sarah had anticipated dinner would be pleasant, but she enjoyed herself and Natalie's company way more than she expected to. If anybody had said to her six months earlier that she and Natalie would become good friends, she would have expressed much surprise. On the surface, they didn't seem to have much in common—the workaholic business executive and the cashier at the local coffee shop—but Sarah was having a blast. She couldn't remember the last time she'd laughed so much and she gave Natalie much-deserved credit for that. The girl had a knack for cracking Sarah up. Not many people could say that.

"So," Natalie said over the rim of her wineglass. "Tell me more about this super date you had last night." Her eyes twinkled and Sarah wasn't sure if it was mischief or too much *vino*, but

Natalie's cheeks were adorably rosy and she was grinning like a schoolgirl as she held the glass nested in her fingers.

"Suzanne," Sarah said. "Her name is Suzanne." She took a sip of her own wine and grinned. "And she was incredibly sexy. Tall. Blond. Assertive."

"Assertive?" Natalie's eyebrows furrowed. "You go for that?"

"No," Sarah said with a laugh. "I usually don't."

"I didn't think so," Natalie said with a wink. "Because *you're* the assertive one."

Wanting to protest but knowing a denial would be pointless, Sarah nodded. "Correct."

"So. Suzanne. Like her?"

Sarah pursed her lips, thinking about it. "Yeah. I think so."

"A lot?"

"I'm not sure yet." With a shrug, she clarified, "I only spent a couple hours with her."

"She a good kisser?" Natalie sipped from her glass again, apparently to hide the playful grin on her face.

"Hey!" Sarah said by way of protest, then followed Natalie's lead and hid her own smile with her glass.

"She is, isn't she?" Natalie pointed at her, mockingly accusatory.

They both burst into laughter. When each caught her breath, Sarah said, "Yes. She is a *very* good kisser. *Very* good."

Natalie held up her glass for a toast. "Good for you." They clinked and sipped.

"I'm having such a good time," Sarah said suddenly. "I can't remember the last time I had this much fun."

"Was it, um, last night, perhaps? With Suzanne the Tongue?"

"No." Sarah snorted a laugh at the nickname. "I mean like this." She waved her hand between the two of them as they sat. "No pressure to impress, no pretenses. Just enjoying somebody else's company."

Natalie cocked her head to the side. "Don't you have any friends, Sarah?" Her voice was teasing, but Sarah wondered if there wasn't a small amount of honest curiosity to the question.

"Truth is I lost most of them in the divorce." Sarah gave a half-grin, half-grimace. "The ones who stuck around, I made miserable with my whining, my disdain for my ex, my constant extolling of the unfairness of life, blah, blah, blah. I think they got sick of me. I drove them away."

"Well, then they weren't very good friends to begin with."

"No?"

"No. You went through a breakup, for Christ's sake. How did they expect you to act? You were in pain. They should have cut you a little slack."

"Where were you a year ago?" Sarah said, grinning. "I could have used you then."

"She really hurt you, huh?"

"Understatement of the century."

"You told me she's getting married. To a man, I assume?"

"Yep." Sarah tried to keep her answers light, to act like it didn't bother her, but she knew by the sympathy in Natalie's eyes that she was failing miserably. And then she realized she didn't have to pretend. She didn't need to fake it with Natalie. She could be herself.

"Ugh. God, that must have sucked."

Sarah laughed then. She couldn't help it, it just burst out of her at the complete and totally perfect accuracy of the statement. "That was exactly it. That's *exactly* how it was," she said. "It *sucked*. Karen fell out of love with me—though frankly, I suspect she was never in love with me in the first place—and in love with Derek and I had no freakin' idea she even liked guys. How's that for not knowing your spouse?"

"You're not sitting there telling me you blame yourself for Karen leaving, are you? It had nothing at all to do with you."

Sarah blinked at her in disbelief. "Of course it did! How can you say it didn't? I mean, if I'd been home more, if I'd spent more time with her and less in the office or something, maybe she wouldn't have been so quick to leave. Maybe we..." Her words trailed off when Natalie placed a warm hand over hers and interrupted her thoughts with a firmly quiet voice.

"Sweetie, Karen isn't gay. She prefers to be with a man. It's as simple as that. That's not about you, it's about her. You could have spent twenty-four hours a day with her and it wouldn't have changed a thing. Her leaving is not your fault. Don't you see that?"

Sarah hung her head and fiddled with the stem of her glass. Deep down, she knew Natalie spoke the honest and simple truth. But accepting that she could not change something, no matter what, was a difficult prospect for her. She pressed her lips together and nodded almost imperceptibly. "I guess."

"God, you're stubborn," Natalie said, and squeezed Sarah's hand affectionately in an attempt to break the tension. With picture-perfect timing, the waiter stopped by with the check, which Sarah took from him. "I'm going to visit the little girls' room."

Grinning in self-deprecation, Sarah took care of the bill and left a generous tip, as she always did. Natalie was right. She knew Natalie was right. It was high time she stopped blaming herself for not being able to fix something and started looking forward instead of backward all the time. Wondering exactly how one went about turning over a new leaf, she poured the remains of the wine evenly into their glasses and picked hers up. As she lifted it to her lips to sip, her stomach clenched and her breath stuck in her throat at the sight walking toward her.

Karen and Derek were heading up the aisle between tables, his arm around her shoulders, her laugh audible from several yards away. Looking around in an almost blind panic, Sarah could find no route of escape as they just kept coming.

"Sarah. Hi."

Shit.

Karen's tone of voice was a combination of surprise and

sweetness. She and Derek both stopped at her table, looking the slightest bit uncomfortable, but obviously allowing manners to win out over the stronger desire to run away quickly. "How are you?"

No sound came out when she opened her mouth to speak, so Sarah cleared her throat to try again. "Um, good. I'm good."

"You remember Derek?" Karen gestured to her fiancé, who smiled warmly—if uncertainly—and held out his hand.

Taking her own turn with manners winning out over creating a scene, Sarah shook his hand quickly, hating the gentle warmth of both it and his eyes. He wasn't necessarily a handsome man, but he was ruggedly attractive somehow and for that, she hated him more. Wanting to crawl under the table until they went away, she could do nothing but blink rapidly and drown in the awkward silence.

Suddenly, a warm hand was on her shoulder, squeezing gently. Natalie's voice said, "Hey, there. How're we doing?" As if just noticing Karen and Derek, she squinted at them for a second. "Oh! You're Karen, aren't you? Hi!"

Karen studied her, furrowed eyebrows just barely noticeable, and Sarah felt a stab of confusion poke at her head.

Natalie held out her hand. "Sarah's told me so much about you, it's nice to finally meet you." She shook Karen's hand enthusiastically, then turned slightly. "And you must be…Derek, right?" She gave him the same treatment, continuing to smile in an open and friendly manner.

Her hand shifted, sliding from Sarah's shoulder to cup the back of her neck and massage it gently and—very clearly to anybody looking—possessively. Sarah chewed on her bottom lip happily as she watched Karen watch Natalie, trying not to notice how good Natalie's hand felt on her skin.

"Don't you just love it here?" Natalie asked, looking around the restaurant.

Derek nodded. "We've only been here a couple times, but it's always been good."

"And the wine list," Natalie said. "To die for."

"We had a 2005 Cabernet Sauvignon that was out of this world," he said, apparently enjoying his conversation with Natalie, probably happy to have a tangible subject on which to focus that didn't have to do with his fiancée's history with Sarah.

"We almost ordered that one, too," Natalie said, pushing at his shoulder in an affectionate move that said she'd known him for years. "But we had seafood, and we thought white made more sense, so we went with the Sauvignon Blanc instead." She grabbed the empty bottle from the table and showed it to him. "This one."

Sarah watched the two of them in disbelief, feeling as if all four of them had been unknowingly submerged in some alternate universe. Judging by the look on Karen's face, she felt the same way. Sarah was aware of nothing more specific than the dim lighting in the room, the sound of Natalie and Derek conversing—though she had reached the point where she could hear their voices, but had no idea what was being said—and the comfort of Natalie's warm palm still resting on her neck, absently kneading the muscles there. Everything else seemed to fade away, and she briefly wondered if she was having some sort of existential meltdown.

Finally, as if deciding she'd had enough of this weirdness, Karen tugged gently on Derek's arm. "We should go, honey." Sarah sent up a prayer of thanks, even though she could have lived the rest of her life without hearing Karen call somebody else "honey."

"Oh." He turned to look at her, almost as if he'd forgotten she was standing next to him. "Okay. Sure." He was clearly disappointed.

"I'm so glad we got to meet," Natalie said sweetly, shaking both their hands again.

"Me, too," Derek said.

"Have a great night."

Karen waved halfheartedly and then they were gone. Natalie followed their departure with her eyes before returning to her side of the table, dragging her hand lazily back across Sarah's shoulder, and taking a seat. As she picked up her wineglass, she looked at Sarah, who was staring at her with an expression that mixed pride, annoyance, and jubilation.

"What?" Natalie asked, then sipped.

Sarah searched her brain for the right words to express what she was feeling, but to no avail. After several seconds, she nodded once and said simply, "Thank you."

"You're welcome." Natalie's wide smile told Sarah that little power play had entertained her immensely.

"You enjoyed that, didn't you?"

"Is that bad?" Natalie scrunched up her face as she posed the question.

Sarah couldn't help but chuckle. "No. No, it's not bad." They sipped quietly, watching patrons come and go. "How'd you know that was her?" Sarah finally asked.

Natalie toyed with the corner of her napkin. "You still have a picture of her in your living room."

"Oh." Sarah poked at the inside of her cheek with her tongue. "Yeah, I should probably get rid of that, huh?"

"Might be a good time to put it away."

CHAPTER TWELVE

Sarah didn't spend nearly as much time with her mother as she wanted to. They'd always been so close…hell, they were still very close. But since her breakup, Sarah had let her job take over because it was the only thing that seemed to keep her from going out of her mind. Suddenly, there never seemed to be enough time in the day, or in the week, and sometimes in the month. Before she knew it, weeks would go by without her seeing either of her parents and she was getting to the point where she wondered if questioning her own priorities was something she should be looking into. That was why she'd called and invited her mom to lunch on Wednesday.

Now, scanning the midday crowd and spotting her mother seated at a nicely located table on the patio, Sarah felt a hundred times better, lighter.

"Hi, Mom." She kissed her mother's cheek and took the seat across from her.

"Hi, baby." Her mother held up her soda. "I started without you."

"Am I late?"

"No, no. I got here a little early. I wanted to people-watch." She said the last line in a lowered voice, like she was telling Sarah a secret.

Sarah grinned at her. "Anything scandalous?"

With an exaggeratedly disappointed sigh, her mother responded, “No. I’m afraid everybody’s boring today.”

“That’s too bad.”

For the next hour and a half, they chatted, laughed, listened to one another, and generally enjoyed each other’s company. Sarah was reminded why her friends were envious of her relationship with her mom. They were like the very best of friends and she had always felt like she could talk about anything with her.

“You seem so good,” her mother said to her as the waitress took their empty plates away.

“I do?” Sarah was surprised by the comment. “What do you mean?”

“Just…lately. The past few weeks. You seem…good. I don’t know how else to put it.”

“As opposed to bad?” Sarah said lightly, curious about her mother’s words.

“As opposed to sad and depressed.” Her mother made a face that said she hadn’t wanted to use those exact words, but they were the truth.

“Oh.” Sarah sucked on her straw.

Her mother placed a hand over Sarah’s. “Have I made you angry?”

“What? No. No, not at all. I’m just absorbing what you said, that’s all.”

“I don’t mean anything by it,” her mother said in an attempt to reassure her. “I just wanted you to know that you seem to be enjoying life a little more.”

At that, Sarah smiled. “I think I am.”

“Is it because Bentley’s back? That must have helped.” Sarah had filled her parents in on what had transpired with her dog, and though they weren’t thrilled that Natalie didn’t just give him back, they understood when Sarah explained things to them.

“That’s definitely part of it.”

“What else? Is there more?”

Sarah began tallying up the latest significant events in

her life—the return of Bentley, Regina Danvers telling her the managers noticed her good job overseas, her date with Suzanne Kennedy, her new friendship with Natalie, the run-in with Karen and Derek the previous week. "There's a bunch of stuff, Mom. But it's all good."

"Tell me." Her mother hunkered down over the table like she was getting ready to receive a juicy piece of gossip. Sarah laughed at her.

"Just a bunch of little things." She gave a quick, abridged version of everything that had happened, including the facts that she'd left a message for Suzanne Kennedy that morning, and that she felt seriously giddy whenever she replayed the restaurant scene with Karen and Derek in her head.

"Life has a way of working things out, honey. I've always told you that. You just have to hang in there long enough to make it through the shit so the sunshine can come along. Everything will be fine in the end."

"If it's not fine, it's not the end," Sarah finished, knowing the phrase well. The waitress dropped off the check and Sarah snagged it out of her mother's reach.

"I've always told you that," her mother repeated, tossing a mock glare at Sarah while she pulled some money out of her wallet.

"You always have, and I'm sure you're right."

"Well, it's just nice to see you smiling."

"Thanks, Mom."

"Thank you for lunch."

"It was my pleasure."

Later that afternoon, Sarah found herself having trouble focusing on the second marketing presentation being given in the conference room. The company was trying to find a marketing firm to help them with advertising and promotion and Sarah knew there were at least two more presentations to see. The nerdy guy standing before them didn't have an ounce of Suzanne Kennedy's charisma, not to mention that his faintly pin-striped shirt and patterned tie were wreaking havoc with her ability to focus, like she was looking through a screen and her eyes couldn't decide what was the central focal point.

As if reading her mind, her cell phone buzzed against her hip. She glanced down at it, saw Suzanne's number, and couldn't keep the smile from spreading across her face.

❖

"One more weekend, baby," Andrea said with great exuberance.

"You're not excited, are you?" Natalie teased as they sat at the little break table in the back of the shop.

"I just need to get the hell away, you know?" Andrea shook her head. "I need a little mindless entertainment." Mr. Valenti pulled a tray of hot confections from the oven across the room. "Lookin' good, Leo. You're gorgeous."

Natalie shook her head as Mr. Valenti blushed to the roots of his white hair, a boyish smile decorating his stubbled face. The line of customers had diminished and Mrs. Valenti bustled into the back to get a refill on cannoli. She glanced at the two women at the table and pointed at Andrea as she passed.

"You. You always here. You never work?" Her wink told them she was bantering, and Andrea schooled her expression into mock insult.

"I'll have you know it's Superintendent's Day. Or something."

"I should have been teacher," Mrs. Valenti scoffed.

"It's not all it's cracked up to be, Mrs. V.," Natalie said. "The million days off aren't worth the red tape, politics, and disrespectful kids. Trust me."

"And you wouldn't know how to fill cannoli," Mrs. Valenti said with a grin, carrying a tray out to the front.

"There you go." Natalie smiled tenderly at her and stood. "Here, let me carry that."

Mrs. Valenti held it away from her. "You sit. You're on break."

Natalie sat, well aware that arguing with Angela Valenti was an exercise in futility.

"You're going to own this place one day," Andrea whispered.

"Oh, I don't know about that." Natalie waved her hand dismissively.

"Mark my words."

Since any idea of the ownership of the shop transferring meant the Valentis either retiring or worse, Natalie was anxious to change the subject. "So…are you packed already?" The camping trip was a very safe topic, being something fun that Andrea was really looking forward to.

"Not yet, but I've made my list." Her face lit up with anticipation. "There are going to be a lot of us this year. Like, twelve or fifteen or something."

"It does seem to get bigger every year." The annual trip had started with only four women and had increased exponentially for the past six years. Natalie had joined in three years before and Andrea had come along the previous year. A realization hit her and she smacked herself in the forehead. "Shit. I forgot to tell Sarah."

"Why does Sarah need to know?"

"Because I need her to keep Bentley for the weekend." She stood and crossed to the phone mounted on the wall, then dialed Sarah's cell from memory. She was surprised when Sarah picked up. "Oh. Hey, it's Natalie."

"Hi, Natalie. How are you doing today?"

Natalie smiled at the friendly tone, the voice that had grown so familiar. "I'm good. How about you? Having a good day?"

"I am, as a matter of fact."

"Good. Hey, I need a favor."

"What a coincidence. So do I."

"Interesting," Natalie said, lowering her voice. "Two women

in need. Whatever shall we do?" She waggled her eyebrows even though Sarah couldn't see her.

"It's a conundrum," Sarah played along. "How about you go first and we'll see what we can come up with?"

"Sounds like a plan."

"Perfect. What do you need?"

Natalie turned toward Andrea just in time to see her making a gagging motion with her hands at her throat. Natalie stuck her tongue out at her. Into the phone, she said, "My camping trip is next weekend, over Labor Day. Can you keep Bentley from Friday until Monday and I'll take him on Monday?"

"Not a problem at all."

"Thanks a bunch. Okay, your turn."

"Can you take him this Friday night? I know it's my night, but I can switch with you and take him Saturday instead."

"Suzanne the Tongue back in town?"

Sarah laughed again at the moniker. "As a matter of fact."

Unable to explain the strange and uncomfortable sensation in her stomach, Natalie tried to swallow it away. "Sure. I'll take him. Should I pick him up from your house again?"

She could hear Sarah hesitate. "Is that a big pain for you?"

"No. No, not at all."

"If you're sure you don't mind, it would help a lot. I think we're meeting after work."

"Consider it all taken care of." Natalie's playfulness seemed to dissipate like it was made of mist. She wondered if Sarah noticed.

"Great. Thanks a bunch."

"Sure. Have a good time." Natalie hung up the phone. When she returned to the break table, Andrea was pointing a finger at her, wiggling it around in the general vicinity of Natalie's face.

"What's this?" she asked, still pointing. "What's this about?"

"What's what about?" Natalie asked in return, sounding a bit testy even to her own ears.

"This face you're making. What's it about?"

"What face? Nothing. Stop it." She pushed Andrea's hand away from her eyes. "I don't know what you're talking about."

"Uh-huh."

Andrea stared at her so hard, Natalie thought she could actually *feel* it on her skin. She made a show of looking at her watch, then said, "Break's over. Back to work." She knew Andrea was staring at her the whole way out to the cash register. She didn't look back.

❖

The slats of sunshine beaming in through the top of Bentley's crate must have made a warm and comfy spot to sleep because Natalie was almost at his crate before he noticed. He blinked himself awake and stretched out his front legs—as much as he could in the limited space. His blanket, which looked soft and warm, was balled up in a corner where he'd obviously pushed it. A slobbery tennis ball and a bone with the knuckles gnawed down to mere nubs occupied the area with him, giving him things to do while he waited for the evening to come. His belly rumbled loudly and Natalie laughed as she unlatched the door of the crate.

"It's just about that time, isn't it, buddy?" He nosed out of the crate and pushed into her body, giving her his version of a greeting hug. She scratched his back right at the base of his nubby tail where he liked it and he leaned against her thigh, apparently loving life. "Come on," she said. "Let's do your business."

He zipped to the sliding glass doors, tapping and prancing in place, excited to get out to the yard. Natalie let him out and watched for a couple minutes as he went directly to the same bush he went to first every time, the telltale deadening of the grass there offering proof of his daily visits. Then he walked the perimeter, nose to the ground, checking for any new passersby or markings. She didn't use the leash but kept a close eye on him as he wandered. When he slinked off slowly, watching and sniffing, Natalie slid the door open and called calmly, "Over here, Bentley."

With an audible sigh, he turned back, moseying along at his own pace until he reached the doorway.

"Good boy," she said, scratching his neck.

On her left heel as always, he trailed her into the kitchen where she reached into his cookie jar for one of the chicken treats he loved. He never ceased to amaze her with his smarts and obedience. She stopped in front of the refrigerator, noticing the note she'd jotted for Sarah was tacked there. Trying to understand why that simple thing made her feel all giddy inside, she stared at it for a long time, until Bentley shifted by her feet, letting her know his patience was growing thin. She turned and told him he was a good boy, chuckling at the spot of drool on the floor.

She wandered the house slowly, not quite sure of her destination, but Bentley followed, perfectly willing to just walk along behind her. From the kitchen, she strolled toward the back of the house, taking her time and looking at things on the walls, the photographs and artwork, never touching anything, just looking. Sarah seemed fond of gentle, calming scenes, landscapes, but not at all boring. One painting in the hallway on the way to the downstairs master bedroom depicted a single Adirondack chair poised toward a large pond. Natalie swore she could almost hear the cicadas and smell the summer grass. She stared at it for a long time as Bentley watched her with curious eyes, probably wondering what she was doing.

Moving down the hall several more steps, they stopped in the doorway of Sarah's bedroom and Natalie leaned against the doorjamb. Bentley sat at her heel and looked up at her, waiting for a clue as to where they were going next. As if an invisible barrier stood across the doorway, Natalie didn't step into the room. She knew there was a boundary there that she had no business crossing. She felt weird just being this close. She closed her eyes and inhaled deeply, the musky scent of Sarah's perfume hanging provocatively in the air and doing things to Natalie that she couldn't explain and didn't want to think about. Her eyes popped open and she suddenly had to get out of there. Now.

She turned so suddenly that she startled Bentley, nearly stepping on him and he jumped backward. "I'm sorry, buddy," she said, reaching down to scratch him as she exhaled a frustrated breath, wondering what was going on with her. "Ready to go?"

He knew the G-word well and his whole body waggled as he followed her to the front door. She clipped his leash on him—she'd been doing that a little more often lately, rather than let him run free, out of respect for Sarah—and opened the door.

"We'll go home and have dinner and guess what? Mrs. Valenti made chicken soup today, so guess who gets the scraps?"

She used the playful voice she always did when they were about to have some fun, so he kept on wiggling, even as he jumped into the backseat. When Natalie took her spot behind the wheel, he stretched forward and gave her a loving lick on the cheek. She looked back at him and he cocked his head at her. He actually looked like he was puzzled and she glanced at herself in the rearview mirror to see what he was seeing. She was dismayed to notice that she was scowling slightly, a new crease at the top of her nose between her eyebrows. "Oh, that's attractive," she muttered as she started the car and shifted into gear.

CHAPTER THIRTEEN

"This is a really nice place you've got here." Sarah wandered around the living room of Suzanne Kennedy's loft apartment. A Bombay and tonic in one hand, she dragged the fingertips of the other across the marble mantel of the gas fireplace, admiring the smooth coldness of it. The room looked like it had been lifted from the pages of an Ethan Allen catalog and set directly into Suzanne's space, the furniture made of crystal clear glass, gleaming metal, and angular corners of black leather. It was inarguably beautiful, if not at all warm or inviting.

"Thanks," Suzanne said, taking a seat on the couch, which seemed to be made up of sharp-cornered black leather squares pieced together. "I'm not good at all with decorating, so I hired a guy. Gay guy, of course. No nurturing female could come up with this design. All I'm missing is the leopard-print rug in front of the fireplace." She laughed. "But it looks cool."

"True," Sarah said. Suzanne might have been a failure in the decorating department, but she was stellar in the kitchen. The chicken French she'd prepared had been out of this world and Sarah had cleaned her plate and contemplated asking for seconds before deciding that gorging herself on a date might be considered less than attractive behavior.

"Hey." Suzanne's voice changed, was now whisper soft, and

when Sarah turned to look at her, she was patting the leather next to her. "Come here. Sit with me."

She looked damn good, Sarah thought, her eyes quickly scanning over Suzanne's lithe form. Her long legs were clad in black slacks that hugged her toned ass as if they were tailored just for her—Sarah couldn't help but notice while Suzanne stood in the kitchen preparing dinner. The teal, short-sleeved summer-weight sweater not only showcased her strong shoulders and small, perfect breasts, but really enhanced the color of her eyes. Sexy didn't begin to describe her, but Sarah couldn't figure out why a tiny kernel of hesitation was forming in the pit of her stomach.

"Okay." Sarah crossed and sat down next to her, the couch cushion barely giving half an inch with her weight. She met Suzanne's eyes, which were slightly hooded and looked nothing short of seductive. "Hi."

"Hi, yourself." Suzanne took Sarah's drink from her hand and set it on the glass coffee table near their knees. Pushing a lock of hair behind Sarah's ear, she said, "You're a beautiful woman."

A tiny lump of arousal formed in Sarah's throat at the feather-light touch of Suzanne's fingertips near her ear, while at the same time, that kernel of hesitation combined with a weird nervousness that suddenly set in and caused a tremor in her right knee. "You don't look so bad yourself," she said, trying for humor but not sure she got there.

Suzanne's lips were soft, hot, and thorough, just as Sarah remembered them. As if replaying the night in the parking lot of the bar, Sarah melted, became putty, was unable to do anything but let Suzanne lead. It was completely out of character for her, and that began to niggle at her brain.

Suzanne's warm tongue slid into her mouth as Sarah tried to analyze why she didn't seem to have it in her to push back with her own tongue, to slip her hands under Suzanne's sweater, to scratch her nails down a black-clad thigh. Everything Suzanne did felt so good, so perfect. Sarah's panties were already damp. They had been since she'd arrived and Suzanne had kissed her at the door.

So why do I feel so…disengaged?

If Suzanne had noticed any lack of participation on Sarah's part, she ignored it like a pro. Instead, she pushed forward so Sarah's back was against the hard, sharp arm of the couch.

"Ow," Sarah managed, trying to sit back up.

"Sorry," Suzanne muttered. "Here." She pulled on Sarah, sliding her body so she was lying on the couch beneath her. Her mouth covered Sarah's once again.

Stiffening, Sarah tried to sit up. "Wait." She pushed Suzanne away, trying to be gentle about it, not wanting to insult the woman, but feeling utterly claustrophobic. "Just…wait. Please."

"What's the matter?" Suzanne's tone was steady, but her eyes crackled with a spark of annoyance.

"I…" Sarah blew out a breath of frustration and shook her head. "I don't know. I'm sorry. I just…" She stood. "I should probably go."

"Already? Why?" Suzanne stood, too, and put her hands on Sarah's upper arms, rubbing gently. "What is it?" she asked softly. "Did I do something wrong? Did I hurt you?"

"No. No, not at all." Sarah scratched at her forehead, wishing she had some explanation to give, but just as confused as Suzanne seemed to be. "I'm sorry. It's not you. I promise. It's not you at all. It's me." She managed to suppress the wince that followed such a clichéd line, but it was the truth and it was all she had to offer as she moved toward the door and took her shoulder bag off the hall tree. "Thank you for dinner," she said lamely.

"Sure," Suzanne said, just as lamely, and opened the door.

In the hall, Sarah turned back to her, feeling completely idiotic and embarrassed. "I'm sorry," she said again.

Suzanne nodded and shut the door with a click.

Twenty minutes later, Sarah slid her key into her own front door lock and let herself into the dark and empty townhouse, feeling a slight sense of déjà vu. Her keys clattered loudly in the silence as she tossed them onto a table on her way to the liquor cabinet. She had the drink all mixed and ready for consumption when something made her stop.

It's such a pretty drink, she thought strangely as she stared at it, the bubbles from the tonic water rising slowly to the top, the clarity of the liquor, the splash of color made by the bright green section of lime. *It should always be served in a clear glass so people can see how pretty it is.* She was unsure how long she stood there, simply looking at the drink.

Suddenly, with no thought at all, she picked up the phone and dialed Natalie's number. It was picked up in the middle of the fourth ring, the voice soft, kind, like always.

"Hello?"

"Hi there."

"Sarah? Are you home already?"

Sarah could picture her, could see her as clearly as if she was standing in the room with her. Natalie had probably been lying on her stomach on her bed, maybe reading or watching TV. Recognizing Sarah's voice, she sat up, her voice clearing, increasing in volume just a titch. It all made Sarah smile, a warm tingle seeping through her body.

"Sadly, yes."

"No dice with Suzanne the Tongue?" There was an attempt at humor, but it was gentle, as if Natalie knew Sarah might be upset about something and didn't want to needle her too badly.

"Not for her lack of trying," Sarah said, wandering back into the living room to the chair where she'd dropped her bag. She unclipped it as she talked. "I don't know what's wrong with me, Natalie."

"What do you mean?"

Snorting a little as she pulled a toothbrush and a change of underwear out of the bag, she tried to put her feelings into words.

"I don't know. I just...I wasn't into it or something. The poor woman was doing all the work and I just...didn't want to."

"Well, maybe you're just not attracted to her."

"Then I need my eyes checked."

"It happens." She could hear the smile in Natalie's voice. "Maybe she just doesn't do it for you."

Sarah shifted her pelvis, double-checking the state of her panties, noting their continued wetness. "No, I don't think that's it."

"Then...maybe you're still not ready to move on from Karen," Natalie suggested with tenderness.

Sarah wandered back into the kitchen and stared at her drink some more. "God, it's been over a year. She's marrying somebody else in a few months. I *have* to move on." She shook her head, refusing the possibility altogether. "No. No, that's not it either."

"Okay. Hmm..." Natalie was quiet for several long seconds, obviously thinking. "Maybe you're not the kind of person who can sleep with somebody you don't love."

Sarah flashed instantly to the couple of women she'd picked up while overseas, on how she'd had no trouble at all with no-strings-attached sex, and made a sound that was a combination of a grunt and a hum.

"That's not uncommon. I'm kind of like that," Natalie confided.

"You are?" Sarah wasn't sure why she was surprised.

"Absolutely. I always had trouble with the casual sex thing. I always *wished* I was better at it," she said with a laugh, "but it's just not the way I'm built. Maybe you're like that, too."

"I suppose anything's possible," Sarah said with a sigh, touched by Natalie wanting to make her feel better but not wishing to burst any bubbles. Changing the subject, she said, "So, tell me about your day. How's our boy?"

By the time they'd exhausted all conversation and Sarah caught Natalie midyawn, they'd been on the phone for over an hour.

"I'm sorry, I should let you get to sleep," Sarah said. "I forgot how early you have to get up."

"Don't be sorry," Natalie said. "I'm glad you called."

"Me, too. You made me feel better."

"I did?"

"Definitely."

"Good. I'm glad. Are you meeting us for our walk tomorrow?"

"I think so."

"Why don't you stay for dinner?"

Sarah was oddly touched by the invitation. "That sounds great. I'll bring the wine."

"Deal. I'll see you tomorrow, then. Sleep well, Sarah."

"You, too. Good night, Natalie. Give Bentley a kiss for me." She held the handset for a long time after Natalie was gone, staring into space at nothing, retracing the weird path of her day. Fatigue set down on her shoulders suddenly, like a shawl made of lead, and she wanted nothing more than to fall into bed, sleep for days, and wake up to a life that was at least a little bit different in some way. Grabbing her untouched Bombay and tonic, she dumped it into the sink and turned off the kitchen light.

❖

Saturday was overcast, but still uncomfortably warm and muggy, as if Mother Nature was giving humanity one last blast of summer before dragging it kicking and screaming toward winter. Natalie normally tried to use her air-conditioning unit sparingly—it really ratcheted up the electric bill—but she turned it on just after noon to make sure the apartment would be cool enough once Sarah came for dinner. She was nervous, and more than once during her top-to-bottom cleaning of the place wondered what on earth she'd been thinking inviting somebody as used to elegance and sophistication as Sarah to her tiny little shoebox of an apartment with the mismatched furniture and hand-me-down Corelle dishes.

At the same time, the entire line of worry got under her skin like tiny little ants, making her itchy and uncomfortable all day. It wasn't like her to be concerned about what somebody else thought of her. That wasn't the kind of person she was. She was happy in her life, comfortable in her own skin, and if Sarah Buchanan thought less of her because her flatware was old or her kitchen table was marred, so what? She'd never been self-conscious about her home or her belongings before. Being so now was nothing short of aggravating, and she vowed to push all that angst into a box and shelve it, at least for the rest of the day.

By the time she'd pulled her hair into a ponytail and donned a decent pair of shorts and a T-shirt that wasn't stained or ragged, and she and Bentley made it to the park, the air had only cooled a few degrees and was still thick and heavy. Natalie commended herself for springing for air-conditioning, certain that Sarah's place had central a/c and she was used to it. She threw the ball for Bentley, but not as far or as often as she normally would have, not wanting to overheat him. His fur was thick and he had begun panting almost immediately. She pulled out the bottle of water and collapsible bowl she had in her shoulder pack and poured some out for him, which he slurped down almost immediately.

"Hot, huh, buddy?" she said softly to him as he drank. There were very few other people out today, she noticed as she looked around. *Too damn stifling.* Just as she decided they wouldn't stay long and wiped the sheen of sweat off the back of her neck, Sarah's voice cut into her thoughts and Natalie smiled as soon as she heard it.

"Good God, it's like an oven out here."

"Welcome to late August in upstate New York," Natalie said as she stood and turned around to face her. "Southerners would never believe it…" Her words trailed off as her eyes landed on Sarah. Sarah and her new, very sexy haircut. "Oh, my God."

Sarah's long hair was gone—well, a lot of it was. She must have had a good six inches cut off the overall length. It now fell an inch or so above her shoulders, the cut sleek, stylish, and professional, the front swooped down to the side, the deep dark color shimmering in the sun. "Wow."

A gentle tinting of pink blossomed on both Sarah's cheeks and she raked her fingertips over her temple and behind her ear, tucking the hair there in what had obviously already become a new habit. "What do you think?" she asked, and the shy uncertainty in her voice surprised Natalie.

"I think it's fabulous." She closed the distance between them and reached out gently, using the same tucking motion Sarah had, but on the other side. Sarah's hair was incredibly silky to the touch. "It looks amazing. It's the perfect cut for your face."

"Yeah?"

"Definitely. What made you decide to do it?"

Lifting one shoulder, Sarah said, "I wanted a change."

"You got one." Natalie grinned at her. "Let me see the back." She drew a circle in the air with one finger. Sarah obeyed and turned slowly. "It's gorgeous," Natalie pronounced when she finished.

"Thanks. I almost had a heart attack in the salon. There was a lot of hair on the floor."

Natalie laughed as Bentley pushed at Sarah's leg with the ball. "I bet there was."

"My stylist was happy, though." Sarah took the ball from Bentley's mouth and tossed it.

"I'm sure. They love to chop off a lot of hair and do something new. I'm sure mine's waiting for me to have her do something other than pink."

Sarah smiled down at her and shook her head. "Nah. I like the pink."

❖

Cinammon, chocolate, coffee. The stairwell to Natalie's apartment smelled delicious and Sarah felt like Bentley, sniffing the air as she climbed.

"God, does it smell this good all the time?"

Natalie's chuckle rolled down from a few steps above. "Yeah, pretty much. And sometimes, Mrs. V. makes her dinner for home down there, too. You should come by sometime when she's making spaghetti sauce."

"I lived above a bar for one semester in college. I've got to say, the aroma of cigarettes and stale beer doesn't really compare to this." She followed Natalie into the apartment, pleasantly surprised by the cool air as it caressed her damp, heated skin.

"Make yourself at home," Natalie said, gesturing to the small living space. "Can I open that?" She pointed with her chin at the bottle of wine Sarah held.

"That would be great."

Natalie's living room was tiny, but it said a lot about her, and Sarah enjoyed taking it all in. There were stacks of books that told her Natalie was partial to mysteries and suspense. She squinted at a couple of textbooks on an end table. "Are you taking an accounting class?"

"Next semester, I think," Natalie responded.

"You like numbers?"

"I taught high school math for a few years."

"You did?" The surprise was clear in Sarah's voice before she had a chance to try to catch it and she winced. "Sorry."

Natalie laughed as she pulled the cork. "It's okay. I know I don't exactly look like the teacher type. I hated the politics of the job. It drove me nuts. I wish I'd realized I wasn't cut out for it before I went through four years of college to be a teacher."

"Why accounting now?"

"I keep the books for the Valentis. I just want to brush up on a few things, make sure I'm doing it right, you know?"

Sarah nodded, her wheels turning as she processed this new information about Natalie, realizing that it had never occurred to her that Natalie might have bigger plans and more responsibility than slinging coffee and baked goods for a living. Chewing on that, she went back to exploring the room. Several plants crowded each other near the front windows, trying to soak up the most sunshine. All were green and lush, with rich, dark earth in their pots and no trace of dust on their leaves. Framed snapshots dotted the entire room and every available surface. Two or three were obviously of family. The rest seemed to be people Natalie's own age. Sarah picked one up in particular. There were eight women, counting Natalie and Andrea, all dressed in windbreakers and jeans and surrounded by camping gear, all smiling and with their arms wrapped around one another, as if they made up one living, breathing entity. The pang of jealousy that struck Sarah was so unexpected, it made her flinch.

"Are these the people you're camping with next weekend?" she asked, holding up the picture so Natalie could see it as she brought two glasses of red wine.

"Yep. We've been camping together for years. Well, actually..." She set her wine down and gave Sarah hers so she could point out faces in the picture. "These four have been going for ages. Then she joined them. Then the next year, me and Ellen went. Andrea just went for the first time last year and she's going again this year. And I think three or four newbies are coming this year, too."

"Sounds like fun," Sarah said. "Except for the camping part."

"What kind of lesbian doesn't like to camp?"

Sarah waved her hand in the air. "This one."

"They could revoke your membership card for that offense, you know." Natalie arched a brow.

"So I've been told." Sarah held up her glass. "Cheers."

"Cheers."

Sarah returned her gaze to the photograph, wanting to know more. "And are these people couples?"

Natalie pointed out the original four. "They are. Andrea's

single. I think the new chick is, too. I am and so is Ellen, though sometimes we like to…share a tent." She winked.

"Wait…you? Little Miss I'm Not a Fan of Casual Sex?" She found her eyes pulled toward this Ellen, the high cheekbones, the dirty blond hair poking out from under a baseball cap, her arm locked tightly around Natalie. She was not unattractive.

Natalie laughed, and waved a hand dismissively. "I've known Ellen since college, so we're not exactly strangers. We both decided that as long as we're both unattached, there's nothing wrong with…helping each other out once a year, if need be. You know?" Her eyes twinkled, and they seemed more green than hazel in their mirth today.

"Hey, what are friends for, right?" Sarah set the photo back in its spot and sipped her wine.

"Exactly."

Dinner was delicious. Sarah wasn't sure why she didn't have high expectations of Natalie's ability to cook, but the chicken was tender, succulent, and juicy. When she asked about the spices, she was told it was Mrs. Valenti's secret recipe and if Natalie told her, she'd have to kill her.

"Do you cook?" Natalie asked as she picked up Bentley's dish and prepared his dinner. He sat quietly at her feet, paying very close attention to every move she made.

"Not really," Sarah replied, watching her. "Karen did all the cooking and she was so good at it and she enjoyed it so much that I never felt I needed to pay attention. After she left, I got myself a subscription to *Cooking Light* and started trying my hand at it."

"And?"

"Well, I kind of like it. I don't know that I'm any good at it and I certainly can't wing things off the top of my head like my mother, but I do okay. I'd probably do more if I had more time."

"Working late?"

"Exactly. Sometimes, by the time I get home, I don't have the energy for more than popping a Lean Cuisine into the microwave."

"I understand that."

"What are you giving him?" Sarah watched as Natalie upended a plastic baggie into Bentley's dish on top of his dry dog food.

"Oh, Mrs. V. made chicken soup last week and gave me all the scraps she didn't use. I call it Chicken Blech." Sarah smiled at that, loving how Natalie took such good care of her—of their—dog. "Bentley loves it. And it's good for him."

Sarah rested her eyes on her dog, who waited patiently in a sit, a tiny dribble of drool hanging from his anticipating mouth. "She spoils you rotten," she said to him. He was unable to pull his eyes from the bowl as Natalie set it down for him.

"He's so cute," Natalie said in a baby voice, ruffling his fur. "How could I not spoil him?" She looked up at Sarah, only to find her staring at her. "What?"

Sarah shook her head, unable to put into words what she was feeling. "Nothing. I just…weird and stressful as it all was, I'm happy things turned out the way they did."

The tenderness on Natalie's face nearly melted Sarah's heart. "I'm glad we're friends," she said quietly.

"Me, too," Sarah said. She cleared her throat, embarrassed by her sudden display of weak emotion. "So, tell me more about this camping excursion."

Chapter Fourteen

"What do you think?" Andrea used her eyes to point out Mary Beth Carhart, one of the newest additions to their camping gang. Unbeknownst to either Andrea or Natalie, their friends had invited Mary Beth along specifically because they thought she'd hit it off with Andrea. They hadn't been wrong.

"What do *you* think? That's really what's important here." Natalie kept her voice to a whisper as she and Andrea sat on a log near the fire, their heads tilted toward one another, each gripping a cold bottle of beer. Within the past week, the temperature had dropped significantly enough to announce the impending arrival of autumn, and the campfire was a welcome burst of warmth on the cool evening.

Andrea sighed and for the first time that Natalie could remember in ages, she faltered slightly. "She seems pretty cool."

"I think so, too." Natalie smiled at her feeling giddy inside but not wanting to betray any of that on the outside. It would be too easy for Andrea to get her hopes up and have them shattered by an insensitive soul. But Mary Beth seemed genuine. She was kind, attractive, funny, and knew all about Andrea's history.

"We'll see." They sat quietly for several minutes, and Andrea took a swig of her beer before asking, "How come you and Ellen don't just hook up for good?"

Natalie sucked in a much-put-upon breath and blew it out

slowly in a wordless *here we go again*. "You ask me that every year."

"But you sleep with her every year."

Glancing around, Natalie punched Andrea lightly. "Why don't you announce it to the entire campground? Jesus."

"Oh, come on, Natty. You think everybody doesn't know?"

Of course they knew. It was no secret. Hell, it was practically tradition. Natalie glanced across the site to her friend of more than ten years. A red Melissa Etheridge baseball cap covered most of Ellen's short blond hair, and her eyes crinkled in the corners as she smiled at one of the other women. With her perpetually suntanned face and her preference for hats, she had always reminded Natalie of a professional golfer.

"It's not like that."

"Not like what?"

"Andrea, you and I have had this conversation before, more than once. Ellen and I...we're not...relationship material." Natalie struggled to find the words to best describe what she had with Ellen. "We're just..."

"Good in the sack? Or the sleeping bag, as it were?" Andrea winked.

"In a nutshell, yes." Natalie felt her face grow hot and was surprised that she could become embarrassed in front of Andrea, a woman who knew just about everything there was to know about her. "We...help each other. You know that."

"Is that what they call it nowadays?"

"Shut up," Natalie said good-naturedly, poking her in the shoulder.

"Hey, I'm just looking out for you." Andrea's expression became unexpectedly serious. "I don't want you to be alone, that's all. Life's too damn short, Natty. Believe me, I should know."

Natalie nodded her somber agreement and they took tandem slugs from their beers, mirror images of one another.

"So how's the Hot Business Exec?" Andrea asked after a few minutes.

"She's fine." Though Andrea had taken to being a bit kinder about Sarah, knowing that she and Natalie had become friends, by unspoken agreement they didn't really talk much about her.

"How come you haven't asked *her* out yet?" At Natalie's wide-eyed surprise, Andrea laughed.

"You're kidding, right?" Natalie took another large gulp of her beer, but this one went down the wrong way and sent her careening into a fit of lung-rattling coughs.

"Yeah, I am." Andrea pounded her on the back. "She's hot, though."

Getting a hold of herself after what felt like hours of sputtering and struggling for breath, Natalie replied in a raspy voice. "I thought you didn't like Sarah."

"I didn't say I liked her. I said I think she's hot."

Natalie groaned in exasperation. "You're such a guy."

"Are you saying you disagree with me? You don't think she's hot?"

"Yes, I think she's hot. She's also completely out of my league and *so* not my type." She wiped her tearing eyes, coughing one last time for good measure.

"But you like her."

"Yeah, I do. So?"

"And you've spent a lot of time with her."

"I suppose."

"And you like spending time with her." Natalie just glared at Andrea, willing her to get to the damn point already. Andrea shrugged. "What? I'm just thinking out loud here."

Before Natalie could make another attempt to pinpoint exactly what Andrea was trying to say to her, Mary Beth appeared in front of them. She held her hand down to Andrea.

"I've been ordered to find marshmallow sticks. Want to help me?" The flash in her eyes was unmistakably seductive.

"Go into the deep, dark, scary woods?" Andrea asked. "With you?"

"Uh-huh."

Andrea grabbed Mary Beth's hand. "Hell, yeah."

Natalie shook her head and grinned, wanting to tease Andrea about her lack of skill at playing hard to get, but too happy about Andrea's obvious enjoyment to spoil it for her. She watched as the pair disappeared into the nearby trees, giggling and bumping shoulders, and felt an unexpected pang of envy.

Her thoughts drifted back to the conversation with Andrea and her desire to pair Natalie up. But she didn't focus on Ellen. She focused on Sarah, and for just a fraction of a second, she wondered to herself, *What if I did ask her out? Would that be so crazy?*

Immediately, she snorted at the ridiculousness of it, a resounding *Yes!* echoing through her head. There was no way. It was ludicrous to even joke about it. Sarah didn't think of her that way. Did she? She couldn't possibly. They were so different. Their lives were different, their jobs were different, their habits were different. Sarah was so perfect, so put together, so everything-in-its-place. It was practically a sickness. She imagined Sarah didn't do a lot of things she could hire somebody to do for her, and she had the money to do so. Natalie had never been like that, had never wanted to be. Ask her out? God, Sarah would probably laugh in her face. Besides, she had Suzanne the Tongue now. Unintentionally wrinkling her nose as that thought hit her square in the face, she blew out a breath. Never in a million years. Absolutely crazy idea.

Natalie took a long pull from her bottle and forced herself to admit that she did enjoy spending time with Sarah, more than she'd ever expected to and in spite of their opposite personalities. Sarah was smart, funny, and fun to talk to. And she *listened.* Natalie had discovered during her adult life that because of her youthful appearance and her penchant for things classified as a little "wild" for an adult—the streak of bright color in her hair, for example—people had a hard time taking her seriously, actually paying attention when she spoke. They tended to write her off as a kid, or worse, an airhead. She didn't have that problem with

Sarah. Sarah looked her in the eye and heard her, and Natalie liked that.

She's hot, though.

That was the one thing Andrea was absolutely right about. Natalie squinted into the dancing flames as she wondered if Sarah had any clue how attractive she was, and then she immediately responded in the negative. *She's probably too busy worrying about whether or not her suit's wrinkled to realize that most people would rather see her out of it.* Natalie's libido threw her an unexpected vision: Sarah's tall, beautiful body, lean and muscular yet femininely curved, in full Boss Mode, hovering over Natalie's prone and naked form, pinning her wrists above her head, piercing her with those blue eyes, telling her just exactly what she wanted and how she intended to take it…

"Jesus Christ," she muttered, gulping down the rest of her beer in the hopes of drowning out the sudden scalding burst of desire she felt. *Okay, okay. There's nothing wrong with a little fantasy here and there.* She forced herself to her feet and wandered over to the enormous cooler to grab another cold one and briefly toyed with the idea of shoving it into her jeans to cool herself off.

"Hey." Ellen sidled up to her with a grin and a wink.

"Hey, yourself." Natalie, as always, was happy to see her old friend. Though Ellen only lived two hours away, the annual camping trip was one of the few times they saw each other during the year. In college, they'd gone through the coming-out phase together, and because of that, shared a special bond.

A sharp, stinging whack to her behind suddenly pulled all Natalie's focus away. "Ow!"

"Good one, huh?" Andrea held up a thin switch of a stick for their inspection as Natalie rubbed her ass and glared. "This one's mine."

Natalie reached forward, still glaring, and picked several dead leaves and a small twig from Andrea's spiky dark locks. "Nice hair. Make out in the woods much?"

Andrea feigned an expression of affront, pressing her hand to her chest as if she'd just been insulted. "I never kiss and tell."

Ellen snorted. "That's the biggest crock of shit I've heard today."

"Hey!" Andrea said with indignation as the other two chuckled and walked away.

"So what's new?" Ellen asked as they wandered back to the fire where Natalie had been sitting previously and plopped back down. "How's the coffee shop-slash-bakery biz?"

"It's great. I love it."

"Still doing the books?"

Natalie nodded. "I'm looking into a class at the community college in January, just to brush up. I like it, though."

Ellen shook her head. "I never would have pegged you as a small-business kind of girl, Nat."

"Neither would I," Natalie responded good-naturedly. "But I like doing it."

"It seems to suit you. You look happy."

Natalie grinned at that, valuing the opinion of somebody who'd known her for so long. "I am. I love the Valentis so much and the shop means a lot to them, so I like helping to take care of it."

"You always were a bleeding heart." Ellen patted Natalie's thigh with affection, taking any sting out of the words. "Not that there's anything wrong with that."

"They're good people, El."

"I'm sure they are," Ellen said. "And they're lucky to have you." She held up her beer and Natalie clinked hers against it.

They sat quietly, perfectly content in their companionable silence, watching as their camp-mates got out bags of marshmallows, boxes of graham crackers, and bars of Hershey's chocolate.

"Want me to make you a s'more, Natty?" Andrea asked across the fire, standing so close to Mary Beth, she was almost on top of her.

"I'd love it," Natalie called back. "Thank you, sweetie." She felt Ellen's gaze on her and turned to meet it. "What?" she asked softly.

Ellen's voice was just as soft. "I was wondering if you're up for a visitor tonight, that's all."

❖

The lamp was off in the living room and the light from the television screen sent flickers of strobing color across the walls and ceiling like Sarah was parked on a couch in some sort of funhouse. The only things missing were the wacky mirrors.

Head propped up by her hand, she lay on her side, her other arm hanging off the couch and absently scratching Bentley's fur as he snuffled quietly on the carpet. She was enjoying the film she'd rented, called *Red Eye*. Her mother had seen it several months ago and recommended it to Sarah as a fun, suspenseful, adrenaline-filled ride worth the cost of admission, and she'd been right. Sarah watched as Rachel McAdams ran across the screen and searched in her closet for an unseen weapon with which to fight off the psychopath who was chasing her. Squinting a bit, Sarah mused that Rachel reminded her of Natalie a little bit.

The hair was the same, minus the streak, of course. Their builds were the same, and Rachel seemed to have a similar friendly, everybody-likes-me-immediately face to Natalie's, one that made it nearly impossible to think anything bad about her.

"Do you wish we were camping, too, Bent?" she asked. Bentley's eyes popped open, and not for the first time, Sarah marveled at the dog's ability to go from a sound sleep to wide awake in the space of a split second. His eyes focused on her, but he made no move to get up as she continued to pet him. "Yeah, me neither. Bugs. Dirt. Peeing in the woods. Wearing flip-flops in the shared shower. Sleeping in a bag on the ground. No, thanks. I'm perfectly happy on my couch with my remote and my dog." Making an honest attempt to refocus on the movie, she found her thoughts drifting to camping, to Natalie, to Natalie tucked snugly into a warm, fuzzy sleeping bag. With that Ellen.

She sat up abruptly, startling Bentley to his feet. Refusing to give undeserved attention to her thoughts, she paused the movie and headed with determination into the kitchen. "Hungry, hungry, hungry," she muttered, in order to keep her mind focused on something over which she had control. "What should we have, buddy?" The refrigerator slapped her with its emptiness, nothing but a half gallon of milk, three cans of Diet Pepsi, various condiments that were older than her single status, and a plastic-wrapped plate of leftovers from dinner with Natalie last week. That, of course, was all it took to send her brain shooting back like a laser beam to the image she was trying hard to avoid.

Why should she care what Natalie was doing or who she was with? It made no sense. *She's not mine, I'm not hers, I don't want to be hers, she doesn't want to be mine, and those are all good things because we're too different to ever be together anyway. She is so utterly* not *my type, it isn't even funny.*

To help her argument, she began to tick off all the reasons they shouldn't be together, even though neither of them wanted to so it didn't matter anyway.

"She works in a coffee shop." She said it aloud. With disdain. And then felt terrible that she'd done so. After all, there was the bookkeeping. Natalie was going to take classes. She was a math teacher. She had a college education.

So what if she works in a coffee shop? What if that makes her happy?

"She's a kid, for Christ's sake."

She's not a kid. She's thirty-one. Maybe she seems like a kid to you because you're old for your age.

"I am not."

Getting annoyed with the arguments and simultaneously trying to figure out exactly whom she was arguing with and whether or not she could be considered certifiable, she spat,

"She stole my dog, damn it." Bentley cocked his head like he understood. And disagreed.

She rescued *your dog. There's a difference.*

"This is fucking ridiculous." Snatching a Diet Pepsi out of the fridge, she returned to the living room, Bentley following her and keeping a close eye on her. Thumbing the Play button, she tried to concentrate on the film, but in the back of her mind, two figures continued to roll and tumble in the confines of a sleeping bag, their friendly giggles turning to groans of passion.

Sarah turned up the volume on the TV.

❖

A torrential downpour hit on Tuesday, large blasts of water banging loudly against Sarah's office windows as if somebody was hurling them. The sky was nearly black and angry thunder rumbled through the clouds, shaking the building like an earthquake.

The loud crashing outside her windows didn't distract Sarah in the least. She worked diligently, head bent over her desk like a high schooler taking a test, assessing the figures on the paper before her. The voice that interrupted her, however, made her jump.

"How was your weekend?"

Sarah looked up as Patti Schmidt fell into one of the chairs in front of the desk and grinned. Patti's face was open and the question genuine, but Sarah wasn't in any kind of shape to deal with small talk. She'd slept horribly the night before and the inside of her head felt every bit as dark and ominous as the sky outside. She was in no mood and tried hard to make that point with her eyes.

Patti surprised her by finally seeming to sense her serious state of mind. Rather than dive into details about her weekend or try to pry those about Sarah's out of her, she simply held out a file folder and asked in an uncertain voice, "Can you take a look at this sheet for last month? I'm not sure I did it right."

"Sure." Sarah took the forms and scanned them as Patti nervously fiddled with a button on her sweater. She didn't really want Patti hanging out in her office today, but figured it wouldn't take her long to finish up and give her approval. The admin had actually done a good job and Sarah told her so as she read.

At that moment, the phone rang.

Oh, good, Sarah thought, expecting Patti to go out to her desk and answer it.

Patti furrowed her brows, apparently concentrating on a spot she'd discovered on her sweater, and didn't look up.

The phone rang again.

Knowing better than to scold the poor girl at that moment because in her current mood she'd come down on her like a hailstorm, Sarah instead snatched up the handset. "Sarah Buchanan," she barked.

"Sarah?" The voice on the other end of the phone was uncertain. "Um, hi, it's Natalie."

At the recognition of Natalie's voice, every muscle in Sarah's body relaxed, as if an enormous sigh of relief was released from her lungs. "Hi," she said softly.

"Everything okay?" Natalie asked. "You sound stressed."

"No more so than usual." Sarah threw a look in Patti's direction. Patti was working feverishly on her sweater, picking at the spot with her fingernail. Sarah spun her chair so her back was to her. "You home?"

"Yup. I just wanted to let you know that and…to ask if I could see Bentley. I missed him."

The tenderness in Natalie's voice made Sarah smile. "Of course you can. You know where to find him. As a matter of fact, I think I'm going to end up here late tonight. Why don't you just take him and I'll get him later in the week? Okay?"

"You work too much." Her smile was apparent in her tone, but there was still an etching of worry.

"I know. How was camping?" Sarah didn't want to talk about herself. She wanted to hear more of Natalie's calming voice.

"Not bad. We had fun. It got a little chillier than I like, but what can you do?"

"Snuggle up in your sleeping bag, I guess," Sarah offered as a solution, not necessarily liking it.

Natalie chuckled. "That's what I did."

"It could have been worse. You could be camping in this right now." She gestured toward her darkened windows with her eyes, as if Natalie could see to what she was referring. As if on cue, a rumble of thunder rattled the window panes.

"Oh, no," Natalie said with a laugh. "I draw the line at camping in a monsoon."

"Smart girl." The sound of Sarah's second line ringing distracted her for a moment.

"I'll let you go," Natalie said, obviously hearing it in the background. "Call me when you're ready to make the doggie exchange."

"I will. Be careful driving in this stuff, okay?"

"Yes, ma'am."

"Bye, Natalie." Sarah hung up the phone.

"Who's Natalie?" The innocence of Patti's question took her by surprise.

"A friend."

"Oh." Patti nodded, the twinkle in her eyes saying she thought differently. "She's called here before for you. She seems really nice."

"She is."

Before Patti could comment further, the phone rang again. At the same time, Regina Danvers appeared in the doorway of her office.

Lowering her voice to a whisper, Sarah jerked her head in the direction of Patti's desk and told her, "You need to go answer that."

"Oh!" Patti stood, an expression of shock on her face as if she just realized her duties at that very moment. "Oh, my God. I'm so sorry." Sarah half expected her to slap herself on the forehead. "I'm sorry, Sarah. I'm on it. I'm so on it." She sidled through the doorway, unable to meet Regina's eyes, and practically flew to her own desk. When the ringing of the phone had stopped, Regina shut the office door behind her and took the seat Patti had vacated.

"I swear to God, if her uncle wasn't the founder of this damn company, I'd throw her out on her ass so fast it would make her head spin."

Sarah gave a small smile, but felt oddly protective of Patti. "Nah, she's okay. She's a good kid and she tries hard. She did a great job on last month's reports." Sarah waved the folder she still had in the air as proof. "She's got potential."

"You just have to mine it."

Chuckling, Sarah agreed. "Exactly."

"I hope you have a damn good pickaxe, then."

"As a matter of fact, I do." Sarah made a mental note to set up some time off hours with Patti to start pushing her a bit harder. She didn't want Regina going over her head, thinking she was doing Sarah a favor by reassigning Patti. The woman had grown on her and Sarah wanted to keep her around.

Regina studied her as if trying to figure out a puzzle. "In the meantime, I have something that just may take your mind off that subject for a while."

Sarah narrowed her eyes at Regina's cryptic tone. "Is that so?"

"Curious?"

"Thoroughly."

"I thought you might be." She crossed her legs and folded her hands over her knee. "We need a manager who knows what she's doing to head up the New Zealand branch."

Sarah tilted her head, not fully comprehending.

"On a permanent basis," Regina clarified. "I've been authorized to offer the position to you first."

"The position," Sarah said dumbly.

"Managing director of the New Zealand branch."

"In New Zealand."

"Yes, that's how it would work." Regina's smile said she was amused.

"Permanently."

"Yes."

"Wow."

Regina waited while Sarah processed the information.

"That's a huge move."

"It is. There would be a significant bump in salary. And obviously, the company would cover your moving expenses to Auckland, help get you set up over there, all that good stuff."

"Wow," Sarah said again, not sure she was registering things completely.

"Look, Sarah." Regina sat forward on the chair and leaned her forearms on the edge of Sarah's desk. "Certainly nobody expects you to make a snap decision. This will take a lot of thinking on your part. And you're not in any jeopardy if you turn it down. I know you have family here and this isn't something you'd jump into without consulting them. It's just that you did such a terrific job while you were over there in the spring, and you seemed to really enjoy the area during your stay. It's only fair that you have first dibs on the position." She sat back and added, "It would be one hell of a promotion, that's for sure."

Sarah could only nod slowly, feeling as if her brain was having trouble absorbing the information Regina had just given her.

Seeming to understand, Regina changed subjects. "So, what do you think of the campaign for a new marketing firm? Any favorites?"

Sarah's eyes snapped to Regina's, guilt flooding her as she wondered if her supervisor had any idea of her unethical dalliances. "Oh. Huh. I can't say I've given it a lot of thought. I'm sorry. I've been so busy." She made a feeble sweep of her desk with an arm and hoped she sounded less like she was full of shit than she thought she did.

"I liked the blond woman—Kennedy, was it? She seemed to know her stuff."

"Yeah, she was definitely good," Sarah agreed, thinking shamefully, *I am going straight to hell.*

Regina stood, announcing her departure. "Take some time, think about what I said, and let me know where you stand, all right?"

"Okay. Thanks."

At the doorway, she turned back and touched the back of her own neck with her fingers. "I like the new hair. It suits you." With a wink, she was gone.

Sarah tucked some of her "new hair" behind her ear in a self-conscious motion and tried to return her focus to the pages of numbers spread out on her desk, but her thoughts were still stuck in the previous conversation.

Managing director of the Auckland, New Zealand branch.

Permanently.

The thought wasn't altogether unpleasant.

CHAPTER FIFTEEN

Indian summer.

That's what they always called this kind of weather when Natalie was small. At this time of year, it really should have been starting to cool down, show signs of the impending autumn and winter. But Saturday afternoon was gorgeous—low sixties; brilliant blue skies with puffy, cotton ball–like clouds floating aimlessly through them; bright sunshine that was warming, but not uncomfortably so; the smell of freshly mowed grass combined with newly fallen leaves to create the very distinct scent of September in upstate New York. Natalie loved everything about it, and she inhaled deeply as she strolled through the park with Bentley.

When she approached their usual clearing, her steps faltered slightly and an uncontrollable smile spread across her face. There, about twenty-five yards away, a blanket was spread out on the warm grass in the sun. Sarah was kneeling on it as she emptied a large picnic basket. Natalie tried not to stare at the pleasing shape of her behind cradled in soft-looking denim. It always amazed her to see the difference between Sarah the business executive and Sarah the casual woman. She wondered if Sarah herself was aware of the dichotomy. During the workday, she was so precise and tidy, so put-together with everything as neat as a pin. Today, in addition to the perfectly fitting jeans, she wore a simple, white button-up shirt and left it untucked. She looked relaxed and comfortable and—Natalie had to admit it—damn sexy. Andrea was right on the money with her description of Sarah as "hot."

Bentley pulled at his leash, having also spotted Sarah, jerking Natalie back from her staring. She unclipped him and let him go, and he ran straight to the blanket, his butt wiggling like crazy. Sarah made a sound of surprise when he slipped under her arm and then hugged him as she looked up and grinned at Natalie's approach.

"Hi there," she said happily, her eyes crinkling in the corners.

"Hi yourself." Natalie was surprised and a little confused by how happy she was to see Sarah, the woman whom, barely three months ago, she'd feared and distrusted. "What's all this?" She gestured to the blanket, which now held several small plastic bowls, a tray with two sandwiches, and a bag of tortilla chips. Still inside the wicker picnic basket, a bottle of wine peeked out.

Sarah kissed the top of Bentley's head and scratched behind his ears as he continued to shed love all over her, along with a lot of fur. "It's such a beautiful day. I thought a picnic was in order. I hope you don't mind."

"Mind? You brought me food and wine. Why would I mind?" Natalie laughed as she took a seat. "If you'd called me, I could have brought dessert."

"I did think about that," Sarah said, reaching for the bottle. "But I sort of wanted to surprise you."

"You did?" Natalie cocked her head, pleased at the idea. "Why?"

Sarah turned to regard her with those eyes. "I'm not really sure." They both laughed, then Sarah's face got a little more serious as she continued, "I guess I just felt like being out in this beautiful weather, and you and Bentley were the first ones to come to mind for company."

Natalie felt oddly touched by the remark. "Well, I'm glad

you did. This is great already." She snagged a grape from one of the bowls and popped it into her mouth.

Sarah took lids off the other bowls to reveal green olives stuffed with gorgonzola, small cubes of cheddar cheese, and what looked to be homemade salsa. "*Mangia,*" she said with a grin.

Natalie narrowed her eyes playfully. "Have you been hanging around Mrs. V. and I don't know about it?"

"Believe me, that's all the Italian I know besides *linguini, lasagna, fetuccini*, and *cappuccino*."

"You don't really need to know much more than that. Trust me." She dunked a chip into the salsa and her eyes widened as the flavors of tomato, onion, and cilantro exploded on her tongue. "Oh, wow. Did you make this?"

Sarah nodded almost shyly. "My first attempt."

"It rocks. Seriously, it's delicious. I thought you didn't have the time to cook."

Lifting one shoulder, Sarah responded as she poured wine into two clear plastic cups. "It's Saturday." She pulled a rawhide chew stick from the basket and handed it to Bentley with a flourish. The dog took it and settled down onto the blanket, gnawing happily as Sarah clipped his leash back onto his collar, obviously hoping Natalie didn't notice.

Natalie studied her for several long seconds, narrowing her eyes as she did so. Sarah looked fabulous—a fact that had already been immediately established in Natalie's mind—but her face showed something else, something more subtle. Worry? Concern? She was trying valiantly to hide it, but something was up. Natalie just didn't know Sarah well enough to put a finger on it.

As if feeling the scrutiny, Sarah looked at her. "What?"

"What's up with you?" Natalie asked.

"What do you mean?" Sarah looked away as she inquired, telling Natalie she was very aware of the fact that something *was* up.

"You seem…" Natalie struggled for the right word. "Pensive."

"Pensive, huh?"

Natalie nodded, dunking another chip.

"Well…" Sarah stared off into the clouds as if trying to decide how detailed to get. "I guess I've got some stuff on my mind today."

"Anything you want to talk about? I can certainly listen carefully and nod thoughtfully as I sit here and stuff my face with this sinfully good salsa."

Sarah rewarded her with a chuckle. "I'll let you know."

"I'll be right here."

"Okay."

They spent over an hour chatting about other things, eating, sipping wine, and just enjoying the day. Sarah told Natalie about watching *Red Eye*, which Natalie had seen and loved. Natalie recommended the Ann Patchett novel she'd just read, trying to tell Sarah all about it without giving away any plot details—not an easy feat, but she managed. They ran Bentley around the field with a new Frisbee Sarah had purchased until his tongue lolled out sideways and he collapsed onto the cool grass near the blanket in a panting pile of fur.

Maybe it was the wine. Natalie wasn't sure. Maybe it loosened things up for Sarah, made her feel safer or more courageous or less uptight. Natalie wasn't sure of that either. But as she poured the last of it evenly into their cups, Sarah said simply, "My company has offered me a permanent position in New Zealand."

Sarah was so nonchalant about it, so matter-of-fact, as if she'd just said, "I've decided to paint my kitchen blue." Natalie stared at her.

"I know," Sarah said, then took a sip of her wine. Pointing at Natalie, she added, "I think that's exactly the face I made."

"Permanent? As in, you'd move there and not come back?"

"That's the general idea, yeah. I mean, of course I'd come

back. I have family here. But for all intents and purposes, I'd live there."

"Halfway around the world."

"Yeah."

"Jesus."

"Yeah. It's a huge deal for me, an enormous jump in position and salary. It's quite a promotion."

"Wow. That's…that's great."

"And if I do go, I'd want…" She stopped and cleared her throat. "I'd want you to take Bentley for me."

"What?" Natalie's eyes widened. "Sarah, no."

"Listen to me. I won't put him on an airplane. I just won't. It's too long a trip and there are too many awful things that could happen to him, and I think he'd have to be quarantined for months before I could take him home." She shook her head. "No, I'd want him to stay with you." At Natalie's next attempt at a protest, Sarah stopped her with an upheld hand. "Don't argue with me."

Natalie fell silent, absorbing the repercussions of what Sarah had just laid out. "Have you made a decision?" she asked after several minutes. Her voice felt small, even to her, and she had trouble placing what she was feeling.

Sarah sighed deeply. "No, I haven't been able to. It's been four days and I'm still unsure. I haven't even talked to my family about it." She looked into Natalie's eyes as if trying to tell her something telepathically. "You're the first one I've mentioned it to."

"I am?" Natalie didn't even attempt to hide her surprise.

Sarah nodded and finished off her wine, then looked at her cup as if confused over how it had become empty so quickly. "What do you think I should do?"

Natalie flinched as if Sarah had slapped her. "What do *I* think you should do? Sarah, I can't answer that for you."

Sarah gestured with her open palms up. "Okay. Fine. What would *you* do if you were me?"

"Yeah, because that's a totally different question," Natalie responded with an eye roll.

Sarah leaned close, grasping Natalie's forearm and gripping it tightly. "Natalie. Please. I need…something. Anything to help me make this decision. I'm so confused and that's just *not* like me. At all." She stared into Natalie's eyes, again as if she was trying to tell her something, and their faces were so close that all Natalie had to do was tilt forward slightly and they'd be kissing. *That* thought made her more nervous than anything else going on at the moment, mostly because she could picture it happening with no trouble whatsoever and it sent a pleasantly shivering tingle through her body. "Just…tell me what you think. Please?"

Natalie swallowed and wrenched her eyes from Sarah's to study the cup in her hand. Inside her, there was a battle raging, one between what she wanted to say and what she knew she should say. Finally opting for the latter, she closed her eyes as she spoke softly. "If there's one thing I've learned from the past few years, from Andrea's illness, it's that life is short. And if this is something that you'd regret not doing…you should do it. The last thing you want is to be looking back ten years from now or twenty years from now or even thirty years from now and thinking, 'What if I'd just taken that job in New Zealand?' You never want to have to deal with those words: 'what if.' I think they're two of the most painful words in the English language." She shrugged, signaling the end of her speech.

Sarah nodded thoughtfully. "Okay." She seemed almost disappointed…or was that just Natalie's imagination? "I see your point. That's good advice."

Natalie set her cup down, her appetite for food and drink suddenly gone. "For what it's worth."

"No, no, it's worth a lot. I…I appreciate it. Thank you for being honest."

They sat quietly, each seemingly lost in her own internal thoughts. Sarah went from desperately pleading to almost silent and—again—pensive. Natalie wasn't sure what to do with that, ask more questions or let her be. She felt such a sudden and profound sense of sadness and she couldn't—or more accurately, didn't want to—explore why. Following Sarah's lead, she began to help her clear up the picnic.

They worked in silence for several moments, packing everything back into the basket. Natalie picked up the blanket and shook the grass off while Sarah grabbed the basket and Bentley's leash.

"Here," Natalie said, taking the basket from Sarah's hand. "You guys go on ahead. He's probably got to pee anyway." She gestured at Bentley with her chin. "I'll carry this and the blanket and meet you at your car."

With a nod, Sarah and Bentley headed off toward the little patch of woods.

Natalie folded the blanket into a neat square, tucked it under her arm, and stood there, unmoving, feeling like she'd been punched in the stomach. She knew why it affected her so. She wasn't an idiot and she was more in touch and aware of her own inner workings than most people she knew. The answer was simple: she didn't want Sarah to go. Over the past couple of months, she'd become a close, valuable friend and… Natalie couldn't help but wonder if they might possibly have something more.

"Which is ridiculous," she said aloud. "She's not my type." Flashing back to a mental image of Karen, all classy and neatly put together, she thought, *and I'm certainly not hers, either*.

Though it was becoming quite clear that whether or not Sarah was her type didn't change the attraction to her. It also didn't change the sound of that tiny, distantly annoying voice in the back of her mind that uttered those two words Natalie had just finished warning Sarah away from: "what if?"

Expelling a loud breath of frustration, she picked up the basket and headed toward the woods, shaking her head in consternation, hoping to jiggle these thoughts away. She had just stepped into the trees when she heard a man's loud shout, followed by a surprised curse and rapid, vicious barking and growling, which was answered by a higher-pitched growling bark.

"Bentley," Natalie whispered, adrenaline flooding her system as she bolted through the woods. Bursting out the other side, she barely had time to register anything but a generalized, overall, frightening picture that was trimmed in liquid red. Bentley was in Sarah's right arm as she held him as high up off the ground as she could with one hand while fending off what looked to be some kind of Chow mix that stood as high as her knees and jumped at the Aussie, snapping and snarling. Sarah was using her left arm and left leg to defend Bentley from his attacker, but the Chow mix was determined, and Sarah's white sleeve was already stained an alarming shade of crimson. Natalie dropped everything and sprinted toward them faster than she thought possible.

The man who'd shouted—Natalie assumed he was the attacking dog's owner—raced up to them and reached Sarah at the same time Natalie did. "Oh, my God," he said, grabbing the growling Chow mix and pulling it away by its collar. "*No*, King. Down."

"*What the hell's the matter with you*?" Natalie unloaded on him in a blistering rage, yelling loudly as she put herself protectively between Sarah and the other dog, backing into them until she could feel them against her, hear Bentley's panting—or was that Sarah? "Jesus Christ, why the hell do you let a dog like that run loose?" Only then did she notice the broken leash in the man's hand.

"I'm so sorry," he said, breathing heavily from his run. "I'm *so* sorry." He tied the leash around his dog's collar, yanking savagely to tighten the knot. "I didn't realize he'd chewed through part of the lead. It just snapped as we were walking. God, I'm sorry." The dog was suddenly docile as a lamb, as if he'd just strolled up rather than made an attempt to rip another dog apart.

Knowing she shouldn't tear the man a new asshole but feeling the desire to continue to do just that, Natalie turned away from him to look up at Sarah. Her face was white as a sheet, her lips dry, her eyes blinking rapidly. "Okay," Natalie whispered, noting the tremor that seemed to shudder through Sarah's body. "It's okay now." It was impossible to see exactly what kind of damage had been done. Sarah's leg seemed okay. The jeans had been a fortunate fashion choice today. Her arm, though… Natalie knew the fact that Sarah's shirt was white was possibly making it look worse than it was, but there seemed to be an awful lot of blood. She fought back a panicked queasiness. *Stay calm. She needs you to stay calm. She's in shock right now and you need to take control. Just do it. Just take care of her.* Swallowing down the lump of anxiety in her throat, she turned to face the man and asked quietly, "Do you have a cell phone?"

He nodded. "Yeah."

"Would you call 911?" She gestured at his dog, who was a bit too close for Natalie's comfort, and Bentley's, too, judging from the low-pitched warning growl coming from Sarah's arms. "And move him back. Please."

Swiping at his forehead, which was beaded with sweat, he tugged the dog several feet away and pulled his phone out of his pocket.

Turning back to Sarah, Natalie kept her voice calm. She focused on her face, on the blue of her eyes, rather than the blood all over her arm and the front of her shirt. "Hey," she said, forcing a smile onto her lips. "How we doing?" She took Bentley from her and set him on the ground, checking him quickly, but finding no injuries. She tied the end of his leash to her own belt loop, told him to stay, and then looked up at Sarah's face, which was still abnormally pale. She stroked Sarah's cheek, and brushed her hair behind her ear as she said her name. "You okay?"

"I…" Sarah's voice cracked, so she cleared her throat and swallowed, cradling her left arm in her right. "I think so. My arm hurts."

"I know. How 'bout we sit down? Hmm?" Natalie held Sarah's good arm and helped her lower herself to the grass. Then she sat next to her, very close, and wrapped a protective arm around her waist. Reaching for the sleeve of Sarah's left arm, she said quietly, "Let's have a look at that, okay?" She unbuttoned the cuff and gingerly began rolling the fabric away from Sarah's skin, apologizing as Sarah winced.

Several people had begun to mill around in their general vicinity, having heard the commotion. A college-age young man approached them and gallantly pulled his T-shirt off.

"You should probably wrap that up," he suggested gently as he handed the shirt to Natalie. "Direct pressure?"

She smiled her gratitude at him. "You're absolutely right. Thanks." She wrapped the cotton around Sarah's forearm tightly and held it there, this time wincing along with her at the pain. "Sorry, sweetie."

Sarah leaned her head on Natalie's shoulder. "I don't feel so good."

"I know. Just a few more minutes, okay?" She scanned the area, her eyes landing on the man, and raised her eyebrows in question.

He approached them, having handed his attack dog off to a woman. He was still sweating and his skin was as deathly pale as Sarah's. "The ambulance is on its way," he said, his face sheepish. "I am so sorry." His eyes were kind, and Natalie abruptly felt bad for him, despite her anger. The broken leash was proof that maybe he wasn't just some irresponsible pet owner.

"Will you come with me?" Sarah asked her suddenly, sounding almost like a frightened child.

"Of course I will." Not wanting to leave her side to search for Sarah's cell, Natalie looked back at the man and asked, "Can I borrow your phone?" He handed it over without a word and she quickly dialed Andrea's number, ordering her to the park immediately, offering little explanation other than, "I need you here. Follow the ambulance."

Though it was only a few minutes, it felt like years before Natalie could hear the siren in the distance. She kept a tight hold on Sarah's arm, her gaze shifting from the woman to the dog and back again. Bentley seemed to understand the seriousness of the situation, lying in the grass next to Sarah with a worried look in his eyes. He rested his chin on her thigh and watched her carefully.

The parking lot was visible from where they sat, and Andrea's car pulled in just after the ambulance. Natalie felt a rush of affection, not wanting to know exactly how fast Andrea had driven in order to get there so quickly. Andrea exited her car and sprinted across the field, skidding to a halt next to them as the ambulance beeped its announcement that it was backing toward them.

"My God, what the hell happened?" Andrea asked, taking in the scene with wide eyes.

"Sarah decided to play with a new dog today." Natalie was relieved to see a small smile cross Sarah's lips.

"Holy shit." Looking at Sarah's face, she said, "Dog didn't want to play nice, huh?"

"Not so much," Sarah responded.

"I need you to take Bentley," Natalie said, untying the leash from her belt loop. "I'm going to go to the hospital with Sarah." She handed over her car keys as well as Sarah's. "And take care of our cars. I'll call you and let you know when we're home. Okay?"

"No problem. Got it." She took the leash and the keys and pulled Bentley out of the way as the EMTs approached with their gear. "Come on, boy."

The rest was a blur to Natalie. She didn't hear much that the EMTs asked Sarah, but when questions were directed at her, she answered as best she could, dismayed by how much she actually *didn't* know about Sarah and then wondering why that bothered her. No, she didn't know if Sarah had any allergies. No, she wasn't sure of her birth date, though she did know the year. Yes, she could give them Sarah's address and phone number while they examined her injuries. When asked her relationship to the injured party, the word "friend" had never sounded so meaningless and unimportant in her life, and she looked down at her shoes when she said it.

The only solid thing she was sure of was the feel of Sarah's good hand in hers, their fingers entwined tightly, clutching one another like lifelines. Even when led to the back of the ambulance for the ride to the hospital for treatment, Sarah never let go of Natalie's hand.

For Natalie, it seemed the most natural thing in the world to simply hold on.

CHAPTER SIXTEEN

Sarah blinked several times, trying to focus her vision and figure out where she was.

She had been fading in and out of sleep for what felt like hours, but since she'd completely lost track of time, she had no idea. A total of seventeen stitches in four different gouges in her arm and several painkillers later, she lay in her own bed with no idea of how long she'd been there. Turning her head to see the clock on the nightstand proved to be no easy feat, but she managed.

6:41.

P.M.? she thought, uncertain. *Must be.* The blinds on the windows were closed and she couldn't see what kind of light there was outside, but she could only assume it was evening. Willing her brain back in time, she tried to remember exactly what had happened after the ambulance ride.

Her thoughts were interrupted by the unmistakable sound of retching coming from the adjoining master bathroom, the door closed but ajar. A soft groan followed, then coughing. Somebody tilted the earth on its axis as Sarah tried to sit up, and she pressed her hand to her forehead and flopped back down to the pillow.

"Jesus, what the hell kind of pills did they give me?" she wondered aloud.

The bathroom door opened and Natalie stood there with a

towel pressed to her lips. "You're awake." She smiled in spite of the slightly gray tint of her skin.

"Are you okay?" Sarah's voice was raspy and she cleared her throat.

"I'm fine."

"You were throwing up."

"Yeah." Natalie grimaced sheepishly. "I guess the adrenaline finally cleared out of my system and made way for the wave of raw fear." She half-grinned. "You don't have an extra toothbrush around, do you?" She stuck out her tongue and made a face.

Sarah smiled. "In the linen closet in the hall."

"Thanks. How do you feel?"

"Like a train ran over my arm."

"I'll bet. Queasy at all?"

"A little."

"Yeah, the doctor said the shot he gave you might make you kind of woozy. We should get something into your stomach. You shouldn't take any more painkillers without some food."

The thought of trying to eat something caused a fresh wave of nausea and Sarah had to swallow several times. "I don't know…"

"We'll start light. Just some broth. See how it goes. Okay?"

"Yes, boss."

"That's what I like to hear." Natalie winked and left the room, then returned with the new toothbrush in her hand. "Let me take care of this and I'll make you some dinner."

Try as she might, Sarah couldn't seem to stay awake. She wanted to. She wanted to talk to Natalie, to keep her mind off the pain in her arm by listening to Natalie's soothing voice, to ask her what she meant by "raw fear." But her eyelids felt like they were made of lead and there was no way she could keep them open. She drifted off, dragged unwillingly into sleep.

The next time she looked at the bedside clock, it told her it was 7:55. She blinked her still-heavy eyelids and felt like she was drunk. Her limbs were made of concrete, her thoughts were jumbled, and her ears seemed stuffed with cotton. She had to work hard to adjust her focus, but beyond the nightstand only a couple of feet was her comfy, overstuffed reading chair. Curled up in it, legs tucked underneath her body, opened book abandoned in her lap, was Natalie. Her chest rose and fell in deep, even breaths, her arm pillowed her head. Her jeans looked old and soft, probably a favorite pair worn over and over judging from their faded color, and she swam in Sarah's red Adidas sweatshirt, which was a size too big. Sarah vaguely remembered directing Natalie to that drawer earlier, Natalie's own shirt being spotted with Sarah's blood. Natalie's shoes had been kicked onto the floor and Sarah could see the toes of one foot peeking out, bright pink nail polish giving them a splash of festive color, almost matching the streak in her hair that now hung over one closed eye. Sarah's fingers itched to touch it, to tuck it back behind Natalie's ear, to stroke what she was sure must be the baby-soft skin of her cheek with her fingertips. She looked so peaceful, so vulnerable and sweet, Sarah suddenly saw with absolute clarity why other people, Andrea for example, wanted to protect her. Felt the need to shield her from those who would try to steal that innocence, that kindness, try to suck her spirit out of her and keep it for themselves. But what was most surprising to Sarah was that on top of the vulnerability, layered over the surface of it like a sheer piece of fabric, was an undeniable sexiness. As she slept curled up in Sarah's chair, the first impression Natalie made wasn't one of childlike innocence, it was one of womanly sensuality. Sarah swallowed hard, trying to focus her thoughts but having little luck.

Her vision blurred again, and in a short blast of coherency, she vowed to give the emergency room doctor a piece of her mind for whatever weird drug he'd given her. She squeezed her eyes shut tightly, then opened them again, hoping to clear things up, but still felt like she'd had too many Bombay and tonics, her inhibitions having fled, her common sense in hiding, her rationality nowhere to be found.

When she looked back at Natalie, her eyes were open and she was watching her.

"Hi." Her voice cracked and she cleared her throat, dry from sleep. "Are you okay?" she asked, just above a whisper. At Sarah's nod, she asked, "Are you hungry? You fell asleep before I could heat up your soup."

"Come here," Sarah requested, gesturing with her non-bandaged hand, amazed she could finally lift it.

"What is it?" Natalie uncurled her legs, stood, and stretched. She took a step toward the bed.

Sarah continued with the gesture, urging her closer.

"Can I get you something? Some water maybe?"

"Closer."

Natalie bent over the bed. "What, sweetie?"

Sarah hooked her finger in the neck of Natalie's shirt and pulled her forward until their faces were scant inches apart. Natalie's hands flew out to catch her as she tipped, balancing on the mattress. Her soft cry of surprise was muffled by Sarah's mouth covering hers.

If she was shocked, she hid it well, because instead of pulling away from Sarah, Natalie sank into her with what sounded like a relieved hum, returning the kiss with unhurried determination, slowly and gently allowing Sarah to coax her lips apart, and Sarah took her good old sweet time about it. They kissed for what seemed like hours to her and when their tongues finally did meet, it was as if an electric jolt zapped through them. Natalie jumped back quickly as if she'd been electrocuted. She brought her fingers to her lips, like she was wondering if they'd been scorched by Sarah's.

"I'm sorry," she said, her eyes wide with surprise and blackened with dilated pupils. "I shouldn't have…the drugs they gave you…I'm sorry."

"Don't be sorry. You're a damn good kisser." Sarah focused hard on not slurring her words, on not sounding like she was on her seventh cocktail, but she wasn't sure if she'd been successful.

Goddamn painkillers. She rubbed at her eyes with her good hand and decided the room spun less if she just kept them closed. "Damn good kisser," she muttered again before she gave in to the blackness and let it envelop her once again.

❖

When Natalie opened the front door of Sarah's townhouse only a couple minutes later, Andrea's smile was so big it seemed to take up the entire doorway. She spoke before Natalie could say a thing.

"I've got a date!"

"What?" Natalie stared at her, trying to catch up. "With who?" She squatted down and wrapped her arms around Bentley, whose butt was wiggling like crazy, he was so happy to see her. "Hi, handsome," she whispered in his ear.

"Mary Beth." The unspoken *duh* was obvious.

"Oh. That's great, Andrea." She was happy for her, she was. She knew since the camping trip the previous weekend, Andrea had been taking things slowly, chatting on the phone with Mary Beth, wanting to see her, but refusing to do the chasing for once. That they'd actually set something up and would be meeting face-to-face again was very good news for Andrea and Natalie knew it. But she had so much on her mind at that moment and her tone was less than enthusiastic. Andrea noticed. Natalie could feel Andrea's eyes on her as she unclipped Bentley's leash and he sprinted off through the house, presumably to find Sarah.

"Are you okay?" Andrea asked.

"Yeah. Fine." Andrea's studying of her made her feel like an insect on display and she looked away. "How is Mary Beth? What are you guys going to do on this date?"

Andrea reached out and captured Natalie's chin in her hand, turned her face for a better view. The scrutiny made Natalie want to squirm. Running her thumb over Natalie's bottom lip, she raised an eyebrow and asked, "Are your lips swollen?"

"No."

"Yes, they are."

"They are not." Natalie rolled them in and pressed them together between her teeth, trying to hide them and knowing that by doing so, she'd just confirmed Andrea's suspicions. More annoyed with herself than Andrea, she grumbled, "God, I hate that you can do that."

Andrea gazed at her for a long time before she said anything. When she did, there was no accusation in her voice. It was a simple, soft-spoken question. "What are you doing, Natty?"

"Nothing." *God, sound like a whiny child much?* "I'm not doing anything. I swear." The truth was she had no earthly idea what she was doing. First of all, she'd barely managed to keep breathing as she'd helped Sarah undress and get out of her shredded and stained shirt once they returned from the hospital. Keeping her hands to herself and not running her fingertips over Sarah's lean and creamy-looking torso had taken a Herculean effort, but she'd done it…not to mention that the desire to do so had stunned her. Thank God Sarah had kept her back to her when she divested herself of her bra and slipped on an old Provincetown T-shirt. Once she'd pulled the covers up to Sarah's chin, she'd expelled an enormous breath and was sure she was home free. But then…the kiss. Yes, Sarah had initiated it, but Sarah was also in a painkiller-induced stupor and Natalie should have known better. Regardless of that fact, Natalie had allowed it, allowed their lips to meet, allowed it to keep going on and on and on… God, Sarah's lips were so soft, so warm. Feeling Andrea's stare, she snapped back to reality. "Nothing," she promised again, hoping it sounded a lot less feeble than it felt.

It was painfully obvious that Andrea didn't believe her but had simply let her off the hook for the time being. Gesturing with her chin in the direction Bentley had gone, she changed the subject. "He hasn't eaten much. I tried to give him a niblet here and there, but he wasn't interested."

"He was probably worried. Thank you for taking him. I appreciate it."

"Hey, anything for you." Her half-grin told Natalie she was still loved, despite her stupidity. Not that Natalie had doubted it, but it was nice to have it be clear.

"So…Mary Beth?"

The half-grin became a full-on, smitten one. "We're going out tonight. Dinner and a movie. Get to know each other a bit better."

"That sounds great." Despite the little trysts into the woods with Mary Beth, Natalie knew that Andrea had kept her guard up and hadn't let things go any further. For all her bravado and tough talk, she'd been very careful with this new woman. That told Natalie a lot about how she might really feel. "I expect a full report in the morning, missy."

"As do I," Andrea said, arching one eyebrow to punctuate the point, telling Natalie that the subject was not closed, not by a long shot. When Natalie looked uncomfortably down at her own bare feet, she added, "And, Natty?"

"Hmm?"

"Be careful, okay? I don't want to see you get hurt."

Natalie nodded.

After closing the door behind Andrea, she stood with her forehead against it, just breathing, trying to get her bearings. *You'd think I was the one on the drugs that are making me loopy.* She doubted very highly that Sarah had any recollection at all of the kiss, that she'd had no idea what she was doing at the time. Natalie should just write it off as no big deal. So why was she having such a hard time doing that? Why couldn't she get it out of her head? Why did her lips still feel like they were on fire?

The smart money said that Sarah was heading to New Zealand, that she would take the promotion and be on her way before long. It had been obvious during the picnic that it was a huge opportunity, one she shouldn't pass up. While she wanted to think Sarah had truly wanted her advice on the subject, the truth was, she was probably just being nice. She'd most likely already made up her mind to go. And when she did, once she was gone to the other side of the planet, Natalie would probably hardly ever see her again.

"God damn it," she growled and headed into the kitchen to heat up the soup, realizing that not only did Sarah need to eat, but that she herself was also starving, having put nothing in her stomach since the picnic several hours ago. Reaching for the refrigerator door to get a drink, she noticed again the note she'd jotted off a couple weeks ago, pretending to be Bentley. That Sarah had kept it pinned to the door with a magnet still made Natalie smile.

Within a short span of time, she had soup, a cup of tea for Sarah, and a Pepsi for herself all situated on a tray she found in a low cupboard. She balanced it all carefully and took it into Sarah's room where she felt filled with affectionate warmth at the picture before her. Bentley was stretched out along Sarah's hip, his head perched on her thigh, eyes open and on alert. Sarah looked like she was still asleep and if it weren't for the contented smile on her lips and her moving hand as she gently scratched her dog's coat, Natalie wouldn't have known otherwise. She took a deep breath and entered the room.

"Hey, you're not supposed to be on this bed, mister," she said playfully to Bentley. "That's only at my house. Mama's going to kick our asses."

"No, he's okay," Sarah said smiling weakly, keeping her eyes closed. "I don't mind. I think he was worried about me."

"I'm sure he was. I finally got that soup made. You feel up to eating something?"

Sarah opened her eyes and took a couple of seconds to focus. "Yeah, I think so."

Natalie had found a set of TV trays earlier and now set one up next to the bed as Sarah gingerly pushed herself to a sitting position. "How's the arm?" she asked as she arranged things.

"Throbbing."

"I'm sure." With a quick glance at the clock, she said, "You can take another dose of the painkillers after you eat."

"We'll see. I may skip them if I can. I don't like how they make me feel."

Wanting to comment on whether they affected her judgment, but thinking better of it, Natalie went in a different direction. "You know, you got lucky. I don't know how much you remember about what the doctor said, but it could have been much worse. You only had four deep wounds. The rest were superficial and didn't need stitches." With a wink, she added, "You just bled like a stuck pig."

"Had to protect my boy," Sarah said simply, ruffling Bentley's soft head.

"I know. You were great. I'm not sure I would have thought to pick him up."

"Karen and I made a pact when we first realized he was going to be kind of smallish. There are so many big dogs and owners who don't have a clue. We decided if we ever thought Bentley was in danger, we'd pick him up and hop up on top of the nearest car." She gave a little snort. "Unfortunately, nobody was driving on the grass through the park today."

Trying to maneuver both arms well enough to eat proved to be more difficult than either of them had predicted. After a few minutes of shuffling, Natalie moved the tray away and sat on the edge of the bed with a bowl and a spoon.

"Here." She scooped some soup and held it up. Sarah studied her for long seconds and when Natalie raised her eyebrows, opened her mouth obediently. They worked quietly and after a few bites, Natalie asked, "How're we doing? Feel like it's going to stay down? I'd like to be prepared if there's going to be vomiting." She grinned.

"So far, so good," Sarah said. "Speaking of vomiting, why were you doing that earlier?"

Natalie focused on the soup, spooning it up, feeding it to

Sarah. "I told you," she said, not meeting Sarah's eyes, feeling probed.

"I know. What did you mean by 'raw fear'?"

Natalie shrugged. "You scared me, that's all."

"*I* scared you?" Sarah accepted another spoonful of soup.

"The situation scared me. You know what I mean. You just... that dog was snarling...and you...I didn't know how badly you were hurt, there seemed to be so much blood...I...you scared me. And when I get really scared or stressed out..." She grimaced.

"You puke."

"Sadly, yes."

Sarah smiled tenderly at her. "You were grace under pressure."

"Oh, I don't know about that."

"I do. You stayed calm in a crisis. Not a lot of people can do that. You...kept me from freaking out, because...*I* didn't know how badly I might be hurt and there *did* seem to be a lot of blood and frankly, I was terrified." She held up her good hand to forestall any more incoming soup. "Hey." When Natalie looked her in the eye, Sarah said simply, "Thank you."

"You're welcome."

Their eyes stayed locked, the energy between them almost tangible, until Sarah was surprised by a yawn that sneaked up on her. "God, haven't I slept enough?"

"Rest is the best thing for your body right now."

"Yes, Dr. Fox."

Natalie stood up, feeling the strange sensation of loss as she moved away from the warmth radiating from Sarah's body. She wanted to stay close, wanted to talk to her more, wanted to steer them to the subject of the kiss so she could figure out what, if anything, to do about what had happened. But Sarah still looked so tired, and Natalie herself felt like a body crash was imminent, so she just smiled and kept it all bottled. "Get some sleep. I'll be right outside the door. Do you mind if I watch TV in the living room?"

"You can watch it right here," Sarah said, her eyes pointed at the sizable TV on the dresser across the room at the same time she patted the bed next to her.

"Oh, no, Sarah. I don't want to keep you up."

"I sleep like a rock. I'm not going to hear anything. Besides, it'll be easier on Bentley if he knows the herd is all in one place and he doesn't have to pace from room to room. You'll be more comfortable on the bed than the couch."

Natalie watched her smile and was sure Sarah knew that by using the dog, she'd easily won the argument. With an exaggeratedly defeated sigh, she said, "All right. Let me clean some stuff up and then I'll be in." She took the tray with her as she left the room, calling Bentley to follow, hoping to get him to eat.

Half an hour later, after Sarah refused to take another dose of painkillers, she lay sleeping soundly on her side of the bed. Awash in the blue light emanating from the television, Natalie sat propped against the headboard next to her, the remote in one hand, her other on Bentley as he snored lightly in between them.

The entire scene was blissfully domestic to Natalie.

And frighteningly comfortable.

CHAPTER SEVENTEEN

Sarah's eyes popped open.

She didn't move. She barely breathed. She just lay there, in her bed, blinking in the eerie bluish darkness created by the TV that was still on, the volume so low she could barely hear it. Her arm throbbed and she chided herself for attempting to be Ms. I Don't Need No Stinkin' Pain Meds. It felt like tiny, icy needles were poking at her skin, and she gritted her teeth against the sting, which only served to give her a headache to add to her collection of ills.

The dream she'd been having was fleeting, but something about it had woken her up, scared her, or startled her enough to send her back to consciousness. The weird thing was, she felt better. Mentally. Emotionally. Her arm was killing her, true, but her brain felt almost clear, clearer than it had been in ages. As if she'd been in a fog for the past year, since Karen had fallen for Derek and finally got around to telling her girlfriend, a sudden and strong wind had come through and blown the fog elsewhere, simply dissipated it without so much as a warning. It was just gone. Sarah could see again, breathe again, move again. It was a relief and it was creepy, both at the same time.

She was keenly aware of Natalie's body next to hers in the bed and turned her head to look. Warmth radiated from where Natalie lay, despite the fact that she was curled up on her side, on top of the covers, as if she were cold. Her face was relaxed in slumber, her breathing deep and even, almost hypnotic. Struggling slowly and—she hoped—quietly, Sarah sat up and grasped the corner of the crocheted afghan that covered the foot of the bed. Tugging it toward her, she gently placed it over Natalie's sleeping form, being sure to cover all of her, wanting to keep her from shivering. The lock of colored hair seemed to hang all by itself over Natalie's eye, and Sarah managed to reach for it and brush it tenderly away, despite the awkward angle she was forced to use with her good arm. As it was earlier when she'd watched her sleep, Sarah felt her initial categorization of Natalie as a "kid" slipping far, far into the distance. She was nowhere near a kid. She was a sexy, sensual woman with a kind heart and a kinder soul, and Sarah caught her breath as that thought hit her full-on, right in the face.

With the backs of her fingers, she caressed Natalie's cheek, soaking in the softness of the creamy skin, in awe of the ripe cherry color of her lips, apparent even in the dim light. She tried to focus on them as best she could when she was suddenly hit by a flashback…a flashback that caused an internal explosion, a meltdown of epic proportions as the memory slapped her with its implications.

I kissed her.

"Oh, my God." She said the words out loud without realizing it, and Natalie's eyes fluttered open. She obviously struggled to concentrate on her strange surroundings, wondering for a few seconds where exactly she was. When her eyes settled on Sarah, her face showed concern.

"Sarah? Everything okay?"

"Did I kiss you?" Sarah's voice was hoarse, the question neither accusatory nor confused. She already knew the answer. She just wanted to hear Natalie say it.

Natalie propped her head up on her elbow and studied Sarah for a long time, so long that Sarah began to wonder if she was going to answer at all.

"Mmm-hmm," she finally said. No elaboration, just confirmation.

A thousand things went through Sarah's mind then… embarrassment, anger, disbelief, mortification. She could put none of it into words, though. Deciding to put herself out of her misery one way or the other, she asked a simple question, so quietly it was barely audible.

"Should I be sorry?"

"No."

The relief that filled the room then, emanating from both women, was like another element in the air in addition to the oxygen and carbon dioxide, but it was almost tangible. By unspoken agreement, Natalie moved closer and Sarah extended her good arm so she could snuggle against her, Natalie's head pillowed on Sarah's shoulder, her body stretched the length of Sarah's. A muffled shuffling told them that Bentley was under the bed, aware that they were awake but possibly too tired to make an appearance. Natalie felt around the bed for the remote, held it up without looking, and clicked off the television, plunging the room into darkness. Bentley settled back down, just as they did. They lay quietly, contentedly, neither speaking, Sarah wondering if Natalie was as uncertain what to say as she was. After a while, it didn't matter, as they both drifted off to sleep.

❖

"Just what exactly do you think you're doing?" Andrea asked, flopping down into one of the coffee shop chairs and propping her feet up on a table, crossing them at the ankle.

Sarah squinted at her, wondering what they were doing at the shop and how she'd gotten there. "What do you mean?"

"She means exactly what she said." Karen's voice came from behind her. When she turned, her ex occupied a different table, but her stance was the same as Andrea's. "What do you think you're doing?"

"I...I don't understand." Sarah's gaze ping-ponged back and forth between the two women.

"What they mean is she's too good for you." Sarah turned to see Derek standing behind the cash register where Natalie usually was. He smiled a friendly smile at her and punched some buttons on the register, making it beep and ding.

"What?" Sarah was completely confused. "Who's too good for me?"

Derek rolled his eyes dramatically and Andrea and Karen laughed at his expression. "Who's too good for me?" he mimicked.

"Natalie? Duh?" Andrea stood up and went around the counter, helping herself to a cookie from the glass display case. Derek punched some buttons and when the cash register drawer opened, he pulled out a dollar and gave it to her.

"Don't you think somebody like Natalie deserves better?" Karen asked her seriously.

"Totally," Andrea added. "All you've done from day one is judge her. You judged her level of ambition because of her job, you judged her intelligence level when you first met her."

"You judged her hair, for Christ's sake," Derek tossed in and then tsked, shaking his head in disapproval.

"And all she's done in return is support you and help you and be a friend to you." Andrea finished her cookie with a flourish, then helped herself to another. Derek gave her another dollar bill from the register while Sarah watched in confusion.

"Why are you telling me this?" Sarah was a smart woman, smart enough to realize that something about this entire scenario was fishy. "None of you want anything to do with me, and then suddenly you all appear out of nowhere for the sole purpose of telling me that the person I didn't realize I was falling for is too good for me?" She froze for several long seconds. Then her hand flew to her lips as the meaning of what she'd said hit her right between the eyes. "Oh, my God."

"I'll say it again," Andrea said with an exaggerated roll of her eyes. "Duh."

"Hey." Suddenly, Karen was standing right next to her, as if she'd simply teleported from the table across the room. Pointing at the glass case, she said, "Try one of these cookies. They're delicious." She grabbed Sarah's left forearm and Sarah winced as if red-hot needles were puncturing her skin...

Sarah gasped and her eyes snapped open. She was surprised, as well as relieved, to find herself staring at her own bedroom ceiling, morning sunlight streaming through the window to her left. Her injured arm was propped up on a soft pillow and throbbing, and she was alone in the bed. Uncertain if she was disappointed or thankful for that, she tried to focus on something else. She could just make out sounds coming from the kitchen... silverware against dishes, a pan on the stove, then a soft murmur, the words of which she couldn't quite decipher.

For the first time in what felt like forever, she sat up. Slowly and holding her good hand to her forehead, she swiveled so her feet hung off the bed. She stayed that way, unmoving, and allowed her body to adjust. Her arm injury was making itself known, but she did her best to deal with it, not wanting any more drugs in her system if she could stand it. Worrying that her bladder might burst on her, she managed to stand and shuffle her way to the bathroom, closing the door behind her.

She nearly cried out in horror when she caught a glimpse of her own reflection in the bathroom mirror. Her new sleek and stylish haircut looked like a squirrel's nest on top of her head, with strands and locks jutting out every which way. The dark circles under her eyes told her she'd gotten a drug-induced sleep and not a restful one. Seeing her toothbrush, she snatched it up, pasted it, and began working diligently to erase the little sweaters that seemed to clothe her teeth. Holding the brush in her mouth so she could use her good hand to pull down her panties, she finally managed to relieve herself, expelling a large breath as she did so.

The knock on the bathroom door startled her and she flinched, dribbling toothpaste onto the front of her T-shirt. "Sarah?" Natalie's voice had the slightest twinge of concern. "You okay?"

"Uh-huh." Stretching from the toilet, Sarah spat into the sink next to it, only partially hitting her target. "Son of a bitch," she muttered. Raising her voice slightly, she answered, "Yeah, I'm fine. I'm going to take a shower."

"Do you need help?"

"No," she answered, too quickly. The idea of Natalie's warm hands on her naked body sent way too many confusing feelings rushing through her bloodstream. "No, I'm fine. Thanks. I can do it."

"I made some scrambled eggs. I thought you might be ready for something a little more substantial than broth."

"Oh. Great. That's great. Thank you." Several long, awkward moments of silence stretched out on either side of the door.

"Are you sure you don't need any help?" Natalie asked again, obviously not liking the idea of Sarah in the tub alone.

"No, I'm good. Listen, why don't you head home? You've been a big help and I really appreciate it, but I'm sure you've got other stuff to do besides baby-sit me."

"It's Sunday. I don't really have any plans." The uncertainty was already there, lacing her voice.

"Really," Sarah said. "I'm good. I'm fine. You go on home now." She closed her eyes as she said it, knowing how cold and ungrateful she must sound.

"Um…" She could almost hear Natalie sifting through a mental catalog of reasons to stay, but Sarah knew she was also a highly intelligent woman. She wasn't going to hang out where she felt like she was unwanted. "As long as you're sure…" Her voice trailed off, leaving an obvious opening for Sarah to jump in with a change of heart.

"I'm sure. I'll be fine." Shame crawled across her skin over her relief at having the door between them so she couldn't see Natalie's face.

"You should give your mom a call." Natalie's tone changed so dramatically, Sarah felt as if she'd missed part of the conversation. It was cool, removed. "She called this morning while you were still asleep. You should tell her what happened."

"Okay."

"I'll leave your eggs on the tray next to the bed."

"Okay. Thanks."

Sarah stayed in the shower for what felt like days. It didn't seem like it would be possible to rub herself raw with only one good hand, but she managed to do just that. Tying a small garbage bag from under the bathroom sink around her wounds, she used her good hand to scrub her skin until it was red and sore, staying in the shower until the hot water turned tepid and she was sure she must be alone in the house.

Drying her skin and dressing with one hand proved more difficult than the showering, and she found ways to use her injured hand a little bit here and a little bit there. By the time she was squeaky clean, dressed, and sat down to eat her ice-cold eggs, her arm was throbbing so insistently that she glowered at the bottle of pain pills, mentally cursing them because they were probably going to win out today.

Bentley sighed as he lay on the floor at her feet and stared at her. His eyes seemed vaguely accusatory.

"What?" she said to him.

He continued to stare, as if to say, "You know what." He tipped over onto his side, looking completely relaxed in the beam of sunshine on the floor, except for the eyes that continued to follow her.

"Don't look at me like that," she said. "I need to think. That's all. I need some space to think."

Bentley sighed and if Sarah didn't know any better, she'd say he was emanating a definite air of being pissed off.

❖

"What's the matter with you today?" Leo Valenti asked the question gruffly, but his eyes belied his concern as he looked at Natalie. She was on her midmorning break at the little back table on Wednesday, arms stretched out on it, head pillowed on them, no smile. It was unusual for her not to be smiling and he knew it. "You lose your best friend or something?"

Oddly enough, it sort of feels that way, she thought, even as she sighed and answered, "No."

"Where's the dog? He always make you smile."

At the mention of Bentley, Natalie felt the corners of her mouth lift just slightly. Mr. V. was right. Bentley did always make her smile. "He's with his other mommy today."

"How she doing? S'okay?" He gestured to his own forearm, knowing the details of Sarah's injury from Andrea's storytelling.

Natalie sighed again, dramatically this time. "I wouldn't know."

Mrs. Valenti bustled by just at that moment and she and her husband exchanged a glance. Then, much to Natalie's surprise, she snapped her with the dish towel that was a constant fixture to her shoulder. "Stop it," she commanded as she crossed to the baking rack and took a tray of cookies off it.

"What?" Natalie jumped, startled by the sound more than the sting of the towel. "Stop what?"

"How you say? Moping? Stop your moping."

"I'm not *moping*," Natalie said, sounding far more like a teenager than she cared to admit.

"Oh, yes. You mope." Mrs. V. nodded, arranging the cookies onto a smaller tray suitable for the glass case out front. "You mope all day Monday. You mope all day yesterday and all day today. Is not like you. Is not good. You strong."

"What are you talking about?" A weird sensation filled her then, a little voice telling her that either she wasn't as subtle as she thought she was or the Valentis were *way* more observant than she'd ever given them credit for. Mrs. Valenti continued on with the cookies while Mr. Valenti did up the dishes from the early morning baking. Neither slowed in their work as Mrs. Valenti spoke and her husband nodded along with her.

"You wonderful girl, Natalie. We love you like our own and we know when you happy. Okay?"

"Okay." Natalie drew the word out, trying to follow but unsure of the path.

"You always a happy girl. You never sad. You never pout. You always nice, always smile. Yes?"

Natalie agreed.

"Since you find dog, you smile even more."

The corners of Natalie's mouth turned up once again, proving Mrs. Valenti's point. "Since you find dog's owner, you smile even bigger."

Her grin faltered. The Valentis had hardly seen Sarah at all, just a few occasions here and there when she'd come in for coffee or to say hi or met Natalie at her apartment instead of the park. How could they know this, even if it was true?

More importantly, *was* it true?

Mrs. Valenti stopped what she was doing, obviously seeing the flabbergasted look on Natalie's face. She approached her and took Natalie's chin in a surprisingly gentle hand. "Listen to me, *bambina*. You want something, you must say. Moping? No good. Whining? No good. Waiting? No, no good. You want? You say. Then?" She shrugged her broad shoulders and let go of Natalie's face. "Then you know."

And just like that, she was done. She took her tray of cookies and headed out front just as the little bell over the door pinged sweetly, indicating a customer. Mr. Valenti was still at the huge sink, washing dishes and grinning like the cat that ate the canary.

"What are you smiling about?" she asked him affectionately.

"Who? Me? Nothing. Nothing at all." He feigned innocence and continued to grin.

"Has she always been so wise?" Natalie asked, quirking an eyebrow at him.

"She married me, no?" he said with a wink.

"Good point." Propping her head on her hand, she chewed on her bottom lip while she replayed the past few months in her head, absorbing, analyzing, and wondering what the hell the next step should be.

❖

By the time Sarah got home on Wednesday night, it was after six and she was exhausted. It didn't seem like a day of meetings would be able to suck the life out of her, but that was exactly how she felt as she closed the front door behind her and clicked on a lamp. Dropping her briefcase on the floor in the foyer and kicking off her pumps, she said aloud, "Sorry, buddy," toward the shuffling sound coming from the kitchen. Hurrying in that direction, she felt guilty for leaving Bentley crated for such a long day. She hadn't intended to stay in her office this late, but she'd been zoning out, staring out the window in the last minutes of the workday, and she'd become lost—worrying about anything and everything and knowing that Regina Danvers really, *really* wanted an answer from her soon about the promotion. The next thing she knew, pretty much everybody was gone and she was still staring. Alone and with no more answers than she'd had when she'd started.

She opened Bentley's crate and accepted her usual greeting of kisses and wiggling butt, giving back as good as she got, scratching him and hugging him and talking baby talk to him. As he roamed the backyard to do his business, she watched out the window fondly, thanking her lucky stars above that she'd been able to locate Natalie and get at least some of him back. And while she knew he was technically hers and she could simply take him anytime she wanted, that Natalie would have no recourse, over the past month or two, she'd realized she had no desire to do that. Bentley loved Natalie and Natalie loved Bentley. Separating them would be cruel, it was as simple as that, and she was not a cruel person.

She wasn't, was she?

She changed out of her suit and into flannel pants and a long-sleeve T-shirt as she pondered the question. She hadn't exactly been kind on Sunday when she'd played the role of the coward and sent Natalie away without actually looking her in the eye. Since then, she'd thought about calling, unable to get the woman with the pink streak in her hair out of her mind. She actually picked up the phone more than once and had begun dialing, but always ended up chickening out, embarrassed that she didn't really have a coherent explanation for why she'd treated her so badly. On the one hand, she was surprised she hadn't heard from Natalie by now. She had to be missing Bentley after three days without contact. On the other hand, could Sarah really blame her for not calling? Who wanted to call somebody who'd tossed her out on her ass after she'd done nothing but helped?

"God, I suck," she muttered aloud as she quick-fried some hamburger for Bentley's dinner. As she let it cool on the stovetop, she searched her freezer for something to feed herself. She wasn't really in the mood to cook, but she'd been eating sparsely since Sunday and was feeling the effects of it today, her body logy, her mind a bit sluggish. The veggie burgers in the freezer door could be prepared by microwave, which was quick and easy. She pulled the box out, thinking the burger and a salad would give her some much-needed vitamins, assuming the lettuce hadn't gotten brown and slimy by now, as it tended to do before she got around to eating it.

By 7:15, she was snuggled up on the couch, her legs tucked underneath her, her bandaged arm balanced on the arm of the couch and actually not hurting all that much. Bentley was on the floor near her, gnawing on a Nylabone. She munched on her salad and watched *Jeopardy*, wondering exactly where in their brains these people could possibly store such obscure and trivial factoids.

"I don't know why I bother with this show, Bent," she said to the dog. "It just makes me feel stupid."

He continued to chew, not disagreeing with her.

She was just finishing her last bite when the doorbell rang, startling both her and Bentley. He jumped up, barking, and ran to the door. Sarah followed him, all the while telling him to shush, to no avail. He yipped and barked and jumped at the door until she held him by his collar and turned the knob. Her eyebrows shot up at the sight of the person on the stoop.

"Natalie. Hi." The relief that washed over Sarah must have been obvious to anybody looking.

Natalie stood there fidgeting, looking nervously unsure of herself. "Don't go," she blurted immediately.

Sarah squinted at her. "What?"

Natalie stepped into the house, into the foyer, and shut the door behind her. As Bentley jumped up and put his front paws on her, she scratched the top of his head and repeated herself. "Don't go."

"I don't know—" Sarah sputtered to a halt at Natalie's upheld hand.

"Wait. Just…let me get this out, okay? I've been rehearsing and I think I have it all and I just need to say it, to get it out. Then I'll be out of your hair. Okay?"

Sarah gave a slow, uncertain nod.

"Okay." Natalie took a deep breath and Sarah tried not to notice how adorable she looked in her worn jeans and royal blue Buffalo Bills T-shirt. Her hair was tied back in a haphazard ponytail and when she emptied her lungs, she blew the brightly colored lock of it forward. It settled back where it had been, where it always was, hanging along her right eye. Sarah fought the urge to reach out and touch it, to tuck it behind her ear, even though she knew the attempt would be useless, that it would never stay.

"I'm an independent woman," Natalie began. "I take care of myself. I don't need to depend on anybody. I don't have a lot, but I do okay. And I'm happy. I'm a happy, independent woman."

Sarah felt the urge to nod or say "okay" or something, but managed to stay still and just listen.

"Finding Bentley was an amazing experience for me." She looked down at the dog, who was looking up at her with a softness in his eyes that said he was totally in love, and she grinned at him. "I was never sure if I wanted a dog, but he just showed up and it was like he was meant to be in my life." Natalie paused, seemed to gather her thoughts, and then began to pace in tiny steps around the little square foyer as she continued. "And then I met you. *Really* met you, I mean, not just served you coffee. And you were angry and I was angry and it never crossed my mind that we'd be anything but enemies. Our lives were so different, or so it seemed at the beginning. But once we started spending time together, I realized—and I think you did, too—that maybe we weren't so different after all. I mean, we like the same movies and the same books. We like the park and to walk. We have similar values and morals. And when you told me you wanted me to be a part of Bentley's life…" Her eyes sparkled with unshed tears that took Sarah by surprise. "I knew then that we were destined to be friends, at the very least.

"And then we spent more time together and I started to miss you when I didn't see you for more than a couple days. I didn't really think anything of it until…the dog attack. Well, first the camping trip and *then* the dog attack. No, wait. First Suzanne the Tongue and *then* the camping trip and *then* the dog attack. Suzanne the Tongue because I just cringed when you were with her, but I couldn't understand why. The camping trip because I turned Ellen away at the entrance of my tent for the first time, and again wasn't sure why. The dog attack because…you scared the shit out of me. When I heard that horrible, awful sound, the snarling, the growling, and I saw the blood…" She took another deep breath as if to steady herself and let the memory of that horrific event fade a little. "I know now that it was a silly overreaction of adrenaline, but my God, Sarah, I was terrified for you. I was terrified of losing you and I wanted to rip that guy's arms off and beat him to death with them."

At that, Sarah laughed softly, both touched and entertained by Natalie's words, if not completely stunned by what she might be saying.

"When we got out of the hospital and came here, all I wanted to do was be by your side and take care of you, and when you kissed me…" Her voice trailed off and her eyes seemed to go out of focus, as if she was remembering the moment. "I knew you had no idea what you were doing and that you were a little loopy from the shot, but…" Her cheeks blossomed red. "It was a damn good kiss, and I had no idea what to do with it."

Sarah inhaled as if to speak, but Natalie held her hand up again.

"No. No, I told you not to apologize. I don't want you to be sorry, because the truth is, I'm not. I totally and completely kissed you back and I'd do it again. I'm not sorry. Not for one second."

"Okay," Sarah said with a grin. "Good to know."

"When you asked me to leave on Sunday, it really stung and I wasn't sure why." She snorted then, and added, "Well, I *did* know why, I just hadn't actually thought it through at that point."

"And that I *will* apologize for," Sarah said, this time successfully interrupting. "That was cold of me and I…" She shook her head as if the rest of her thoughts were too poignant to voice. "I'm sorry."

"I wanted to be the one taking care of you. I wanted to be the person getting and giving what you needed while you were laid up. I didn't know that then, but I realize it now." Natalie glanced down at her feet where Bentley still sat, looking adoringly up at her. She smiled and ruffled his ears. "I guess what I'm trying to say is that…" She hesitated for the first time since the words began tumbling from her lips and she swallowed, cleared her throat, and then pushed on. This time, she looked Sarah directly in the eye as she spoke. "I think we could very possibly have something good, Sarah, you and I, if we chose to, maybe, explore it. I'm not asking for a ring, so don't get nervous. I'm not really asking for anything. I'm just telling. Instead of waiting for something to happen like I always have when it comes to relationships, I'm speaking up. These are my thoughts. I think we could have something and it would be cool to be able to give it a try. So, that being said…I'm going to be incredibly selfish right now and tell you that I don't want you to take the job. I don't want you to go to New Zealand. I want you to stay here. With me."

She inhaled suddenly and blew out the breath in one short burst of relief, very obviously thinking, *There, I said it.* "Okay. That's it. That's what I wanted to say. Thank you very much for listening to me." She grasped the doorknob and opened the door, and Sarah got the distinct impression that she wanted to sprint back to her car as fast as possible. Sarah waited until Natalie had taken three steps and was on the front stoop before she spoke.

"Natalie?"

"Yeah?" Natalie spun around, her expression saying she wasn't sure whether to hope or to shield herself from the impending blow.

The only feeling Sarah could coherently put her finger on was warmth. Warmth from the inside out. Everything felt… somehow relaxed and calm as she held out her hand to Natalie. "Come inside?"

❖

Natalie didn't stay long. It was a little weird, but it was a comfortable, at ease kind of weirdness. She'd taken Sarah's hand and gone inside. They sat on the couch—close together and still holding hands—and watched TV for a little over an hour. They chatted, but mostly about superficial, unimportant things like the weather (which was definitely getting cooler), Bentley's favorite toys (the pork chop–shaped chewy, without a doubt), and which actress made the best ADA on *Law & Order* (Angie Harmon, hands down). If either of them had expected more in-depth, emotional discussion, they didn't get it, and Natalie was surprised by how okay that was. It was as if she'd shot her proverbial wad on her little speech in the foyer and hadn't the energy to delve into the subject any deeper, at least not tonight. Sarah seemed perfectly all right with that, perfectly all right to just sit quietly on the couch together and share time and space. She even managed to almost hide her flinch when Natalie called Bentley up onto the couch with them. Natalie teased Sarah that she was proud of her.

When Sarah tried unsuccessfully to stifle a yawn around nine, Natalie took that as her cue.

"Not that it isn't absolute bliss to sit here all warm and toasty with you," she said and meant it, "but I should probably get going." Much as she wanted to stay, she thought it would be a good idea for the two of them to absorb the events of the evening, have some time to just roll things around. She wondered if Sarah agreed, but was afraid to ask.

Expelling a sigh that sounded almost like disappointment, Sarah gave a quick nod. "Okay. I'm sorry about that. It was just a really long day at work and I didn't sleep well last night. I think it's all catching up with me."

"Hey, don't apologize for being tired." Natalie hushed her as she stood and pulled Sarah to her feet. "We've all been there. Besides, you're still recovering from the events of the weekend," she reminded her as they strolled to the front door. "And you weren't expecting company."

"No, I wasn't. But I'm glad I got some."

"Yeah?"

"Yeah." They stood somewhat awkwardly for several seconds before Sarah leaned down and placed a gentle kiss on Natalie's lips. She kept it soft and almost chaste, but it still sent an electric tingle along Natalie's spine, giving her flashbacks of the more thorough kiss Sarah had given her in her bedroom several days ago, and she swore she could feel it sizzle all the way down to her toes.

"Good." Natalie felt like a teenager on her first date, all mushy and giddy inside.

"You should take Bentley tonight," Sarah said suddenly, as if remembering that Natalie hadn't had him all week.

Natalie looked down at the dog, who yawned widely at her. "Nice," she said with a laugh. Looking back up at Sarah, she said, "No, you keep him tonight. He's all ready for sleeping anyway. I can swing by and grab him tomorrow after work…if that's okay with you."

"That works." Then she asked, "Are you free Friday night?"

"Depends on who wants to know," Natalie said.

"I do."

"In that case, yes. I just happen to be free."

Sarah grinned at the lilting tone as she reached around and opened the door for Natalie. "Well, lucky me."

CHAPTER EIGHTEEN

Did you shave your legs?" Andrea was lounging on Natalie's futon, running her fingers through Bentley's thick, silky fur, squinting at Natalie as she asked the question.

"What?" Natalie made a confused face as she searched the tiny living room for her brown leather mocs.

"Did you shave your legs?" Andrea asked again, this time annunciating each word carefully. "You know you're going to sleep with her tonight and you don't want to have stubbly legs. It's just yucky."

Natalie was crouched on the floor looking under the futon. She snapped her head around and glared at her. "Why are you here? Is it just to harass me?"

"Entertaining as that is, no. I told you I'm meeting Mary Beth at SoHo's and thought I'd stop by first to say hi to you." She nuzzled her face into Bentley's neck. "And to see my boyfriend."

"And to give me a hard time."

"I simply asked if you'd shaved your legs. It's my job as your best friend to save you from embarrassment that can be easily avoided, that's all. Just doing my sworn duty."

"I am *not* sleeping with her tonight."

Andrea snorted, a sound that made Bentley cock his head in curiosity. "Yeah, okay."

"You know, not everybody jumps in the sack immediately." She'd moved to a chair and was peering under it as she spoke.

"Um, it's the twenty-first century, Natty. Yes, everybody *does* jump in the sack immediately. Where have you been? Under a rock?"

Her arm stretched under the chair as far as it could possibly go, Natalie clamped her fingers around her shoe and pulled it out, puffing her cheeks out with the effort. As she put it on her foot, she squinted at Andrea. "I don't get you. You hate Sarah. You've always hated Sarah. You've tried your best to steer me away from Sarah. And now you're practically throwing me into her bed."

Andrea said nothing.

"Why the change of heart?" Natalie asked, standing with her hands on her hips and studying her.

"Maybe I just want you to have a little fun once in a while," Andrea said, her voice devoid of any tone of confidence. It made Natalie squint at her some more, trying to figure her out. When it dawned on her, her eyes flew open wide.

"You think she's leaving, don't you? You think she's going to take the job, go off to New Zealand and never come back and I'll be rid of her once and for all, don't you?" The way Andrea glanced down at her hands told Natalie all she needed to know. "I can't believe you," was all she could say.

"You said yourself she hasn't said she's not going to take the job," Andrea said. "Right? She hasn't said those words, has she?"

"So?"

"So, why not?" Andrea sat up straight and ticked off the list on her fingers. "You went to her house, you poured out your heart, you asked her not to go, and she didn't respond. Did she?"

Natalie scratched her neck and looked away. "No."

Andrea grunted a sound that said, "I rest my case," and sat back.

"It's a big deal for her, Andrea. She's not going to make some snap decision just because little ol' me asked her to stay. I'm giving her the benefit of the doubt."

"Uh-huh," Andrea said, cocking an eyebrow.

At the smarmy expression, Natalie felt herself filling with sudden anger. "You know what, Andrea? Fuck you. Okay? Just… fuck you."

Andrea sighed, obviously realizing that she'd crossed a line. "Look, Natty, I'm sorry." She stood up and crossed the room to put a tentative hand on Natalie's shoulder. Natalie flinched away from the contact. "I'm not trying to piss you off. I just don't want you to get hurt. I see you getting all prettied up and I'm worried you have your hopes up and you'll be let down and I don't want you to get hurt. All right? I'm just looking out for you."

"Well, much as I appreciate it," Natalie snapped, "I'm a big girl. I can look out for myself. Okay?"

"Okay." Andrea pulled back and held her hands up like she was being robbed. "Fine. Whatever you say."

Natalie sighed, bothered by the stung look that zipped across Andrea's face. She had never been good at arguing. She hated it, as a matter of fact, and tended to avoid it at all costs—not the best course of action, it turned out. But arguing with Andrea was the worst. They'd been through too much together in their lives to snipe at one another and cause each other pain.

"I'm sorry," Natalie said, rubbing at her eye. "I'm sorry. I shouldn't have snapped like that. It's just…" Her voice trailed off and she tried to put her thoughts into words that would make sense. She stepped closer to Andrea and took her hand. "Listen to me. You've taught me so much. I've learned a *ridiculous* number of life-altering facts from you, my dear." She smiled fondly and to her great delight, Andrea returned the smile, squeezing her hand. "One of the biggest lessons is never put yourself in a position of having to ask 'what if.' And I said that to Sarah when she told me about her job offer overseas. I told her life is too short and she should never pass up an opportunity that might make her ask herself 'what if' down the road. But the more I thought about things later, the more I replayed my own words and recalled how much fun I have just…really doing nothing but spending time with her, the more I realized that I need to practice what I preach.

No 'what ifs,' Andrea. *You* taught me that. No 'what ifs.'" She stared hard into Andrea's eyes, hoping to convey what she was feeling, hoping Andrea understood her need to find out. If nothing else, to at least *find out*. To *know* and not feel the need to wonder, years down the line, "*What if I had just asked Sarah to give us a shot?*" Suddenly, Mrs. Valenti's words echoed through her head. *"You want? You say. Then? Then you know."*

At that moment, she knew beyond a shadow of a doubt that she had done the right thing. That she did exactly what she needed to do by asking Sarah to stay, to give them a try instead of waiting to see if it would happen on its own. She'd taken the bull by the horns. She hoped Andrea understood it, too…that even if Sarah got on a plane to New Zealand tomorrow and Natalie never saw her again, she would never have to ask herself, "What if?"

And she'd shaved her legs, just in case.

❖

When the doorbell rang, Sarah jumped, then laughed at herself for being so nervous. *Seriously, what is it? I feel like I'm a teenager. This is ridiculous.* She'd racked her brains over and over trying to figure out exactly what had happened over the past couple of weeks to make her start looking at Natalie from a different perspective, but she'd had no luck. All she knew was that at this particular point in her life, there was nobody else she'd rather spend time with.

Standing on the front step, Natalie sported a big grin, Bentley's leash in one hand and a bottle of wine in the other. "Hi."

"Hey, you." Sarah's eyes gave her a quick once-over of their own accord. Sarah couldn't seem to control them. Natalie wasn't dressed up per se, but she was wearing nicer clothes than Sarah had ever seen her in before. A feminine and soft-looking pair of khakis was the basis of the outfit, belted in dark brown leather. Her shirt was a deep burgundy, lightweight ribbed turtleneck that was perfect for the cool autumn weather. Her hair was pulled neatly back off her face, and even the rebellious streak seemed to be making an attempt to behave itself, tucked neatly behind one ear. Modest gold hoops adorned her ears and Sarah thought she looked casually beautiful, like she'd stepped out of an Eddie Bauer catalog and onto her front step. "Come on in," she said, stepping aside as she realized she was staring. She bent to ruffle Bentley's ears and unclip his leash.

"I really do love that hair on you," Natalie said, pointing a finger at Sarah.

As she did every time somebody commented on her new 'do, Sarah raked her fingers through it self-consciously. "Thanks. I'm getting used to it, I think."

"It looks great." Natalie held out the bottle. "Here. I don't know very much about wine, but I noticed you had this kind on your counter last time I was here."

Sarah was flattered that Natalie took note of such a thing. "Would you like some?"

"Is it good?" Natalie asked with complete innocence.

"No," Sarah deadpanned. "It's awful. Total crap." At Natalie's stricken look, she laughed and squeezed her upper arm. "I'm kidding. It's excellent. So you don't know about wine, huh?"

Natalie's shoulders dropped a bit as she relaxed. "Not much beyond there being red and white and some is dry and some is sweet. But I like it. I'm willing to learn."

Finding the thought of playing teacher to Natalie's student suddenly and alarmingly erotic, Sarah cleared her throat and said, "Well, I'm no expert, but I'm happy to tell you what I know."

They fell into a rhythm that seemed more than natural, like they'd been having dinner together for years and years. They worked in tandem, getting dishes served and placed on the dining room table, talking about their respective days at work, simply enjoying one another's company. Bentley watched them from a spot in the far corner of the kitchen floor and seemed more content to Sarah than he had since Karen left. She wasn't sure what to do with that, she only knew that it made her feel oddly restful inside. A strange description, but the right one, and she realized that Natalie seemed to have a similar effect on both of them.

When dinner was finished, Natalie insisted on cleaning up the table and loading the dishwasher, brushing off Sarah's protests by picking up a glass of wine, taking Sarah by the arm, and dragging her physically to the living room couch.

"Sit right here and talk to me," she ordered, pushing on Sarah's shoulder until she sat obediently on the couch. "You're injured."

"But it doesn't even hurt anymore," Sarah whined, taking the glass Natalie offered.

"You cooked, I clean. Just talk to me. I can see you while I work."

The open design of Sarah's kitchen allowed for just such a thing and she let herself sink into the softness of the furniture, coming to the realization that arguing with Natalie and winning was no easy task.

"Dinner was delicious, by the way," Natalie said from her place behind the sink. "Thanks so much for inviting me."

"You're welcome. I'm glad you came. I figure living alone, neither of us eat a regular meal as often as we should." Sarah brought her wineglass to her lips and said over the rim, "Maybe if we eat together once in a while, we can fix that."

If Natalie caught the innuendo of the statement, she didn't let on that she had. She continued rinsing dishes and loading them into the dishwasher, her focus on what she was doing. Then she filled Bentley's bowl with some chicken scraps she'd brought with her—Sarah assumed she'd gotten them from Mrs. Valenti again—and added a scoop of cottage cheese from Sarah's refrigerator. She set the bowl down, bending out of Sarah's view, and was gone for several seconds. When she stood back up, she refilled her wineglass, took a healthy sip, and looked Sarah straight in the eye from across the room.

"I'd like that," she said simply and—Sarah was almost certain—hopefully.

Sarah felt caught in Natalie's gaze, feeling captured and liking the unfamiliar sensation. "Good," she said finally. "Because with me not going to New Zealand, I'll probably want dinner company a little more often."

Natalie froze, hand in midair, mouth filled with red wine, and stared at her wide-eyed. Forcing the swallow down, she stared some more, before finally asking, "You're *not* going?"

"No."

"You're really not?"

"I'm really not."

"You turned down the promotion?"

"I did. Today, as a matter of fact."

"How come?"

Sarah leaned forward and set her wineglass on the coffee table. Then she sat back, stretching her arms out along the back of the couch. She crossed her legs and studied the ceiling as she searched for the right words to describe her thoughts of late. "Well, there were a lot of factors to consider. It's a pretty big decision, you know."

Natalie snorted her agreement.

"I had to decide if the things I would miss were bigger than the things I would gain by being there."

"What would you have gained?"

"A hefty raise. That was the big thing. A title promotion. I would have been a bigwig in a big company, which is something I always thought I wanted. The chance to live in a completely new place, explore, discover, meet new people, all that stuff."

"Mmm-hmm." Natalie nodded. "And what would you have missed?" Sarah saw Natalie's throat move as she swallowed and looked down at the countertop.

"My family, of course. Bentley."

"Of course."

"My friends and the familiarity of a city I know like the back of my hand."

Natalie nodded some more.

"And what I think might be a golden opportunity with a woman I met recently."

The nodding stopped and Natalie looked as if she were trying to hold back a grin. "A woman you met recently?"

"Yup. I didn't really like her at first. As a matter of fact, I wanted to hate her. She stole my dog."

"Really?" Natalie arched a brow. "Because I heard she *rescued* your dog."

"Potato, po-tah-to," Sarah said with a dismissive wave.

"But you ended up not hating her?"

"I really wanted to, but she made it impossible. She's way too sweet to hate. I didn't really think we had much in common, but the more I got to know her, the more I realized I was wrong, that we have a lot in common and that I admire her."

Natalie's eyes widened in shocked surprise. "You *admire* her? Why?"

"Why?" It was Sarah's turn to be surprised. "Because she had the balls to ask for what she wanted. She had the courage and the strength to say, 'Hey, make sure you think about this before you make a decision, okay?' That kind of bravery is sorely lacking in most women. Most women are too afraid to speak their minds, too afraid to ask for something they want or something they think they deserve. I know. In the past year, I've become one of them. But you…" Her voice got quiet and she smiled tenderly. "You weren't afraid to tell me not to go. You just put it out there. Just like that."

"I was worried I was being reckless," Natalie confessed with a nervous chuckle.

"You were being ballsy," Sarah corrected with a chuckle. "It told me everything I needed to know."

"Yeah, well." Two rosy circles blossomed on Natalie's cheeks, making Sarah smile.

"Come here." She motioned for Natalie to come into the living room with her. As she approached, Sarah held her arms out. "Come here," she said again.

Natalie didn't wait for a third invitation. She nearly threw herself into Sarah's arms, then pulled back immediately, concern on her face. "Oh, God, I'm sorry," she said as she gingerly touched Sarah's bandaged forearm.

"I told you it doesn't even hurt anymore," Sarah said, taking Natalie's face in her hands and pressing their lips together, effectively silencing her. A sudden flashback from her drug-induced daze the previous weekend threatened to melt her into a bubbling puddle right there on the couch. She tried to take things slowly, but sense memory urged her forward, the softness of Natalie's lips nearly undoing her as she pushed herself deeper into the warm wet of Natalie's mouth. The groan that rewarded her sent a rush to her groin and kicked her heart rate up three or four notches. She gripped the back of Natalie's neck, the skin there hot to the touch, and used her other arm around Natalie's waist to pull her closer, hold her tighter.

The next thing she knew, she was leaning backward, Natalie pushing into her until her back hit the couch cushions and Natalie was stretched out on top of her. She moaned into Natalie's mouth, reveling in the feel of the weight above her.

"Am I hurting you?" Natalie asked, pulling away.

"No!" Sarah said, too loudly, making them both laugh. "No. Stay right there. You feel great." Natalie moved her mouth over Sarah's chin and down to her throat.

"So do you." Natalie bathed Sarah's skin with her tongue, hot and sensual. After several long minutes of such treatment, Sarah was nearly panting.

"You know," she said through ragged breaths, "we probably shouldn't sleep together so soon."

"You're right. We probably shouldn't."

"Sex on the first date is rarely a good idea."

"Rarely," Natalie agreed just before she crushed her mouth

to Sarah's, kissing her roughly, plunging her tongue into Sarah's mouth and laying claim to it.

Oh, my God, was the only coherent thought Sarah could muster as her body went into sensation overload. Natalie gently grasped her bandaged arm and moved it up over her head.

"Keep this here," she ordered. "I don't want to hurt you accidentally."

"But you'll hurt me on purpose?" Sarah teased.

Natalie leaned closer so her lips brushed Sarah's ear. "If that's what turns you on," she whispered, punctuating her words with a swipe of her tongue, forcing a muffled cry from Sarah.

"Christ, you're going to be the death of me," she muttered, not at all worried.

"Oh, no, no," Natalie said. "Where's the fun in that? I have far too many plans for you to kill you this early on." With that, she slid a hand up Sarah's torso and squeezed the handful of breast she came across, running a thumb over the already-erect nipple and earning a startled gasp from Sarah.

Never having been the kind of woman to be led, Sarah couldn't believe she was letting it happen now. *When did I become so damn submissive?* she thought with confusion, even more baffled by how much she was enjoying it. Sure, Suzanne had taken the reins in their few make-out sessions, but Sarah had been slightly uncomfortable with that, never quite feeling as relaxed as she should have. She was used to leading, to taking control, to setting the pace. She'd always done so with Karen. Therefore, she was shocked at how easily she allowed Natalie to take over. For the first time in her life, she was perfectly content, happy even, to let somebody else have the sole responsibility of making her feel good.

And damn if Natalie wasn't a pro at it already.

It was a little surprising, if Sarah was totally honest. As Natalie deftly unbuttoned the front of Sarah's blouse, Sarah thought it interesting that she'd never pegged Natalie for a take-control type. She seemed more like an avoid-conflict, let-somebody-else-handle-it kind of girl. Maybe that was because she'd seen Andrea protect her, stand up for her and take the heat. Sarah had mistakenly assumed that meant Natalie was weak, but what it really meant was that those who cared about Natalie simply wanted to shield her from harm or pain. It had nothing to do with Natalie being timid or helpless. *No. No, she's certainly not either of those.* Sarah arched into Natalie's mouth, which had closed over one now-bared breast, and moaned with pleasure at the shock waves that zipped through her torso.

"God, you're beautiful," Natalie said around the flesh in her mouth.

Sarah's head was thrown back into the couch cushions, her eyes squeezed shut as she coasted along the ripples of bliss Natalie created in her body.

"Sarah." Natalie's voice was hoarse. Sarah lifted her head and almost flinched at the calm reverence reflected in Natalie's eyes. "I think you're beautiful."

Grasping her face in both hands, filled with a pounding desire she hadn't felt in years, Sarah pulled Natalie up so they were nose to nose, and kissed her deeply, pushing her tongue far into Natalie's mouth, responding to the compliment the best way she knew how. The resulting whimper that issued from Natalie's throat was enough to ensure Sarah's panties were not just damp, but soaked. As if reading her thoughts, Natalie slipped a hand between their bodies and fumbled with the fastening of Sarah's black slacks. Not bothering with any attempts at actually pulling them down, Natalie simply thrust her hand down the front, into Sarah's panties, and slid her fingers into the growing wetness that was waiting for her, that she'd created. Sarah pushed against her, unbelievably close to climax already, and did her best to open her legs as wide as she could despite the obstacle of the couch. When the rhythmic rocking began, she knew it was only a matter of minutes. Natalie toyed with her as they continued to devour one another, pressing here and circling there, but not giving the full-on pressure that they both knew would send Sarah careening over the edge and into the abyss. When Natalie finally pulled back and held Sarah's gaze, Sarah was sure she'd never, ever been looked at in quite the same way ever before. Not breaking that eye contact, Natalie lowered herself to Sarah's chest slowly—painfully slowly—and ran the flat of her tongue over one pebble-like nipple at the same time she slipped her fingers inside the moist warmth of Sarah's body. Sucking the nipple firmly, she pulled her fingers out and then thrust them back in, only once, and that was it. The growl that ripped from Sarah's throat was unrecognizable to her as she arched completely up off the couch. Surely she didn't make such noises during an orgasm. Did she? Every muscle in her body contracted and she felt like an overstretched rubber band, about to snap any second. Natalie continued to push her fingers in and pull them out, milking every second of the pulsing, pounding climax, taking everything Sarah was willing to give her and more.

When Sarah finally dropped back onto the cushions, flat on her back and beaded with sweat, all words escaped her. She couldn't formulate a single one as she lay there trying to catch her breath, Natalie's head pillowed on her shoulder, Natalie's fingers still tucked snugly inside her. All she knew was that she felt full, filled, loved like she never had before. Emotion suddenly welled up, and to her own horror, she sensed her eyes pooling with unshed tears. Before she could collect herself, Natalie pulled her hand slowly from Sarah's pants and lifted her head to meet her embarrassed gaze. But instead of alarm, as Sarah expected her reaction would be, Natalie simply smiled and her eyes sparkled wetly, too.

"I...I just..." Sarah thought an explanation was in order, but she had none, the description of what she was feeling too complex, a little awkward, too confusing to verbalize.

Natalie placed a finger over Sarah's lips, her voice a whisper. "It's okay. I know."

The relief Sarah felt, the contentment and comfort at not having to explain herself was almost immediately overshadowed by the pang of arousal that hit her when her own scent, which coated Natalie's fingers, hit her nostrils. Suddenly, there was nothing in the world Sarah wanted to do more than touch this woman, to see her naked, to feel her skin, to make her groan and whimper and beg. Nothing. She took Natalie's chin in her hand and held her gaze.

"I want you. Come to bed with me."

❖

"Oh, that's nice." Natalie spoke softly, something about the dim candlelight of the room creating an atmosphere she didn't want to disturb. "A little mood lighting."

"Exactly," Sarah said, setting the large candle she'd just lit on the nightstand nearby. Natalie watched as she slid onto the eggplant-colored bedspread and propped up a couple of matching pillows. Quickly shedding what remained of her clothing, she slipped beneath the covers and sat with her back against the pillows. Waving a directing finger at Natalie, she commanded in a hoarse voice, "Off."

Natalie stood before her, fully dressed with the exception of her shoes. Granted, her hair was disheveled and her turtleneck wrinkled from their session on the couch, but otherwise, she was entirely overdressed and they both knew it. "You're a bossy thing, aren't you?" Natalie commented with a wink.

"Hey, I let you have your way with me in the living room. Now it's my turn." She made the same gesture with her finger. "Off."

The commanding tone of Sarah's voice sent an erotic tingle up Natalie's spine and she wet her lips with her tongue. "Yes, ma'am," she said quietly and began to do as she was told.

"Slowly."

Natalie swallowed hard, her arousal almost painful. She unclipped her hair and let it fall around her shoulders, brushing her fingers through it to fluff it. The belt came next, and unbuckling it proved to be difficult with her suddenly trembling hands, but she managed, unfastened her khakis and slid them down her legs. She didn't meet Sarah's eyes again until she'd stepped out of them and kicked them to the side.

Sarah's gaze wandered slowly up her legs, so intense that Natalie was sure she could actually *feel* it, as if it was Sarah's hand and not her eyes traveling along Natalie's skin. When Sarah's focus returned to Natalie's face, she arched an eyebrow as if to ask, "And? Why are you stopping?" Astonishment filled Natalie as she tried to reconcile how she'd been so brazen and commanding twenty minutes ago and now felt like a virgin on her wedding night, wanting nothing more than for her partner to find her body pleasing. She grasped her turtleneck by the hem and pulled it up and over her head, certain she heard a small gasp come from Sarah. She dropped the shirt on the floor and stood before Sarah in a black satin bra and matching panties, and when she saw the expression of undeniable excitement etched across Sarah's face, she silently congratulated herself for taking a risk and wearing the only truly sexy underwear she owned, despite having no idea where the evening would go.

"My God," Sarah whispered. "You're stunning."

A warm sensation filled Natalie from the inside when she heard the words. "Stunning, huh? Okay, I'll take that."

"Come here," Sarah ordered, throwing the covers back and indicating the space between her knees. "Sit right here."

Still in her bra and panties, Natalie did as she was told, crawling onto the bed and sitting between Sarah's legs, her back to Sarah's front. Sarah wrapped an arm around her torso and pulled her back tightly. The sensation of Sarah's bare breasts against her back, of Sarah's warm legs alongside her own, caused her to moan softly as she leaned fully back, feeling surrounded by Sarah's body and reveling in it. Sarah's chin rested on Natalie's shoulder, her lips brushing Natalie's ear as she spoke in a breezy whisper.

"You are so unbelievably sexy," she said, her tone underlining her surprise. "I want to touch you everywhere." Her bandaged arm was tight across Natalie's middle, the gauze scraping against the sensitive skin of her stomach. With one easy shift, Sarah closed her hand over Natalie's satin-covered breast, kneading it gently but firmly, coaxing the nipple to stand at attention, which it did in a matter of mere seconds. Natalie's breath hitched.

"You like that?" Sarah asked, her breath in Natalie's ear only ratcheting her excitement up another notch.

Natalie nodded, not trusting herself to speak.

Sarah continued to massage Natalie's breasts through her bra, first one, then the other, first with one hand, then with both. Natalie tried to keep her squirming to a minimum, but the sensations were so strong, she was sure if she didn't move at least a little, she might simply implode right there in Sarah's arms. Her own hands were on Sarah's thighs, which were stretched out on either side of her. She gripped them tightly, the heat of Sarah's skin warming her palms. If she wasn't certain how wet she was after making love to Sarah in the living room, she was definitely certain now. She could feel herself sliding inside her satin panties and absently wondered if she'd ever been so wet in her entire life. She didn't think so.

Sarah slid her right hand up Natalie's throat, grasped her chin, and turned her head. The next thing Natalie knew, they were kissing, hard, Sarah's tongue deep in her mouth, her left hand still in ownership of Natalie's breasts, pushing the bra up and out of the way, focusing all its attention on her aching and now-bare nipples. Prying her fingers from Sarah's knee, Natalie brought her hand up and grasped the back of Sarah's neck, trying to pull her impossibly deeper, wanting more of her, just...*more.*

Sarah made a sound then, a cross between a grunt and a growl, as she squeezed Natalie's body more tightly, pulling her even closer. Then she was moving, her legs were moving, and Natalie felt Sarah's feet, heels pushing between her shins, separating them, so that when Sarah slid her own feet along the sheet in opposite directions, she pulled Natalie's legs apart, spreading them wide and pinning them that way. Natalie whimpered at the sudden feel of cool air on the most heated part of her, at the knowledge that she was helplessly exposed and open to Sarah, who had full and easy access to just about every part of her body. The thought sent a thrill through Natalie, the idea of being at Sarah's mercy nothing but astonishingly erotic.

Fastening her lips onto the pulse point at the side of Natalie's neck, Sarah ran her fingernails up and down the inside of Natalie's thighs, leaving trails of red, causing the eruption of goose bumps. Natalie was almost embarrassed by the needy cry that tore from her voice box.

"What's the matter?" Sarah asked in her ear, the teasing lilt unmistakable. "Do you need something?" She raked her fingernails up and down the opposite thigh, and when Natalie's muscles twitched, Sarah pulled her own feet apart another inch, spreading Natalie even more.

"God, Sarah…"

"What, sweetheart?" Sarah squeezed a nipple, rolled it firmly between her fingers. "Is there something I can do for you?"

"Please…" Natalie was rapidly losing any coherency at all. The only thing she could focus on was the myriad of sensations rolling through her body on a wave of liquid heat. Sarah totally owned her at that moment. And it was obvious to Natalie that Sarah totally knew it.

"Please what?"

"God, touch me. Please. Oh, Sarah. Please?"

Pressing her lips against Natalie's ear, Sarah hummed. "Ooh, begging. Now *that's* what I like to hear." The hand that had been torturing Natalie's thighs moved higher, insistent fingertips rubbed against the fabric that covered Natalie's drenched sex. Both women groaned at the same time and Natalie threw her head back against Sarah's shoulder.

"Jesus Christ," she muttered through clenched teeth, arching as much as she could in her captured state to push herself more firmly against Sarah's hand.

Sarah squeezed around her middle tightly, pulling her closer, and Natalie gasped when she felt the wetness from Sarah's center against the small of her back. Natalie's orgasm was racing up on her quickly, and Sarah seemed to understand that. Shifting her position, Sarah slipped her hand down the front of Natalie's panties and plunged her fingers into the liquefied passion that evidenced her need. "My God, you're so wet," she murmured, sending a shiver through Natalie's body.

"For you," Natalie whispered, her entire system sizzling, ready to combust.

Sarah pressed her forehead to Natalie's shoulder and picked up the pace of her hand, their bodies moving in the same rhythm. It only took a few more seconds before Natalie convulsed and her orgasm hit her full force. Colors exploded behind her eyelids as a primal groan ripped from her throat and her body arched like a bowstring in Sarah's arms. Her fingers tightened on a fistful of Sarah's hair, her other hand digging into Sarah's thigh. She vaguely wondered how her molars didn't crack, so tightly clenched were her teeth.

Sarah's hand continued to move between Natalie's legs until Natalie grasped her wrist and whimpered breathlessly, "Okay… stop…stop." Sarah complied and stretched out her legs, freeing Natalie to close her own. They lay together silently, quietly panting, for long moments, the haze of their lovemaking still swirling almost visibly around the room.

"Wow," Natalie said simply after a while.

"I'll say," Sarah agreed.

"You're…" Natalie's voice trailed off and she shook her head. "Amazing. It's the only word I have."

"Besides wow."

"Right. Wow and amazing. That's all I've got." She felt Sarah's body shake gently as she laughed behind her.

"I'll take those. Those are good words."

"They are." More silence followed as Natalie absorbed the events of the evening, the things that had been said, and where they would go from here. She wondered if Sarah was thinking about the same stuff. "So…what now?" she asked timidly, almost afraid to break the spell by bringing reality into the mix.

"Now?" Sarah asked. "Well, let's see. Now, I think we stretch out under the covers…" She adjusted their positions so they were no longer a tangle of limbs. "We cuddle, and we stay warm, and we rest." She lay on her back and lifted her arm so Natalie could curl up into her body.

"And then what?" Natalie asked, lifting her head from Sarah's shoulder so she could look into her eyes.

"And then we do it again."

Natalie grinned, knowing she was being teased. "And after that?"

"After that, we go forward. Together."

Natalie held her gaze for long seconds before giving a quick nod. She leaned down and kissed Sarah softly on the mouth. "I like that."

She lay back down and snuggled in comfortably, allowing herself to be surrounded by the warmth of Sarah's body and the heady scent of sex still hanging in the air. Just as she began to drift off, she heard a shuffling from under the bed. Popping her head up, she said, "Bentley?" More shuffling and he was out, his head propped on the edge of the bed, his butt wiggling. Natalie patted the mattress. "Come on. Come on up."

"Here we go," Sarah groaned, rolling her eyes. "It's starting already."

Bentley was looking at her, obviously waiting for permission.

"Fine," she said resignedly. "Come on up."

He jumped onto the bed immediately and curled up in the crook of Natalie's knees.

"Thank you," Natalie said, kissing the tip of Sarah's nose.

Sarah snorted. "Like you ever *won't* get your way with me."

CHAPTER NINETEEN

Sarah awoke in the wee hours of the early morning, her ears conditioned to hear the gentle sound of Bentley wandering the darkened house. She listened as he padded into the kitchen to get a drink of water, and slid out of the warmth of the covers to check on him, wondering if he needed to do his business. She found him at the sliding glass door and moved silently to stand beside him. The yard was dark and would be for another couple hours, the whole world asleep except for the creatures that moved under cover of the blackness. Raccoons, possums, mice. She was sure Bentley knew they were out there and even though he was a herding dog by nature and not a hunter, she wondered if he still felt the itch every now and then to give chase, if that desire was in his blood.

"Do you need to go out?" she whispered.

He looked up at her, then turned away from the door and headed into the living room. A pair of shoes lay scattered on the living room carpet and he gave them a happy sniff. They were Natalie's, and he knew it. Sarah was sure if he could smile and tell her he told her so, he would do just that. It seemed kind of strange, but it was almost as if he was happier with two people in his house now.

He gave the shoes a nuzzle with his nose, then headed back into the bedroom, Sarah following behind. The candle was still flickering on the nightstand, sending soft and fuzzy shadows along the walls. Natalie was sleeping deeply, snuggled into the covers as if she slept there every night, as if she belonged there. The sound of her even breathing sent such a wave of comfort and happiness over Sarah that she almost wept.

Bentley hopped up onto the bed and stood looking at Natalie for a moment. He didn't settle down, though. Instead, he looked at Sarah as she continued to stand in the middle of the room as if to say, "Are you coming back to bed?" Sarah padded across the carpet and gently eased back under the covers. Natalie stirred, shifting her position so she was touching Sarah, tossing a warm arm across Sarah's middle, snuggling closer but never waking. Her knees still made a V shape and Bentley settled back down where he had been, sure the herd was safe and sound. He laid his head on Natalie's knee and continued to watch Sarah. After a few moments, he exhaled a deep, meaningful sigh of contentment and let his eyes drift peacefully closed.

Sarah knew exactly how he felt.

About the Author

Born and raised in upstate New York, so close to the border she's practically Canadian, Georgia Beers has been writing since she was old enough to hold a pen. Her first romance novel, *Turning the Page*, was published in the year 2000. Since then, she's written five more and has no intention of stopping anytime soon. Her fourth novel, *Fresh Tracks*, was presented the Lambda Literary Award, as well as a Golden Crown Literary Society Award, for Best Lesbian Romance of 2006.

She lives in North Carolina with Bonnie, her partner of fourteen years, and their two dogs. The eldest of five daughters, she has a slew of nieces and nephews to keep her on her toes. She is currently hard at work on her seventh novel.

Books Available From Bold Strokes Books

Finding Home by Georgia Beers. Take two polar-opposite women with an attraction for one another they're trying desperately to ignore, throw in a far-too-observant dog, and then sit back and enjoy the romance. (978-1-60282-019-7)

Word of Honor by Radclyffe. All Secret Service Agent Cameron Roberts and First Daughter Blair Powell want is a small intimate wedding, but the paparazzi and a domestic terrorist have other plans. (978-1-60282-018-0)

Hotel Liaison by JLee Meyer. Two women searching through a secret past discover that their brief hotel liaison is only the beginning. Will they risk their careers—and their hearts—to follow through on their desires? (978-1-60282-017-3)

Love on Location by Lisa Girolami. Hollywood film producer Kate Nyland and artist Dawn Brock discover that love doesn't always follow the script. (978-1-60282-016-6)

Edge of Darkness by Jove Belle. Investigator Diana Collins charges at life with an irreverent comment and a right hook, but even those may not protect her heart from a charming villain. (978-1-60282-015-9)

Thirteen Hours by Meghan O'Brien. Workaholic Dana Watts's life takes a sudden turn when an unexpected interruption arrives in the form of the most beautiful breasts she has ever seen—stripper Laurel Stanley's. (978-1-60282-014-2)

In Deep Waters 2 by Radclyffe and Karin Kallmaker. All bets are off when two award winning-authors deal the cards of love and passion… and every hand is a winner. (978-1-60282-013-5)

Pink by Jennifer Harris. An irrepressible heroine frolics, frets, and navigates through the "what ifs" of her life: all the unexpected turns of fortune, fame, and karma. (978-1-60282-043-2)

Deal with the Devil by Ali Vali. New Orleans crime boss Cain Casey brings her fury down on the men who threatened her family, and blood and bullets fly. (978-1-60282-012-8)

Naked Heart by Jennifer Fulton. When a sexy ex-CIA agent sets out to seduce and entrap a powerful CEO, there's more to this plan than meets the eye…or the flogger. (978-1-60282-011-1)

Heart of the Matter by KI Thompson. TV newscaster Kate Foster is Professor Ellen Webster's dream girl, but Kate doesn't know Ellen exists…until an accident changes everything. (978-1-60282-010-4)

Heartland by Julie Cannon. When political strategist Rachel Stanton and dude ranch owner Shivley McCoy collide on an empty country road, fate intervenes. (978-1-60282-009-8)

Shadow of the Knife by Jane Fletcher. Militia Rookie Ellen Mittal has no idea just how complex and dangerous her life is about to become. A Celaeno series adventure romance. (978-1-60282-008-1)

To Protect and Serve by VK Powell. Lieutenant Alex Troy is caught in the paradox of her life—to hold steadfast to her professional oath or to protect the woman she loves. (978-1-60282-007-4)

Deeper by Ronica Black. Former homicide detective Erin McKenzie and her fiancée Elizabeth Adams couldn't be happier—until the not-so-distant past comes knocking at the door. (978-1-60282-006-7)

The Lonely Hearts Club by Radclyffe. Take three friends, add two ex-lovers and several new ones, and the result is a recipe for explosive rivalries and incendiary romance. (978-1-60282-005-0)

Venus Besieged by Andrews & Austin. Teague Richfield heads for Sedona and the sensual arms of psychic astrologer Callie Rivers for a much-needed romantic reunion. (978-1-60282-004-3)

Branded Ann by Merry Shannon. Pirate Branded Ann raids a merchant vessel to obtain a treasure map and gets more than she bargained for with the widow Violet. (978-1-60282-003-6)

American Goth by JD Glass. Trapped by an unsuspected inheritance and guided only by the guardian who holds the secret to her future, Samantha Cray fights to fulfill her destiny. (978-1-60282-002-9)

Learning Curve by Rachel Spangler. Ashton Clarke is perfectly content with her life until she meets the intriguing Professor Carrie Fletcher, who isn't looking for a relationship with anyone. (978-1-60282-001-2)

Place of Exile by Rose Beecham. Sheriff's detective Jude Devine struggles with ghosts of her past and an ex-lover who still haunts her dreams. (978-1-933110-98-1)

Fully Involved by Erin Dutton. A love that has smoldered for years ignites when two women and one little boy come together in the aftermath of tragedy. (978-1-933110-99-8)

Heart 2 Heart by Julie Cannon. Suffering from a devastating personal loss, Kyle Bain meets Lane Connor, and the chance for happiness suddenly seems possible. (978-1-60282-000-5)

Queens of Tristaine by Cate Culpepper. When a deadly plague stalks the Amazons of Tristaine, two warrior lovers must return to the place of their nightmares to find a cure. (978-1-933110-97-4)

The Crown of Valencia by Catherine Friend. Ex-lovers can really mess up your life…even, as Kate discovers, if they've traveled back to the eleventh century! (978-1-933110-96-7)

Mine by Georgia Beers. What happens when you've already given your heart and love finds you again? Courtney McAllister is about to find out. (978-1-933110-95-0)

House of Clouds by KI Thompson. A sweeping saga of an impassioned romance between a Northern spy and a Southern sympathizer, set amidst the upheaval of a nation under siege. (978-1-933110-94-3)

Winds of Fortune by Radclyffe. Provincetown local Deo Camara agrees to rehab Dr. Bonita Burgoyne's historic home, but she never said anything about mending her heart. (978-1-933110-93-6)

Focus of Desire by Kim Baldwin. Isabel Sterling is surprised when she wins a photography contest, but no more than photographer Natasha Kashnikova. Their promo tour becomes a ticket to romance. (978-1-933110-92-9)

Blind Leap by Diane and Jacob Anderson-Minshall. A Golden Gate Bridge suicide becomes suspect when a filmmaker's camera shows a different story. Yoshi Yakamota and the Blind Eye Detective Agency uncover evidence that could be worth killing for. (978-1-933110-91-2)

Wall of Silence, 2nd ed. by Gabrielle Goldsby. Life takes a dangerous turn when jaded police detective Foster Everett meets Riley Medeiros, a woman who isn't afraid to discover the truth no matter the cost. (978-1-933110-90-5)

Mistress of the Runes by Andrews & Austin. Passion ignites between two women with ties to ancient secrets, contemporary mysteries, and a shared quest for the meaning of life. (978-1-933110-89-9)

Vulture's Kiss by Justine Saracen. Archeologist Valerie Foret, heir to a terrifying task, returns in a powerful desert adventure set in Egypt and Jerusalem. (978-1-933110-87-5)

Sheridan's Fate by Gun Brooke. A dynamic, erotic romance between physiotherapist Lark Mitchell and businesswoman Sheridan Ward set in the scorching hot days and humid, steamy nights of San Antonio. (978-1-933110-88-2)

Rising Storm by JLee Meyer. The sequel to *First Instinct* takes our heroines on a dangerous journey instead of the honeymoon they'd planned. (978-1-933110-86-8)

Not Single Enough by Grace Lennox. A funny, sexy modern romance about two lonely women who bond over the unexpected and fall in love along the way. (978-1-933110-85-1)

Such a Pretty Face by Gabrielle Goldsby. A sexy, sometimes humorous, sometimes biting contemporary romance that gently exposes the damage to heart and soul when we fail to look beneath the surface for what truly matters. (978-1-933110-84-4)

Second Season by Ali Vali. A romance set in New Orleans amidst betrayal, Hurricane Katrina, and the new beginnings hardship and heartbreak sometimes make possible. (978-1-933110-83-7)

Hearts Aflame by Ronica Black. A poignant, erotic romance between a hard-driving businesswoman and a solitary vet. Packed with adventure and set in the harsh beauty of the Arizona countryside. (978-1-933110-82-0)

Red Light by JD Glass. Tori forges her path as an EMT in the New York City 911 system while discovering what matters most to herself and the woman she loves. (978-1-933110-81-3)

Honor Under Siege by Radclyffe. Secret Service agent Cameron Roberts struggles to protect her lover while searching for a traitor who just may be another woman with a claim on her heart. (978-1-933110-80-6)

Dark Valentine by Jennifer Fulton. Danger and desire fuel a high-stakes cat-and-mouse game when an attorney and an endangered witness team up to thwart a killer. (978-1-933110-79-0)

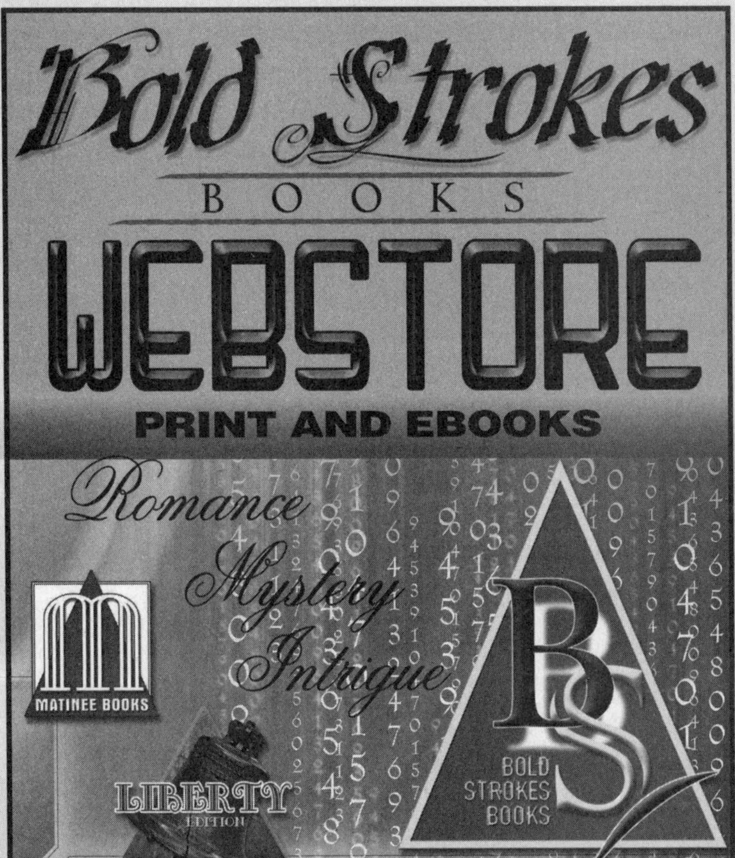
Bold Strokes
BOOKS
WEBSTORE
PRINT AND EBOOKS
Romance
Mystery
Intrigue
MATINEE BOOKS
LIBERTY
EDITION
BOLD
STROKES
BOOKS
Adventure
victory
EDITIONS
ECLIPSE
Erotica
Fantasy
Sci-Fi
http://www.boldstrokesbooks.com